MW01286680

# VILLAGE POLITICS
# CAN BE MURDER

# VILLAGE POLITICS CAN BE MURDER

Jeanne M. Dams

SEVERN
HOUSE

First world edition published in Great Britain and the USA in 2024
by Severn House, an imprint of Canongate Books Ltd,
14 High Street, Edinburgh EH1 1TE.

severnhouse.com

*British Library Cataloguing-in-Publication Data*
A CIP catalogue record for this title is available from the British Library.

ISBN-13: 978-1-4483-1097-5 (cased)
ISBN-13: 978-1-4483-1098-2 (e-book)

*All Severn House titles are printed on acid-free paper.*

MIX
Paper from
responsible sources
FSC www.fsc.org    FSC® C013056

Typeset by Palimpsest Book Production Ltd.,
Falkirk, Stirlingshire, Scotland.
Printed and bound in Great Britain by
TJ Books, Padstow, Cornwall.

# Praise for the Dorothy Martin series

"Thoroughly engaging, with plenty of twists and
a solid dark streak"
*Booklist* on *The Bath Conspiracy*

"A treat for fans"
*Booklist* on *A Deadly Web*

"Old-fashioned British mores take some very modern twists in
this charming mystery"
*Kirkus Reviews* on *A Deadly Web*

"Intriguing . . . Cozy fans and Anglophiles will be satisfied"
*Publishers Weekly* on *Death Comes to Durham*

"Tension runs high until the surprise ending"
*Kirkus Reviews* on *Death in the Garden City*

"Perfect for fans of Rhys Bowen and
Alexander McCall Smith"
*Booklist* on *A Dagger Before Me*

# About the author

**Jeanne M. Dams**, an American, is a devout Anglophile who has wished she could live in England ever since her first visit in 1963. Fortunately, her alter ego, Dorothy Martin, can do just that. Dorothy has featured in twenty-five previous novels. Jeanne lives in South Bend, Indiana, with a varying population of cats.

# ONE

I was in one of those moods when nothing was right. They don't seize me very often, thank the Lord, but when they do, I'm impossible to live with. I can't even live with myself. Whatever occupation presented itself, I didn't want to do it. I didn't want to eat any of the food that was available. I didn't want to pet the dog or any of the cats. Nothing I picked up to read was of any interest. I didn't feel at home in my skin. Psychologists probably have a name for the scourge, but I've never heard of a cure. On those rare occasions when I'm in the grip of it, Alan has learned to leave me strictly alone, and the animals avoid me.

Of course, such is the perversity of human nature (at least mine), being left alone simply added to my grievance. They were treating me badly. Nobody loved me, not even the pets. If there had been any worms to eat, I might have dug them up for lunch.

There were, however, no worms readily available. The summer had been warm and dry (at least dry for England), and now that August was upon us, the worms in my garden had burrowed deep under the dry top layer of soil. The birds weren't especially happy about that, but there were plenty of other bugs for them to eat. My next-door neighbour Jane Langland had begun to breed mealworms and put them out in her feeders, so I could watch the delightful little English robins, so much perkier than our big American version.

Just thinking about the cheeky little birds was threatening to improve my state of mind, and our youngest cat, Mike, completed the exorcism. He gambolled into the room, still a kitten in temperament though grown-up physically, and jumped into my lap.

'And what do *you* want, you little nuisance?'

He batted first at my hand, then at my face. What he wanted, apparently, was attention. None of the other animals were immediately to hand, so I was his choice for playmate. Now, there are people who can resist the blandishments of a cat. I am not one of them, even when I'm trying to nurse a blue funk. I obediently tore a leaf off the notepad on the end table, wadded it up, and threw it on the floor.

A cat can be silent on its feet when it wants to be, but when it's intent on the chase, galloping madly around the room to the imminent danger of lamps and other breakables, it can sound like a herd of small elephants. The ruckus fetched the other inhabitants, feline, canine, and human.

'Feeling better, are you, love?' Alan leaned over and kissed me on the cheek.

'Mike decided it was time I snapped out of it,' I admitted. 'I don't know what was wrong with me.'

'I diagnose a bad case of being human, and of boredom. Life has perhaps been a trifle routine lately, I admit. But as you're back to nearly normal, suppose we go find some lunch? I have a proposition for you, and it would go well with a pint and a ploughman's.'

My second husband, Alan Nesbitt, who entered my life some years ago when we were both widowed, is as English as I am American. We have different ideas about a lot of things, but he is an utter darling, and we rub along together very nicely, thank you. Our love for animals helps a lot, as does his background of police work. He retired a while back from his position of chief constable for our county of Belleshire but still has many connections with the force. And since my preferred reading is the mystery, or crime novel as they're called here in my adopted country, we share that interest.

We also both love pub food and good beer, and there are two or three lovely pubs quite near our home near Shierebury Cathedral. A new one in the High Street, the Dark Horse, has become our favourite for a quick meal. So we put Watson on the leash, since he insists on accompanying us for walks, and headed out.

This was one of the pubs that admitted well-behaved dogs, and Watson knew perfectly well where we were going as soon as we got near. His tail started to wag with enthusiasm. He's a sweet dog, and handsome in his own mongrel way, and he was almost always offered treats at the Dark Horse. We try to discourage the generous impulses, as he has a tendency to embonpoint, but Watson's pleading eyes usually win the day.

Once seated with our beer and plates of cheese, pâté, crusty bread, and pickle in front of us, I prompted my dear husband. 'Okay, a proposition. Don't keep me in suspense.' I cut a bit of pâté, put it on a morsel of bread and conveyed it to my mouth, Watson's eyes following every movement. I slipped him a tiny piece of meat.

'That dog is going to weigh a hundred pounds one of these days,' said Alan in mock exasperation.

'You feed him just as much as I do,' I retorted. 'Who was it gave him the last of the leftover lamb yesterday? We can neither of us resist those eyes.'

Alan held up his hands in surrender. Watson observed that the hands held nothing of interest and subsided under the table. For the moment.

'Yes, the proposition. I've had an email from an old friend who's moved to Grasmere, a very pleasant village in the Lake District. Did you and Frank ever visit those parts?'

My first husband and I travelled extensively in England before his untimely death. 'No, we always meant to, but somehow we never got there. Everyone told us it was *the* beauty spot of the whole UK. It was one of the places we were going to go when we moved to Sherebury, but . . .' But he had died and I'd ended up moving alone into the house we had rented. Happy as I was with Alan, I still had some trouble talking about that time.

Alan gave me an understanding smile. 'Helen and I never did that bit, either, though people told us we must, raving about the beauty. So the point is, Christopher has invited us to come for a visit. He's from Cornwall, like me, and we worked together for a while in Penzance. He never married, and we lost touch when we both moved on, but now that he lives in one of the prime tourist destinations, he wants to show it off. At least that's the impression I got from his note. He's a pleasant chap; I think you'd like him.'

'Well, then, I don't see any reason why we shouldn't go.'

Watson's ears pricked up at the word 'go', which often meant a car ride.

'No, dog, we're not going anywhere, at least not now.' I patted him and gave him a sliver of cheese to make up for the disappointment. 'Did he say when?'

'He said any time but that we might find the end of the month especially interesting. I gather there are some special village doings then.'

'All right, as soon as we see about dates I'll write him a proper letter to thank him and accept the invitation. What's his last name?'

'Prideaux.' He spelled it.

'That doesn't sound very Cornish. Was he a transplant, like you?' Alan's family were originally from Northumberland, a few generations back.

'No, Cornish since the Ark. The area came under French influence at some point. This is an old country, you know. We have names that have changed over the centuries, unlike you Americans, wet behind the ears.'

It was a familiar jibe. I aimed a friendly kick under the table but managed to connect with Watson instead. The poor dog looked up with a questioning whine, drawing obvious disapproval from some of the other patrons. Alan offered some lame explanation, and we finished our meals and left rather quickly.

'So tell me about Grasmere,' I said as we walked home.

'As I said, I've never been there either. All I really know is that William Wordsworth lived there for quite some time and called it "the loveliest spot that man hath ever found".'

'I've never been all that fond of Wordsworth, or any of the Romantic poets, for that matter.'

'You won't want to say that in Grasmere. Rank heresy. It is, as I said, a prime tourist destination, mostly because of the poet and his mates, and tourism is virtually their only industry, I'm told. Myself, I know very little of his poetry, mostly the paean to daffodils.'

'That and "The World Is Too Much With Us". I do like that one, or at least the first few lines. It's true that we lay waste our powers in so many futile pursuits,' I said.

'Mmm. Perhaps we should find a volume of his poems and educate ourselves a trifle before we go.'

'Wouldn't hurt. I may have some in an anthology somewhere. No point in buying something that will just take up permanent residence on a shelf and gather dust.'

After making certain that our dear neighbour Jane would look after the animals, we arranged to travel to Grasmere in the last week in August and booked a room in a hotel recommended by some friends, The Inn at Grasmere. For I told Alan firmly that I was not prepared to impose on his old friend for several days, and anyway we'd be more comfortable in a good hotel and have more freedom of movement. Alan decided to drive, though it was a stiffish piece of work, because the train connections were awkward. 'Anyway, more rail strikes are threatened. And I like to have my car ready to hand.'

So it was that we pulled up to The Inn late on a Thursday afternoon, tired and a bit stiff, but favourably impressed with the look of the hotel and the friendly reception. Alan took care of the details of checking in and then phoned his friend.

'Christopher? Alan Nesbitt here. We've arrived, and we wondered if you'd care to join us for a drink. Splendid! We'll be in the lobby.'

He left me in a comfortable chair with a comfortable glass of bourbon in front of me while he took the luggage to our room, and had just returned when a round, cheerful-looking man came in the front door, spotted Alan, and greeted him with enthusiasm. 'My dear chap!' He clasped Alan's hand in both of his. 'How good to see you after all these years! You haven't changed at all, you know.'

'You always could tell a convincing lie, Christopher. I've gained forty years or so, and hundreds of grey hairs.'

'At least you still have hair,' said his friend with a grin, running a hand across his shining pate. 'And you haven't lost any of your impressive height. Still towering over me by a foot. But you haven't introduced me to this lovely lady, who must surely be your wife.'

'Dorothy Martin.' I put out my hand. 'I kept my name when we married. Confusing, I know.' He waved that peculiarity aside, and the formalities over, the men ordered drinks for themselves and we settled in the large lounge to make plans.

'First things first,' said Christopher. 'Tonight I'm taking you out to dinner. There's a restaurant just a little ways along that I've found to be excellent, and they offer a bit of everything – English, French, even Asian. It's a small place, so I've booked a table, but if you'd prefer somewhere else, it's no problem.'

'That sounds lovely,' I assured him, 'but will there be time to put my feet up first? It's been a long day.'

'Of course. It's only just after five now, and we're booked in for eight.'

He still sounded a bit anxious, and again we told him that was just fine. I promised myself a bag of crisps or something to allay stomach rumblings meantime.

Reassured, the bouncy little man began to lay out an itinerary. 'We can talk more over dinner, but I thought tomorrow I could drive you around and give you a feel of the village and the countryside. I know I sound a bit like Visit Britain, but this part of England truthfully is the most beautiful place I've ever seen. Well, you'll have caught glimpses driving up. Then at some point of course you'll want to see Dove Cottage.'

I tried to look eager, while having no idea what Christopher was talking about. He wasn't a trained policeman for nothing, though. He caught the look and grinned. 'Sorry. Wordsworth's home. Our big tourist attraction.'

It was true confessions time. Alan cleared his throat in an embarrassed sort of way. 'I'm afraid neither of us is a Wordsworth enthusiast, except for a few lines here and there. We'd be happy to see the house, if you think—' He broke off at Christopher's guffaw.

'Truth is, I don't care for his stuff myself! Give me a good Cornish poet like Charlie Causley, someone you can understand. Maybe a mite grim sometimes, but no nonsense about clouds and daffodils!' He finished his drink and stood up. 'Mind, I don't say so to most people. Old Willie's their bread and butter here. Now you two go have a nice lie-down, and I'll pick you up a little before eight, right?'

'Who's Charlie Causley?' I murmured on our way upstairs.

'No idea.'

We were still chuckling as we stretched out on the comfy bed.

# TWO

Our meal was, as promised, delectable, from a starter of scallops through the local lamb to the sticky toffee pudding I always order when it's on the menu. The cheese board that the men ordered looked wonderful, but I couldn't have eaten another atom of anything.

The men still had some room, I think because they'd done more talking than eating all evening. There was a good deal of 'do you remember?' and then of catching up on the forty years since they'd last seen each other. I listened, and smiled and nodded when appropriate, and enjoyed seeing my husband having such a good time.

They had started on their cheese and I was toying with a brandy when Christopher cleared his throat and launched on a new topic. 'Well, that's enough of that. We're boring Dorothy to tears.'

I hastily disclaimed any boredom, but Christopher smiled and shook his head. 'You're too polite, ma'am! Old boy talk is of interest only to the old boys in question, and we need to decide what to do while you're here. We've agreed to give Dove Cottage a miss. You'd love the garden in spring – positively paved with daffodils – but at this time of year it's nothing special. I do want to take you to at least one of the lakes, so you can see for yourself what all the fuss is about, and I'll let you decide what else you'd like to see. But there are two events that are cut in stone. The first is a party tomorrow evening. I'm inviting my friends to meet you, and I think you'll find them congenial. At least most of them.'

He grinned and left that tantalizing gambit on the board for us to pursue if we wanted, but Alan, an old hand at the game, simply smiled and waited.

'Not to be drawn, eh, you sly old fox! You'll see. But the other must-do is the Grasmere Sports Day on Sunday.'

He registered my look of limited enthusiasm. 'So you're not a sports fan, Dorothy? Just wait. These are not your usual sports.

Grasmere has held this event every year since 1868, except when the two wars intervened and then Covid-19 shut down everything. Because I've lived here for only three years, last year was my first experience of the sports. And experience is the word!' His smile filled his rosy little face. 'You've never seen anything quite like this. All very amateur, but serious. You've not seen ten-year-old girls wrestling, I'll warrant. Nor dog shows featuring puppies and rescue dogs. Nor grey-beards racing up a hill. Truly, it's super fun, something you'll not forget, I promise.'

His eagerness won me over. I conceded (I hope with grace), and the pleasant evening ended with plans to meet tomorrow.

'Ten-year-old girls wrestling?' I commented to Alan as we went to bed.

He shrugged. 'When in Rome, dear. Christopher's a sound man. I think we can trust him.'

'He's a dear, anyway, even if he does have some peculiar tastes. I like him a lot. This is going to be an interesting holiday.'

The next day, Christopher took us on the promised tour of Grasmere and vicinity. Grasmere itself didn't take long. We went on a walk of the 'business district', which consisted almost entirely of hotels and pubs and cafés and restaurants and other establishments dedicated to tourism. Most of them were built of local slate in striking colours, including rose-coloured stones such as I'd never seen before. We were treated to a slab of Grasmere's famous gingerbread, and peeked into the church with its rather odd arrangement of roof beams.

Then Christopher drove us out of town to the highest point accessible by car. 'To get farther up, for a really good view, you have to climb, on foot. But you can get an idea from here.'

Spread out below us were the village and the lake, embraced by the green hills all around. Lush pastures and fields, farms, trees – all made me wish I had some vestige of artistic ability, so I could paint the scene and have it with me forever. There was no point in trying to take a picture on my phone; it couldn't capture the sweep of the scene or its peace. We were too close to the valley to see the highest surrounding peaks, but we could watch the sheep working their leisurely way across the pastures, the very essence of pastoral tranquillity.

I heaved a deep sigh. 'I find myself agreeing with Wordsworth. This is perfectly lovely.'

For once Christopher had nothing to add. He had shown us the serene perfection, and as his pride in it was as great as if he had created it, he was content to let it speak for himself. In silence, we drove back to the hotel, where he said he'd pick us up at seven. 'It's a cocktail party, with ample food, so you won't need dinner. See you then.'

I made some tea in the room and unwrapped the packet of biscuits (Brit-speak for cookies) provided by the hotel, not wanting to face cocktails on an empty stomach. 'Why do you think Christopher wanted to move here, so far from his home?' I mused. 'Does he have family here?'

'None that I'm aware of, though as you know we've been out of touch for years. No, it was probably the fabled beauty of the Lakes. He was always a lover of nature. In Cornwall, it was the sea and the sands, the woodlands, the hills, the peat moors. Every moment of his time off duty was spent wandering, soaking up nature. It was inevitable, I suppose, that he would eventually find himself in this fabled place.'

'And, Alan, the beauty isn't just a fable. It's a pity that so many tourists have come to enjoy and perhaps spoil it.'

'They won't be able to spoil it very much. Do you know about Beatrix Potter?'

'Her books, of course. And oh, didn't she live around here for a time?'

'Most of her life actually, and once Peter Rabbit became popular and the books started making a great deal of money, she began buying up property in the Lake District. Some years before, she'd met the man who became one of the founders of the National Trust. Thus when she died, she left four thousand acres of farmland and countryside to the Trust, as well as fifteen farms.'

I began to laugh. 'You didn't always know this. You've been mugging it up!'

Alan acknowledged my accusation with a grin. 'You admit it's interesting. And it means there are great swathes of land that will never be "developed" out of recognition. All thanks to a famous bunny.'

'Then here's to Beatrix – and Peter!' I raised a teacup in salute.

A woman of my age and figure looks simply ridiculous in showy evening clothes. Long ago, I decided to rely on one good 'little black dress' that could be dressed up or down, depending on the occasion. Mine has a high neck and long sleeves, hangs from the shoulder and fits loosely, thus covering up years of unwise indulgences – and just plain years. I never travel without it. For Christopher's party I added the pearls Alan gave me one Christmas and a silver mesh jacket I'd found at a sale in London, and considered myself quite adequately arrayed.

'Very nice,' said Alan with a hug, and escorted me downstairs to meet Christopher.

He had picked us up in good time to be back home before his other guests were to arrive, so we were able to get a good look at his home. A typical Grasmere cottage, it was small and scrupulously clean, but without much character. 'You can tell no woman lives here,' I murmured to Alan while Christopher was pouring us drinks. 'No knick-knacks, no cushions, no decorative touches of any kind.'

'Functional,' Alan murmured back, and turned to thank Christopher for his glass of whisky. Then there was no more opportunity for private conversation, for guests began to arrive all in a bunch. We were introduced, of course, but my memory for names and faces, never good, was soon overwhelmed. Alan's trained memory did better. As we moved to the lavish buffet table, he provided me with a recap, *sotto voce*.

'The sexy piece with the red hair is Lilian Sullivan, and that's her husband Brian, over there talking to the grey-haired man who looks like one of your American Secret Service men.'

I nodded. 'Blends into the background and is always glancing in all directions.'

'Right. His name is Harold, and he doesn't seem to have a wife, at least not here. I think I remember that he's a solicitor.'

'He looks sneaky. I wouldn't trust him with *my* business affairs, that's for sure. I wonder why Brian finds him of interest.'

'No idea. With a last name like Sullivan, perhaps it's just his Irish curiosity about everything.'

I took another quick survey of the room, which was filling up rapidly. 'And that young man talking to – Lilian, was it?'

'That,' said Alan, 'is Brian's son Kevin.'

'I see.' I did, too, or thought I did. 'Brian was married before.'

'And his handsome son by his first marriage looks to be just about the same age as his gorgeous second wife.'

'Hmm.'

'Perhaps not. We both have suspicious minds.'

I made a face. 'Speak for yourself. I prefer to think of myself as interested in people.'

I would have pursued the subject, but one of the other guests came up to help herself to some little crab quiches. 'Sorry to interrupt, but I've been dying to talk to you. Dorothy, am I right? I'm Ruth.'

'And you're American! Oh, it's great to hear a familiar accent!'

'Well, Christopher told me you're American, too, but you certainly don't sound like it.'

'That's what Americans always say. I've lived here a long time now, and I guess I sound English to American ears. Every Englishman can spot the Yank underpinnings, though, the minute I open my mouth. But whatever I sound like, I'm a real American – a Hoosier, in fact. Where are you from?'

We took our food and found a place to sit down for a good 'down home' talk, while Alan smilingly excused himself to mingle. I learned that Ruth, last name Williams, was a widow who, like me, had moved to England after her husband died. 'I've been living in a village in Kent, and it's nice enough, but I began to need real country. I'm from a farm in Vermont, and Kent seems awfully flat by comparison. Somebody told me I might like the Lakes, and boy, were they right! This place feels like home.'

'How long have you lived here?'

'Only since spring. I rented a house for a year, just to see how I'd like it, but I'm hoping to buy it, if they'll sell and if I can afford it. Housing is really steep here!'

'That's only to be expected in a famous beauty spot. But the other consideration is the atmosphere. A village can be awfully close-minded towards incomers. Have the villagers accepted you?'

'I worried about that, too, so I jumped into everything the minute I could. Joined the Women's Institute, got on the flower rota for the church, asked if I could get into a painting group and a book group – well, you get the idea. Christopher helped. He does a lot for the village, so he's known and loved all over. And when people figured out they could count on me for an extra hand, even with the dirty work, they soon stopped being snippy. You don't find willing volunteers under every rock, you know!'

I latched on to one particular. 'A painting group, you said. You paint, then?'

'Not at a professional level, but well enough to satisfy myself. Watercolours, mostly. The only trouble with trying to paint around here is that there's a paintable scene everywhere you look. A person could go crazy trying to choose!'

'I do know what you mean. This morning Christopher – he's an old friend of my husband's – took us on a tour of the area and I was wishing every minute that I had some paints to record the glorious views. And I can no more paint than my cat can!'

'Oh, you have a cat? I did, before I moved here, but I couldn't bring him when I didn't know where I was going to live or anything. A ginger tom. I miss him.' She sighed, and I was about to commiserate when an odd silence fell. I automatically looked for a clock, expecting the legendary twenty-past lull.

The clock read seven minutes to eight. But a couple had walked in through the door, apologizing for being late. They both looked to be in their thirties, but where he was burnished to a high gloss, handsome as all get-out and well aware of it, she looked, as the saying goes, rode hard and put away wet. His well-cut brown hair was as smooth as a thoroughbred's; hers was mousy, of no particular colour, and needed styling. His skin was bronzed; hers was pasty. He stood with a proud grace that made him seem taller than he really was; she slumped. Her dress was unflattering and too big for her; his suit and tie were impeccable.

The odd silence lasted no more than a second or two before conversations resumed, at perhaps a somewhat higher level than before.

'Who,' I asked my new friend, 'are they?'

'He's a would-be politician, and is of course God's gift to women. She is my best friend in this village. Excuse me.'

# THREE

I got a better introduction a few minutes later when Alan rejoined me. Their names, he told me, were Donald and Sarah Atkinson. He was an accountant who worked in Carlisle. 'I'm told he has political ambitions,' Alan said drily. 'Harold over there, the middle-aged chap you didn't take to, is the local king-maker. It's said he's grooming Mr Atkinson to stand for Parliament in the next general election. The incumbent is planning to retire, and it seems this constituency is a safe Lib Dem seat.'

I understand the parliamentary system about as well as I understand cricket, which is to say almost not at all. In either case, I think you have to be born and bred British to get it. But a safe seat? 'Does that mean that if they find a congenital idiot to stand as a Liberal Democrat, he's bound to get elected?'

'He or she, dear. Let's not be sexist.'

'I refuse to admit the possibility of an idiotic female politician. Well, in England, anyway. But am I right?'

'To a degree, yes.' He cast a long look across the room to where Mr Atkinson was talking to— What was his name? Brian, that was it. The exchange didn't seem to be cordial.

'Alan, what was the deal with that funny reaction when he and his wife got here? Is he so important that everyone must pay him silent obeisance?'

'I wouldn't say so, no. It didn't feel like respect to me.'

'Me neither. I'm going to go talk to my new American friend.'

She was deep in conversation with Donald's wimpy little wife, who was actually showing some signs of animation. I shouldn't have interrupted, but I was feeling nosy – no, 'interested in people' – and I badly wanted to know more about this glamorous wannabe politician. Who better to tell me than his wife and a relative stranger who plainly wasn't inclined to genuflect?

I drew near enough to make it obvious that I wanted to join them, and Ruth obligingly stepped aside.

'Oh, good! I wanted you two to meet. Sarah, this is Dorothy

– can't remember her last name. She's a transplanted American like me, only she's lived in England a long time. I don't know where you live?' She turned to me.

'Sherebury, down in Belleshire. I'm from Indiana originally. You live in Grasmere, Sarah?'

'For now.' Her voice was an apologetic murmur.

'Oh, yes, I heard your husband may be going into politics. I suppose that means you'd have to move to London, poor dear.'

'You don't like London?' queried Ruth.

'I love London but not to live in. Too noisy and busy. Three days is about my limit. What about you, Sarah?'

'I hate London.' Her voice had risen, though only a trifle, and she looked around guiltily. 'I suppose I shouldn't say that. Donald loves it.'

'Of course he does,' said Ruth. 'He can strut there, and look important, and get his picture taken. Even before he gets into the government, he's good at that stuff.' She spoke quietly, but her tone could have stripped paint.

Sarah giggled, then raised her hand to her mouth like an embarrassed child.

Ruth laughed in reply. 'You say anything you want, Sarah. You're a free woman.'

'No, I'm not,' she whispered. The laughter was gone, the slight ease wiped out of her face. 'I'm not free at all.'

This time it was Ruth who looked around, and none too soon. Donald came striding toward us. He addressed himself to me, cutting Ruth dead. 'We haven't met. My name is Atkinson.'

He extended a hand, which I was able to avoid shaking, as both my hands were occupied with food and drink. I smiled and shrugged. 'Dorothy Martin. I'm visiting Grasmere for a few days, with my husband. How do you do?' The formula allowed me also to avoid the usual 'so pleased to meet you'.

He didn't bother to smile in reply. I didn't live here. I could be of no use to him. Even while I'd been speaking, his eyes had been sweeping the room to see if anyone was worthier of his time.

Deciding on his next encounter, he took his wife by the arm, none too gently. 'Come, dear, Lilian was wanting to talk to you. Dora, I hope you and Mr Morgan enjoy your stay in the Lakes.'

'He'll never make a politician if he can't remember names,' I commented.

'Oh, he remembers useful people. I can't vote, so I don't matter, and the minute he found out you're not a constituent here, you don't matter, either. Even if you might be a voter somewhere down south.'

'I am, in fact. I became a British subject some time ago. It makes a lot of things easier. But Ruth, how on earth did such an odious man decide to get into politics? Who would vote for him?'

'I don't know. Sarah and I have become friends. Heaven knows she needs a friend, married to that man! He doesn't like our friendship. You saw how he hustled her away. Anyway, I've asked her that very question, and she didn't have an answer. If you ask me, I think he has some kind of hold on a lot of people, but I don't know what. I'd like to find out, because I'm trying to help Sarah work up the courage to leave him, and if his supporters can be chased away, she might be able to do it.'

'Couldn't she get the law involved? If he abuses her . . .' I was thinking about that firm, probably painful grip on her arm.

'He does, but not physically. Bruises would show. It's all emotional. And then of course there are his adulterous exploits. Lilian–oops! Here he comes again. He's going to try and brain-wash you now.'

His progress through the room was slow and deliberate, since he stopped to talk to everyone along the way, smiling and posturing with each couple or group. 'He looks like he's leading a parade,' I said. 'Or perhaps a coronation processional.'

Ruth choked on her drink. 'I love it!'

And then he was upon us, or rather me, since Ruth had rapidly taken herself off.

Atkinson watched her go with a slight frown. 'I hope, Ms Morgan, that you'll take what Ms Wilson says with several grains of salt. I'm sure she means well, but I'm afraid she's apt to get the wrong end of the stick. My wife is a lovely person, but her mind – well, she is not always strictly accurate in what she says. Her doctors haven't actually said she's suffering from early-onset Alzheimer's, but . . .' He spread his hands and arranged his face in a mask of brave resignation. 'I know you think I took her away somewhat abruptly, but I could tell by her face that she was off on one of her imaginary tales, and I wanted to soothe her and bring her back to reality. If possible.' He sighed dramatically. 'I'm sure you understand.'

'I do, and I have every sympathy.' I carefully didn't say for whom. 'If you'll excuse me, I believe my husband is trying to get my attention. Thank you for explaining.'

I moved away and tried to spot Alan. I needed to get away from the buffet table and the smell of food, as I was afraid I might soon be sick. Sick of one Donald Atkinson.

My husband materialized at my side, by some alchemy that he has practised for years. He always seems to know when I need his support. 'Had enough?' He knows my limited tolerance for cocktail parties.

'Not enough of the party quite yet, but definitely enough of Mr Donald Atkinson. The man is a— I can't think of a polite word for what he is. He just told me I shouldn't pay any attention to his wife, because she's crazy. Or words to that effect. By all that's holy, if she's crazy, I know who drove her to it! And a woman I just met implied something about him and the red-headed bombshell. Yuck!'

Alan led me to a quiet corner. 'Simmer down, dear. Your opinion seems to be general, from what I've picked up. To put it at the most charitable, the man is not well liked.'

'And that explains the reaction when he walked into the room. I'm willing to bet he came late on purpose, in order to make an entrance. And he sure did, but not the sort he intended. And yet he seems to think he's a shoo-in when he runs – stands, I mean – for Parliament. Alan, there has to be more to it than simple loyalty to the party. How can anyone who's cordially hated get himself elected?'

'I'm not sure the prevalent feeling goes as deep as hatred. That isn't the same as just intense dislike. And even if he is, as you put it, cordially hated, there could be a number of reasons for him to be fairly certain of political success. One could be pure pragmatism. The average Englishman approaches life pragmatically. What works? Not necessarily what is right or good or beautiful, but what's in my self-interest? If Atkinson looks like delivering what his constituency needs, they'll vote for him. I've known men who would have voted for the devil incarnate if he'd guarantee a living wage, or improve the health system, or control inflation.'

I thought about that for a while. 'I think I need a drink.'

After I'd had a sip or two of some watered-down bourbon and circulated among the other guests, I felt mellow enough to approach our host. 'You said we'd find most of your guests congenial,' I said with a smile, 'and I agree that most of them are delightful, but I think I've met the exception.'

'Well – certainly I like some people here better than others. But yes, there is one I can't seem to warm up to.'

'So why did you invite him to your party?'

'I didn't. I invited his wife Sarah, because I wanted to give her a chance to have a good long chat with Ruth. Donald came along uninvited.'

'I see. So he's a social boor as well. Does the man have any redeeming qualities at all?'

Christopher thought for a moment. 'He can be generous, when generosity will gain him something. He's contributed quite a lot to local charities. Making sure, of course, that he is properly recognized in the media.'

I sighed. 'He has money, then.'

'Sarah does. Or at least did.'

I finished my drink rather quickly and looked around for Alan.

Before we could make our escape, Ruth cornered me. She studied my face and said, 'I know. Me, too. But give me your phone number. I want to take you to lunch before you head off home.'

She pulled out her phone, and I recited the number. 'Soon,' she said. 'Tomorrow?'

'I don't know what Christopher might have in mind for us tomorrow, and Sunday he's taking us to the sports day. Monday?'

'Good. I'll call.'

We were outside before we remembered that Christopher had brought us here and could hardly leave his guests to run us home. I knew our hotel wasn't far away, but neither of us was quite sure how to get there. Uber seemed to be the answer, but before Alan could summon a car, the youngest guest came out, began to light a cigarette, and spotted us looking a trifle forlorn. 'Lost your car?' he asked with a smile.

'Lost our ride,' said Alan. 'Christopher drove us from our hotel, and we can't quite recall—'

'Ah. My car is right here, and I'd be happy to get you back to your digs. Which hotel?'

'The Inn, and it's very kind of you, but we don't want to impose—'

'Not to worry. I was just taking a smoke break, and this won't take long. No place in Grasmere is more than ten minutes from any other place. Hop in.'

As I might have expected, the young man – Kevin, was it? – drove a low-slung Jaguar that I had trouble folding into until Alan gave me a lift and a twist. It was comfortable enough once I was installed, and with the aid of Alan's strong arm, I didn't need a can opener to get out.

Kevin seemed inclined to stay and chat, but my husband knows me very well. 'Afraid we two oldies are for our bed,' he said with a smile. 'Thanks again for the lift, and off you go, back to the party!'

'Whew!' When the Jag was out of sight, I shook my head. I needed to get it clear of the unpleasantness of the evening.

'Would you like another drink?'

'Yes. But tea this time. Good, honest, English tea.'

Alan laughed and took my arm. 'That's my American transplant. The graft has taken. Very well, come into the lounge and I'll order tea.'

'Why,' I asked when I'd finished one restorative cup, 'did Christopher want us to come tonight?'

Alan shrugged. 'To introduce us to his friends, don't you think?'

'But they weren't all friends. Okay, maybe Donald crashed the party, but then there's that political guy, Harold, who is . . . well, odd, to say the least.'

'Dorothy, my love, this is a very small village, though it may not seem so in high tourist season. If you have a party, you really must invite virtually everyone you know, or risk offending anyone who isn't on the list. And most of them are interconnected. A works with B, and his wife is C's sister-in-law and niece to D, and so on. You know how everyone knows almost everyone in Sherebury, and we've easily ten times the population.'

'Okay, given all that, I still think he was up to something. He's a cop, after all, with his ear to the ground.'

'A retired cop – and from Cornwall. Where the ground noises are far different from those in the Lakes.'

'Hah! Who's always telling me that people are the same every-where, so crime is the same everywhere? I realize you know him well, and I don't, but I'm sure he was trying to hint at something, only I haven't the slightest idea what.'

'I knew him well many years ago. Your insights, seeing him from a fresh point of view, may be right. You can see through a brick wall as well as most, and much better than some, I admit. Now, why don't you have a little brandy in that second cup of tea, so you'll have some chance of sleeping tonight.'

# FOUR

Christopher called the next morning as we were just finishing an excellent breakfast. I don't know if heart trouble is more prevalent in England than anywhere else, but if it is, much of the blame should be assigned to the Full English Breakfast. I love every cholesterol-laden bite of it except for the baked beans, which seem to me to be both redundant and disgusting. But eggs, sausage, bacon, mushrooms, grilled tomatoes, fried bread – who couldn't go for that?

So I was just mopping up the last of my egg with a triangle of fried bread, and trying to ignore the guilt, when Alan's phone rang. He listened for a moment or two and then turned to me. 'Christopher wants to know if you'd be up for a visit to Beatrix Potter territory today.'

'I'd love it. I always did like Peter Rabbit and Mrs Tiggy-Winkle better than daffodils.'

So we were off on what was for me a tour of my childhood fantasies. Hill Top Farm, which Beatrix bought with her first royalties from *The Tale of Peter Rabbit*. Wray Castle, where she stayed for a summer at the age of sixteen, and met the man who was to become one of the founders of the National Trust. The Beatrix Potter Gallery in Hawkshead, where I had to be dragged away from the enchanting originals of the illustrations for her books, and the photos of some of the pets that inspired Peter and Benjamin and Jemima and the rest. We skipped lunch, after that enormous breakfast, but I was more than ready for my tea when Christopher drove us back to Grasmere. He insisted that the Wordsworth Hotel was the place to go, and anyway he had booked us a table. So we indulged in more delicious carbs and went back to our hotel for a nap and then a walk. No need for dinner!

We were early to bed Saturday night, so woke early Sunday morning to the sound of rain pattering against our window. There is no better lullaby. We turned over and went back to sleep for another hour. But, lullaby or not, there are certain aspects of old age that tend to wake one before one would prefer to get up. When I came back from the bathroom and Alan had run the same errand, I yawned and asked, 'When did Christopher say these sports are supposed to start?'

'Ten, he said. He planned to pick us up a little after half nine. But as the events are all out-of-doors . . .'

'Exactly. I'm prepared to go, if only to make him happy, but definitely not in the rain. Why don't you call him and tell him we'd prefer to go to church this morning and then go later if the rain lets up?'

It was a good plan. We had a light breakfast to make up for yesterday's indulgences, enjoyed the church service and went out into a world that sparkled with raindrops under a clear sky. The sun was somewhat watery and tenuous, but it looked as though it intended to stick around for a while.

We had wanted to drive to the sports day on our own, so we could leave if I got bored, but Christopher explained that parking would be at a premium, and he'd already bought our tickets, so I resigned myself to sticking it out no matter what. And to my considerable surprise it proved to be fascinating.

The first event we watched was the wrestling. Forgetting what Christopher had said, I had in my head a disgusting image of large sweaty men pretending to attempt murder. What I saw, first, was a pair of ten-year-old girls, arms clasped around each other's head and shoulders, trying not to slip on the wet grass as each struggled to push the other down. When one of the pair hit the ground, that was the end of the encounter. The winner brushed the loser off and they went off amicably to let the next pair contend.

When that palled, we went to the next ring to watch the dog show. Again there were images in my head: Crufts or Westminster, highly trained, highly pedigreed dogs, groomed to within an inch of their lives, competing for coveted prizes, the dogs and owners both seeming to look down their aristocratic noses at animals kept as mere pets. Again, Grasmere was unique. There were various classes.

The puppies were just finishing when we sat down on the rather damp bleachers, and the winning cocker spaniel exuberantly led his owners back to seats next to us. I don't remember which class came next, but pretty soon the children's class was up. Children as in handlers, that is. The dogs were adults and plainly keeping an eye on their young owners. One little boy was leading a dog easily twice his weight, or else the dog was leading him. Whoever was in charge, the dog went through his paces very nicely, and the pair were warmly applauded when they took a prize. Of course, in that class, all the exhibitors took prizes!

'This is fun!' I said to Alan, and Christopher manfully refrained from *I told you so*.

Mine were probably not the only teary eyes in the crowd when the rescue dogs were shown. Every one of these creatures had a horror story to tell, and all were told. The ones who had been abandoned. The ones who had belonged to hoarders, half-starved, diseased, kept in tiny cages, even abused. The ones from puppy farms. The only thing that kept me from outright bawling was that these were the lucky ones. They had been rescued and nursed back to health and now lived with loving families. I clapped for all of them until my hands hurt.

I was feeling a bit peckish by that time, so Alan went in search of sustenance and came back with hamburgers and donuts, which we munched while watching a display of falconry. I fell in love with raptors years ago when Alan and I visited the marvellous raptor centre on Vancouver Island in British Columbia. My favourites will always be the magnificent bald eagles, but all raptors are amazing, and this Cooper's hawk was fascinating to watch.

First the handler simply gave a glove to someone from the audience and flew the bird to him, changing the 'catcher' every time and increasing the distance with every flight. The bird knew none of these people except its handler, but did exactly as it was told, and returned home perfectly.

Then he asked two people to come into the field and form an arch by facing each other a few feet apart and joining their hands overhead, between the handler and the person at the other end of the flight. The hawk never faltered but swooped under the arch to get to its destination and back. Another couple joined the first. Still no problem. More couples, no problem. Finally the handler asked everyone who wanted to come and form arches. By the end there were at least twenty couples, making a tunnel probably forty feet long for the bird to fly through. Which it did without skipping a beat, garnering huge applause.

'And they talk about bird brains,' I commented. 'I've known lots of people not nearly as smart as that bird.'

'Or as well trained,' said Alan the cop – feelingly.

The afternoon was well advanced, and I was getting tired, but Christopher said we really needed to watch the last of the fell races. The fell, it turned out, was the large, steep hill – almost a mountain – at the edge of the field. The racers were to run up the hill then back down, a relatively short but arduous run. Several groups, in various classes (by age) had already finished when we turned our attention to them, but the culminating race of the day was about to begin. 'The senior guides,' I read in the programme, and looked around for a flock of grey heads in running shorts.

'Senior, in this case, means over eighteen,' Christopher explained. 'Though there are some wrinklies in the group. And the rules are different for the seniors. They run up the same track as everyone else, but then they go farther up and into the wooded area, and back down over there.' He pointed. 'It's a real endurance test. The best time ever recorded is twelve minutes and twenty-one seconds, back in 1978, so of course some of the runners are keen to break that.'

I looked at the course. 'I couldn't do it at all, even at a walk, but if I tried it, my time would be counted in hours. Are there prizes?'

Christopher consulted his programme. 'One hundred and sixty-five pounds to the winning man and to the winning woman. And five hundred pounds to anyone who breaks the old record.'

'Nice,' I said.

'Yes, nice, but chicken feed compared to the real money changing hands. This is a famous race, with competitors and audience from all over the kingdom, and even abroad. You, Dorothy, as an American, might find it hard to believe the betting that goes on.'

I laughed a little ruefully. 'I have over the years learned that an Englishman will bet on anything, so it doesn't surprise me that they'll bet on a famous race. Oh, look. They must be almost ready to start. And – Alan, isn't that—?'

It was. Our least-favourite fellow guest from Christopher's party was warming up, jogging in place and stretching, showing off excellent legs and impressive delts in his brief running gear, and smiling his conceited smile at the crowd.

'I hope he trips and rolls all the way down the hill and makes a fool of himself!' I said in a vicious whisper.

'I'll second that,' said a voice behind me, equally soft, equally venomous. I turned to see my new American friend Ruth, Donald's wife Sarah beside her. Sarah, to my surprise, was giggling into her hand.

'Now, ladies,' Alan chided, but the twinkle in his eye was clearly visible. 'It's Sunday. Where's your Christian spirit?'

'Shall I quote some Psalms that express the same sentiment, only in much stronger terms?' I retorted. 'A public humiliation would do that man a lot of good, and you know it as well as I do. Sarah, I don't know if you remember me – Dorothy Martin. We met at Christopher's party. Oh, they're off!'

The grass was still damp and somewhat slippery, which slowed the pace. One man fell halfway up the slope, but recovered instantly and charged ahead. 'Not Donald, sad to say,' Ruth commented.

'Don't despair. It could still happen. Gosh, look at that tall guy leading the pack, number forty-seven. He has to be sixty at least, but look at him go!' I forbore to mention Donald, who wasn't far behind the front runner. I didn't want to call attention to his maddening skill.

It wasn't long before the first ten or twelve runners disappeared into the trees.

'It'll be a little while before we see them again,' said Christopher, the old hand. (Having attended exactly one previous sports day.) 'Does anyone want a beer? Or whatever?'

Alan thanked him and chose beer. The sun had strengthened; the air was growing warm and muggy and bringing on a thirst that only one thing could quench, for me. 'I'll have water, please. Sparkling if they have it.' I knew better than to ask for ice. Ruth and Sarah opted for the same.

By the time Christopher got back, the last few runners were well away from the starting pole. They were slower than the rest, loping easily. With no chance at the prize, they seemed content simply to enjoy the exercise and feel the pride of finishing eventually.

And there came the winner, that same tall, lanky, grey-haired man, still running well – and fast! A couple more men, and one woman, were close behind him, but not close enough to steal the lead. He passed the end marker to a round of applause, slowed to acknowledge it, and accepted the towel someone gave him. He was obviously tired but not exhausted.

'What must it be like to be so fit at that age,' I marvelled.

'There was a time,' Alan began, and I grinned.

'You were in very good shape when we married,' I retorted, 'but I'll bet you never in your life could run like that. Even chasing a crook!'

He and Christopher exchanged glances and fell about with laughter but wouldn't share the joke.

The second- and third-place runners accepted their applause, and then stayed with the winner to welcome in the slower ones as they came trotting in. There was no visible 'I'm a winner and you're not' but instead a spirit of camaraderie.

'I can't imagine American athletes behaving like that,' I commented to Ruth. 'The winners would be crowing and ignoring the rest. This kind of good sportsmanship seems to me to be entirely English. One of the reasons I love this country so much.' I looked back at the hill, down which the last few stragglers were drifting, at a walk. 'They're totally beat but congratulating themselves on making it to the end. As well they might!'

'Christopher,' said Alan in an odd tone of voice, 'I don't remember seeing Atkinson come in. Did I simply miss him?'

'If you did, so did I. Number fifty-four, wasn't he? I'll just check with the judges.'

I thought of my silly jibe at the beginning of the race and began to feel cold, remembering that old saying: You better watch what you hope for; it might come true.

Christopher returned, a worried frown on his face. 'No. He hasn't come in. I'm wondering if he could have sprained an ankle or something.'

I glanced at Sarah, pale and clinging to her friend. 'Surely someone would have seen him if he fell. Some of the other runners?'

'The trees are fairly dense over part of the run. If he somehow got separated from the others, he could have had an accident out of view of witnesses.'

'Don't they have watchers along the way?' Alan was becoming more and more concerned.

'Yes, of course they do, and I think someone's going up to check with them right now. Except— No, here they come. The last of the runners have come down, so the watchers have given up their posts.'

'But the last of the runners has *not* come down!' Sarah startled me with the urgency in her voice. 'Donald is still up there! Something's happened to him! I'm going up to see!'

'No, you're not.' Ruth grabbed her arm. I was reminded of Donald's gesture. Ruth was much gentler but just as determined. 'Someone needs to check, but not you. You couldn't get halfway up that hill. Christopher, can't they send someone up in a golf cart or something like that? You're a policeman; do something!'

Alan stepped in. He has a commanding presence when he wants to. People listen. 'Ruth, we're neither of us acting policemen anymore, but yes, we can do something. Stay put. Dorothy, take care of them.'

And the two of them, looking oddly official even in their summer holiday clothes, strode off to speak with the race organisers.

Sarah refused to sit down. She was strung tight as wire.

I mouthed 'Tea?' at Ruth, who nodded. Myself, I thought brandy might be more effective, but I doubted any was available on the premises. I didn't know where to find tea, either, but a kindly man who had heard our conversation came up and volunteered to get some for all of us.

As the day grew old, the clouds set in again, and there was now a distinct chill. Hot tea helped warm our bodies. Our feelings were another matter.

The man lingered after he brought us our tea. Our gazes were fixed on the field where the race began, watching as men talked and gestured. It seemed to take an hour, but I suppose it was only a few minutes before Alan came back to us.

'A crew will go up there and search, and they've called the mountain rescue dogs to help. We're going to be here a while,

I'm afraid. Christopher gave me his car key, so you can at least sit in it and be warm.'

'Sir, are these ladies your family?' The kindly man put out his hand for Alan to shake. 'It's easy to see something has gone wrong, but need they stay here? I'd be happy to drive them to a hotel, or your home, or wherever you say.'

Alan can size up people at a glance. He sighed in relief. 'That's an excellent suggestion, sir, and I'm grateful for the offer. Only one of these ladies is mine, so to speak, but the other two are friends. I don't live in this part of the country, but if you could take them all to my hotel, my wife would make them comfortable until I can join them.'

'No!' said Sarah. 'I'm not leaving till they find him.' Her voice was low but determined.

'Yes, you are.' Ruth again took charge. 'I live in a small flat, or I'd offer, but the hotel is obviously the best place. Room to be private, all amenities, and comfortable beds, if it comes to that. Sarah, there's no point in staying here. We're as close as our phones; they'll let us know as soon as anything happens. Thank you, sir. Lead the way.'

# FIVE

S arah had been conditioned by Donald to follow orders, so although she didn't want to leave the scene of his disappearance, she went obediently to the car with Ruth and me. She sat tense and silent, but she got out at the hotel and went up to my room with never a complaint.

I had forgotten to get the room key card from Alan, but the efficient Ruth had remembered. I called room service at once, ordering tea and scones and a small bottle of brandy. Sarah wasn't the only one who needed a little liquid comfort.

I made sure she didn't see me pour the tiny tot into her tea. She was so thin, and (I surmised) so unaccustomed to alcohol that it took only that little bit to loosen her muscles – and her tongue.

'It's very good of you, Mrs— I'm sorry, I can't remember your name.'

'Just call me Dorothy,' I began, but she burbled on in her whispery voice.

'Very good of you to take me in, but I don't need looking after, and really I'd much rather be there when they find Donald and bring him down the hill. He'll be annoyed with me for leaving, and if he's somehow been hurt, he'll need me to tend to him.' She stood. 'I think I'd better—'

'Sit, love,' Ruth commanded. 'The men and dogs looking for Donald are much better able to find him and treat what ails him than we are. Have another cup of tea.'

I poured her a second cup, with a little more artificial courage, and stronger ones for Ruth and myself. With a nasty suspicion about what those searchers might find, I had a feeling Ruth and I might shortly need considerable help dealing with Sarah.

'You don't understand. He needs me. Ruth, I know you think he bullies me, and maybe he does sometimes, but he'd be lost without me. I'm the only one he can depend on to be on his side, always. He has enemies, you know, people who are jealous of his looks and his accomplishments and his easy way with women. Oh, I know I'm not his only woman, but I'm the one he comes back to in the end.'

She went on praising him and saying, over and over again, how important to him she knew she was. Ruth and I exchanged raised eyebrows now and then, but we let her talk. She needed to believe what she was saying, and who knew? There might even be a grain of truth in it. Donald wouldn't be the first man to hide profound insecurity under a brash façade.

The dreary trickle of words stopped abruptly when my phone rang. Sarah clasped her hands tightly in what looked almost like prayer. Her knuckles were white.

I listened while Alan gave me the news I'd expected – and dreaded. I nodded once or twice, forgetting he couldn't see me, said something, and clicked the phone off, wishing desperately that I didn't have to be the one to say the words. I caught Ruth's eye; she sat down next to Sarah, ready to offer a hand or an arm as needed.

I took a deep breath. There was no way to make it easy, so I made it quick. 'I'm sorry, Sarah. It's bad news. Your husband is dead. They're bringing him here, so you can see him and say goodbye.'

'No,' she said quietly. 'No, you didn't hear properly. No, Donald can't be dead. People like him don't die. No. No. *No-oo*!' The words turned to a wail and finally the tears started.

Alan and Christopher brought a doctor with them. Donald's body had been removed to a mortuary van. They let Sarah see him, and then the doctor gave her a sedative before escorting her to Ruth's apartment, as no one wanted her to be alone. I assumed a nurse would be found soon, but at the moment I just wanted to know what had happened. Christopher had left with the body and the official police, so Alan and I were finally alone.

Alan eyed what was left of the brandy, queried me with raised eyebrows and, when I shook my head, poured it out for himself into a spare teacup. I waited.

'It was grim, Dorothy. None of the watchers had seen anything unusual; nor had the rest of the runners, or so they said. That meant the search team, men and dogs, had to explore every inch of the small wood. It's pretty dense, and a small tarn lies the other side of the trees. What with the searchers and their dogs, there was no hope of preserving footprints or that sort of thing, but in any case, no signs of traffic off the path were found. The searchers were looking for signs, of course, hoping to find a trail to follow, but the leaf mould is thick and wouldn't show prints well.'

'So it was the dogs that found him.'

'Yes, they traced his scent to the tarn. He was right at the edge. The mud there showed that he'd tripped and fallen, face down, and then couldn't get out and save himself.' Alan stopped.

I gave him a long look. 'And that's it? A young man in perfect condition wanders away from the race he'd probably hoped to win, stumbles and falls into an inch or two of water, and can't save himself from drowning. Presumably he didn't even cry out when he fell, or someone would have heard and gone to his rescue. I flat out don't believe it, and neither do you.'

'No, I don't. But that's what happened. If there'd been any kind of scuffle near the pond, the leaf mould would have been disturbed. It wasn't. There's not the slightest evidence that he was pushed into that water.'

'Then he had a seizure or a heart attack or something that made him fall.'

'That's actually what we're all thinking. *We* being Christopher and I and the local police. There'll be an autopsy, of course, and we're hoping the coroner will be able to determine the cause of death.'

'Well, I could tell them that! He was found face down in the water. Duh!'

Alan sighed. 'We don't think he drowned.'

'You mean – he was dead before he went into the water?'

'Probably. Dorothy, we don't know anything at all yet, and it's been a very long day. I propose we order a small meal from room service and then go to bed. Tomorrow, as Scarlett famously said—'

'Is another day. Sounds good to me. But oh, poor Sarah!'

Sarah, predictably, was first in my thoughts upon awakening in the morning. It was a beautiful day, the sort that makes getting up a joy, even at my age.

'I wonder if she managed to get any sleep at all,' I said while Alan made coffee.

He didn't have to ask who. 'I'm sure she did. The doctor said he was giving her a strong sedative.'

'Yes, but that's not the same as real sleep. That poor woman! She doesn't have anyone to dictate her every moment. She's going to fall apart.'

'No, she isn't. She has her friend Ruth, who is just as bossy as Donald.'

'But she's a benevolent dictator. There's a difference.'

'Agreed. But it's still a case of one dominant personality and one weak one. I agree Sarah will need someone to lean on for these first difficult weeks, but in time, she's going to have to stand on her own feet and make her own decisions, and begin to realize how fortunate she is.'

'Ruth will certainly help with that! She can't stand Donald. Couldn't, I mean.'

'His detractors form a large club. If the assortment at that party the other night is any indication, he hadn't one friend in the village.'

'The red-headed bombshell?'

'I don't know that I'd describe their probable relationship as precisely friendly.'

'Aha! So you drew the same uncharitable conclusion.'

'Didn't take much drawing, did it?'

His phone rang. I looked at the bedside clock. 'That'll be Christopher. Nobody else would be calling before eight.'

But it wasn't. Alan answered and then turned the phone over to me. 'Ruth.'

'I'm sorry, Dorothy, I misplaced your phone number, but I suppose Alan or Christopher might be the one to help, anyway. I'm in a bit of a dither. Sarah is very insistent that she wants to go back home, but she doesn't have a house key and the police have everything that was in Donald's pockets. Do you have any idea how she could go about getting his key?'

I snorted. 'Of course she wouldn't have one. Mr In-Command would have kept all the keys to himself. And you're right. She'll have to go through the police, and Alan and Christopher would both know the best way to do that. Here you are.'

I handed the phone back to Alan, who said he'd take care of it, right away. They made arrangements, and then Alan said, 'Do you think she'll be all right by herself? She was quite upset last night.'

I didn't hear her reply, of course, but Alan nodded several times and said, 'Good. I think that's wise. We'll see you soon.'

He clicked off. 'Ruth is bringing Sarah here. I'm going to the police to get Donald's keys.'

'Will they give them to you?'

'I think so. In a village this size, the words "chief constable" carry a little clout, even with "retired" in the title. It may take a little while, though. When the women get here, try to get Sarah to eat some breakfast, if Ruth hasn't already done that.' He dressed hurriedly and sketchily and flew out the door.

I took a quick shower, pulled on some clothes, and got downstairs in time to meet Ruth and Sarah just coming in.

Sarah always looked so woebegone that it didn't seem she could look much more miserable. Tear stains on her cheeks and red eyes were the only differences I noted.

I chose matter-of-fact over bright and cheery, thinking the nanny treatment might be the last straw. 'Oh, good,' I said. 'Glad you're here. I was just about to get myself some breakfast. They do an excellent spread here. It's this way.'

Someone was showing her what to do, and she obeyed, as usual. I ordered for her, choosing a small but healthy selection, with (I hoped) nothing that she absolutely couldn't face. A boiled egg and toast and marmalade, with fruit and tea, ought to give her a little fuel to face what was bound to be a terrible day.

And I refused to talk about her husband. Ruth picked up my cue, and we babbled on about our American backgrounds, why we moved to England, what we loved about our new home. I thought it was perhaps safe to mention our deep sorrow when the Queen died, just about a year ago, and how the country reacted, and whether we thought King Charles was going to do a good job.

'I'm sorry,' I said with a little giggle, 'but I can never say "King Charles" without thinking of the adorable little spaniels.' That brought a momentary smile to Sarah's face.

We were beginning to run out of innocuous conversation when

Alan appeared, to my great relief, a keyring in his hand. 'Success,' he said. 'They took a bit of convincing, but they acknowledged that you needed to get into your own house. You'll want to get fresh clothes, for one thing.'

'I want to live there,' Sarah said flatly. 'It's my house, not Donald's. I have a right.'

That was the first inkling that a backbone lurked there somewhere, and I was delighted.

Alan's face clouded. 'I'm afraid the police don't want you to live there just yet.'

'They can't stop me. It's my house,' she repeated. Her quiet voice was nonetheless determined.

'No one's questioning that, Mrs Atkinson, but it's not a good idea for you to be alone just now.' He saw Ruth open her mouth to speak and shook his head. 'I'm sure your friends will want to help, but for the time being, you'll be better off with skilled care.'

'I don't need a nurse, or whatever you're talking about. I need my home.'

I knew that weak people can sometimes be amazingly stubborn. 'But, Sarah,' I began, as Ruth said, 'My dear—'

Alan overrode both of us. 'I hoped I wouldn't have to say this, Mrs Atkinson, but the fact is, the police are not satisfied about the way your husband died, and until they know, they want to make sure you're safe.'

'What do you mean? He fell in the tarn and drowned.'

'Yes.' He looked at me and shook his head ever so slightly. 'The question is, *why* did he fall in the tarn? We've talked to his doctor. He was in excellent health. He was taking no medication that could have made him dizzy. No one has ever seen him drink to excess, and in fact he had drunk nothing but sparkling water since breakfast yesterday.'

'He hated beer. He hated most alcohol. We never had any in the house. I don't understand. Why do you think I might not be safe?'

'Until we're sure that Mr Atkinson was not . . . assisted to his death, we can't be sure that you are not also under threat.'

It must have sounded as lame to Sarah as to me. She shook her head. 'I don't see how I could be. If you're saying that my husband was murdered, I think that's nonsense. I know that some people, jealous people, didn't like Donald. He was a success in business. He was a very handsome man. He was going to be a great success in Parliament. But jealousy doesn't make someone kill. And it doesn't make someone hunt down a wife. I want to go home.'

Ruth was tired of the fencing. She knew as well as I did why the cops didn't want Sarah to go home, at least not for a while. 'Sarah, there's a possibility that Donald took something, maybe by accident. I have no idea what. Maybe just something to make him drowsy, so he'd stumble and fall, and it just happened to be into the water. The point is, the police want to know where that whatever-it-was came from. If it was from your house, they want to get rid of it before you fall victim to it yourself. So they need to search the place, and that's a whole lot easier to do with you not there. So would you rather come back home with me for a few hours, or get a room for the two of us here? Either way, I'm not leaving you alone until I'm sure you can cope.'

Sarah was still not firing on all cylinders, but she could understand that argument. 'Well – whichever you think is best. But I'll need some things from home.'

Alan said he'd take her home to fetch what she needed, and the two of them went off. She still wasn't happy, but she accepted what Ruth had told her.

'And it's almost true,' I commented after they'd gone. 'You just left out who they think might have administered whatever it was.'

She snorted. 'The idea is absurd. That poor woman would never have the guts to kill anyone, let alone plan something elaborate. And she adored him.'

'Even though she knew he wasn't faithful to her.'

'Even so. She had decided he was so wonderful, and she was so insignificant, he was entitled to other women.'

'Women, plural?'

'Good Lord, yes. At least three, just since I've lived here. Those women's groups I'm involved in don't just sit and knit in silence, you know.'

'So his fun and games are common knowledge in the village? I can't imagine Sarah enjoyed that.'

'They never talked about it in front of her, the few times she was ever with them. He didn't let her off the chain much. No hobbies, no charities, nothing to take her away from her full-time job of looking after him and his house.'

I suddenly remembered something. 'She said this morning that it was her house. Slip of the tongue? Hers because she lived there?'

'No, it actually is hers. She's the one with the money. She and I have talked quite a lot, you know. The one thing he would let her do was church work.'

'Because it reflected well on him.' I made a face.

'Of course. What other reason did she have for existing? Anyway, she sometimes does the flowers, and so do I, so we could chat now and then. And she sings in the choir, a nice alto. Little by little, I've wormed my way into her confidence. Her father was a businessman and left her a pile of money when he died young. She's spent almost none of it, because she's a thrifty little thing and she had some money of her own. She had a good job, secretary to a solicitor here in the village. But of course Big D made her quit that when she married him.'

'Why *did* she marry him? She must have been really pretty when she was younger. She has good bones. Surely there must have been other men.'

Ruth made an exasperated shrug. 'Who knows? Yes, she was beautiful, actually. I've seen her wedding pictures. A porcelain doll, fragile and lovely, with long golden hair. Her money wasn't the only attraction, though for Donald I'm sure it was the primary one. I'm reading between the lines here, but I think he simply went after her full speed ahead, using all his weapons. And they're considerable, let me tell you. I don't like him. Didn't, I should say. But I can see that he has glamour when he cares to use it. Those looks that anyone in Hollywood would kill for— Oh dear. I didn't mean to say that. Terrible taste, under the circumstances.'

'Yes, I could see it, too. But so shallow. He could probably act gallant, but I'm willing to bet there was only one person he ever cared about in his whole life.'

'No bet. I don't throw away money. Yes, he was the complete egotist. And maybe that's why he's dead.'

# SIX

When Alan walked in with a small suitcase and Sarah, we had to stop talking. There was still so much I wanted to know, but it would have to wait. Alan left us, saying he had some errands to run. Maybe Sarah took that at face value. Ruth and I were pretty sure he was going to join the local cops in searching Sarah's house. A local force can be very protective of its territory, but when an experienced man with no official ties offers his services, gratis, they're not apt to turn him down.

So I went about getting adjoining rooms for Sarah and Ruth, for one night with the option of extending the stay. I proffered my credit card, but Sarah saw and insisted on using her own. I was about to argue when I remembered that she 'had money' and let her have her way.

Now the question was how to spend the rest of the day. A meal is a good way to kill an hour or so, but it wasn't even close to lunchtime. Sarah, I was sure, would want to talk about Donald, his sterling qualities and his so-impossible death. Women can always go shopping, but except for touristy gift shops, there wasn't much scope for that in tiny Grasmere, which one website had described as 'wholly given over to the tourist industry'.

It was Ruth who had the inspiration. 'It's such a beautiful day,' she said. 'Why don't we walk over to St Oswald's? It's well worth seeing.'

'Alan and I went to church there yesterday, but we were eager to get to the sports day, so we didn't spend much time there.'

'Oh, then Sarah and I can show you around. Well, mostly Sarah, as I'm an incomer. She's the expert.'

That put a little brightness in Sarah's eyes. 'Not an expert, but I do love the church. I've spent a lot of time there over the years.'

A bright oasis in the grey wilderness of marriage to Donald, I thought. I was glad she'd had at least those moments of joy.

Maybe now she could take control of her life and find some measure of happiness.

I worried, as we walked, whether there would be lots of other church workers there, people who would want to corner Sarah and talk. I should have had more faith in English restraint. There were people in the church, certainly, who knew Sarah and greeted her with nods and smiles, but they offered no fulsome sympathy, certainly no painful curiosity, just friendliness. *We're here if you need us*, their manner seemed to say, *but we won't bother you.* They went about their business, and Sarah led us around the church.

The first thing to strike a visitor was the very peculiar roof, which had a lopsided look to it. Sarah explained the historical reasons for the re-roofing which caused the asymmetry and did so in such a clear, sympathetic way that I was immediately aware of two things: just how much she loved the place and how talented she was as a narrator. I picked up a leaflet about the church. She wasn't reciting something she had memorized. She gave us the same facts, but burnished by her love and spoken in her lovely, quiet voice, the facts shone with life.

It was the same with every feature of the church. The beautifully carved pulpit. The needlepoint kneelers, done by members of the congregation, some of whom had even signed and dated them. The clear glass east window, designed to give a view of the fells. On my own, I would have skimmed the leaflet, been bored, and forgotten everything five minutes later. With Sarah explaining, I began to fall in love with her church, too.

We worked our way back from the chancel to the font and thence to the inevitable gift shop, where I bought up every booklet and souvenir on offer, so enamoured had I become of the place. Somewhat apologetically, Sarah pointed out the new computer screen that one could use for donations to any one of a number of church projects, including the organ appeal. I could have dropped a two-pound coin into the nearby box, but I was so enchanted with the church, as well as with the notion of electronic processing of contributions to a thirteenth-century church, that I pulled out my credit card and keyed in a reckless amount. Alan would understand.

That had taken us around to lunchtime, so we peeked into

several restaurants along our way, but finding them too crowded
went back to the hotel – where, to my joy, Alan was waiting for
us.

He looked at the bulging bag I was carrying and raised his
eyebrows. 'I've been to church, love,' I said, and snickered.

'And collected a bagful of grace, it appears.'

'And worked up a healthy appetite. Let's find a table for lunch.'

We had to wait for a few minutes, and Ruth decided to leave
us to it. 'I'm going home for my jammies,' she said, giving us
a look that made it plain she was handing over the care and
feeding of Sarah to Alan and me for a while. 'Order me a dessert.
I'll be back in half an hour or so.'

'So what is actually in that bag, my dear?'

'Books and cards and pictures and everything I could find
about St Oswald's. Alan, it is the most amazing place! Sarah
took Ruth and me on a tour this morning, and the things she
doesn't know about that church never happened, anyway. She got
me so fascinated, I bought out the shop. I've never had such a
wonderful guide, and, Sarah, I'm not just saying that. You have
a real gift for storytelling – and such a beautiful voice!' When
she could be heard. I didn't voice that thought. 'I'm sure you
must have done some acting at some point in your life.'

There was actually some colour in her cheeks. 'Oh, nothing
to speak of. I was in one or two plays in school, but that was a
long time ago.'

'Titania, maybe?' *Midsummer Night's Dream* is an almost
obligatory production in English schools, and her fragile beauty
would have been just right for the Queen of the Fairies.

She nodded, looking at her lap.

'And Juliet?' That was Alan's suggestion, and Sarah actually
smiled.

'Scenes from,' she said. 'The whole play was thought to be
unsuitable for pupils our age.'

I laughed. 'Given that it's about a pair of kids just about the
age you were when you played in it, that's a judgement worthy
of Puritan Americans. But it does get a bit steamy, I admit. The
point, though, is that you were a star actress at your school. Did
you never pursue it after that?' I was skating on some thin ice
now, delving into her past. Alan frowned at me, but I wanted her

to hark back to the days when she was a whole person, before she was swallowed whole by a python named Donald.

'I'd have liked to go to drama school, but my parents thought it unwise. Dad was in business and didn't have much time for the arts. He wanted me either to marry well, or failing that to get into a good solid profession that would keep me secure. I didn't want to do that, so I knew I'd have to come up with the tuition myself. I wasn't anything like good enough to win a scholarship, so I thought I could get a job, just any job, and save up enough for a good drama school, if not RADA. But then Mum— Well, she'd never been strong, and she just . . . faded away.'

'Oh, Sarah, I'm so sorry! I suppose you had to stay home like a dutiful daughter and look after Papa.'

'No, not quite. He wasn't that Victorian. He cared a lot about me, but he didn't think much of my ability to deal with the world. No, he found a job for me in a law firm here in Grasmere, a good job with prospects. I took it to make him happy, but it wasn't awful, and I did rather well.' She fell silent.

'Ruth told me your father died young,' I said gently.

'Yes, and left me all his money. All of a sudden, I was a wealthy orphan. And that was when I met Donald, and he just swept me off my feet. Every girl in town would have liked to marry him, so young and handsome and charming – and he chose me. I couldn't believe my luck. I still can't. And he stayed with me, even though I'm not pretty anymore. Mr Martin, what happened to him? Why did he die?' Her face twisted, and she blinked back tears.

Alan didn't correct his name. We're both accustomed to people's confusion, and now certainly wasn't the time to deal with it. 'We don't yet know that, Mrs Atkinson. The police have checked out your house for possible dangers and so far haven't found anything suspicious, but since you're settled in here, we'd like you to wait until tomorrow to go home, just to be sure. I would like to ask you a question or two, though, unless you'd rather wait until you've had a meal and a rest.'

'No. Now.'

'Very well. The police were looking particularly for any medicine that might have caused an unusual reaction in your husband.

Apart from two over-the-counter painkillers, we found no medications at all. Did neither of you use any prescribed drugs?'

'No. We're very healthy. We were.' Her breath caught, but she steadied herself. 'I do get headaches quite often, but I take only aspirin and ibuprofen. Donald doesn't believe in strong drugs.'

*So he made you suffer,* I thought angrily, *when there are drugs that are very effective in relieving pain. Some can even prevent serious headaches.*

I wondered if perhaps the best preventive was the death of her tormentor.

Sarah continued. 'Donald never liked to admit that anything might be wrong with him. He developed a bad rash a couple of weeks ago, we think from a plant someone gave him, and I wanted him to see a doctor, but he refused. He said it was nothing. It wasn't nothing. It started on his arm, but then when he kept pawing at it, he got it on one hand and spread it all over. I insisted then, and the doctor told him Boots had some ointment called Anthisan that would help. I got some, and it did make him itch less.'

'Ointment?' said Alan. 'I don't believe they found any ointment at your house.' His ears didn't prick up noticeably, but I could see he was on high alert.

'Oh, no, he kept it in his pocket, in case he needed it during the day. He didn't want anyone at the office to see him scratching. The places he couldn't easily reach, like the middle of his back, were getting really nasty, like blisters. I knew he should see the doctor again, but he hated me to nag about things like that. He really hated that he had to let someone help him with the ointment in the hard-to-reach places, too.'

Alan made a note. 'I think that's all for now, Mrs Atkinson. Later on—'

'Do call me Sarah. I've never liked Donald's name. It's so long and clumsy. I was a Scott, and I wish I could have kept my own name.'

'That's what I did,' I put in, glad of the chance to set the record straight. 'At least, Martin was the name of my first husband, and when Alan and I married, I decided to keep it. It had been my name for forty-odd years, after all, and Nesbitt just didn't seem to fit.'

'Oh, then I got it wrong. I'm so sorry, Mr Nesbitt.'

'How could you know? Doesn't worry me. As I was saying, when we know more, I'll want to talk to you again, but meantime get some rest. Try not to worry too much. I know you're shocked and saddened, but things really will get better with time. Dorothy and I both lost our first spouses, so we can understand the pain.'

She said nothing to that, nor did she try to eat any of the meal we ordered for her.


Alan finished his meal in a hurry and took off again. We had no chance to talk, but I knew his first task would be to tell the official police about a tube of ointment that should have been somewhere in Donald's clothing. That it hadn't been, I was pretty sure, or Alan would have commented, 'Oh, so that's what it was,' or words to that effect. It would have to be found. A good many substances can be absorbed through the skin, especially when the skin is abraded or blistered.

Ruth came back for her dessert and managed to persuade Sarah to share it with her. Not the healthiest sort of meal, but at least it got some sugar into her bloodstream. Then they went up to their rooms where Ruth, I felt sure, would try to talk Sarah into a nap. Me, I didn't need any persuading. Last night's sleep had been fitful and too short. I was quite sure there were a good many things I ought to be doing, but I kicked off my shoes, and sank into the pillows and was out in seconds.

I slept for about an hour, longer than the experts say one should. The experts are not familiar with my metabolism. I woke up refreshed and ready to tackle whatever came along. The first thing that came to mind was that I needed to know a lot more about the guests at Christopher's party. Well, he'd given me his number too, in case I needed it for any reason, so I called. It went to voicemail.

That was the way of life these days. Modern life also provides very few phone books, in which one used to be able to look up someone's address, but there are ways to track someone down. I tidied my hair, washed my face, and went down to the front desk, making up a good story on the way.

The lobby was quiet during this interval between check-out

and check-in time. I approached the clerk, who was reading a magazine and looked bored.

'I hope you can help me,' I said, using my best helpless-American persona. 'I wanted to visit a friend, but I've misplaced his address and he's not answering his phone. At home, I could use a city directory to find him, but I don't know if you even have such a thing here.'

'We do have an old phone book, if that's any help. Unless he's moved, of course.'

'He's lived here only for two or three years, I think. So he might not be in the book, anyway.'

'We're a village, of course,' the clerk said, glad to have something to do on a quiet afternoon. 'Everyone knows everyone else, more or less. What's your friend's name?'

'He's my husband's friend, actually. His name is Christopher Prideaux.' I started to spell it for her, but she smiled.

'Oh, the Cornish copper! At least, he's retired, but he used to be with the police before he moved here. Oh, yes, we all know Mr Prideaux. A pleasant chap. I don't know exactly where he lives, but Robin would. He works in the kitchen, and sometimes they play chess together. I'll go get him.'

Armed with directions and assurances that I couldn't miss the place, I set out. Even though I'd been there the other night, Christopher had driven us there and I'd paid no attention to where we were going. So I was sure I could in fact miss it. I was not born with a bump of navigation, but Grasmere was so small it really would have taken wilful stupidity to get lost. I walked up and rang the bell.

# SEVEN

M y ring went unanswered for a long time. I was about to give up when Christopher opened the door, clad in a terry-cloth robe, hair dripping. 'Sorry, I just got out of the shower.'

'Oh no, I'm sorry to disturb you. I can come back later—'

'No, no, come in. Give me a moment to dress.'

He was back in a very short time. 'I learned to dress in a hurry when I was in the force, and it's never left me. Would you like some tea?'

'Panting for some, thank you.'

He made tea with the speed and dexterity of someone who's been doing for himself for years, and set the tray down on the table in front of us. After he poured it, he smiled and said, 'Now, Dorothy, I suspect you want to talk about Donald Atkinson.'

'And I want to know why you invited us to your party. You were worried that something like this might happen, weren't you?'

He sighed. 'I never anticipated murder. One doesn't. I simply felt that something was badly wrong, and I couldn't put my finger on it. Back in Cornwall all those years ago, Alan was getting a reputation for a sensitivity to situations, an instinct for where the trouble lay. I really did want to see him again, and to meet you, but I also thought he might be able to sense what was going on. I'd also heard that you possessed many of those same qualities.'

*So you brought us straight into the hornet's nest.* I didn't say it. 'All right, so tell me about your guests at the party.'

'Looking for a suspect, are you?'

I made a face. 'I can't help it. It was so obvious that the man had a number of – well, enemies is a very strong word, but—'

'But apt. You're quite right. I don't know that Donald Atkinson had a friend in this county.'

'What about that man who was trying to get him into politics?'

'Harold Thompson. That has nothing to do with friendship. Thompson is the compleat politician.'

'Oh, is he an MP or something?'

'Or something. He's never held a public office. He's a puppeteer, pulling any number of strings to accomplish his aims. He likes power, but he wants to wield it behind the scenes. He's made a lot of money over the years, and nobody seems to know quite how, except that somehow schemes he promotes have a way of working out.'

'Alan says he's a lawyer. A solicitor, I mean.'

'After all these years, you still speak American?'

'I spent a lot more years speaking my native language. Anyway, at home a lawyer can sometimes earn a lot of money. Do solicitors earn a lot over here?'

'Some do. The general feeling in Grasmere is that Thompson has made his money in other ways, some of them not quite straightforward.'

'Meaning?'

'Meaning extortion, to be blunt. A man in his position learns a lot about people's lives and is expected to keep his knowledge confidential. It's whispered that Thompson's confidentiality comes at a price.'

I made some sort of sound, and Christopher snorted an unamused laugh. 'Yes, nasty practices go on in this country, too. And yes, they're despicable.'

'Couldn't he be disbarred, or whatever the penalty is here?'

'Of course, if anyone was willing to go to the authorities about it.'

'But of course they won't.' I heaved a sigh. 'Because then their dirty little secrets, whatever they are, would come to light. Thompson's got himself a perfect set of victims. And where did Donald Atkinson fit into this cosy little scenario?'

'He was going to promote Thompson's agenda in Parliament.'

'But— I really don't understand the Parliamentary system at all, but surely one member couldn't do much. He'd be from a small constituency, and a member of a minority party at that – at least, the Lib Dems are a minority?'

'Yes, a very small minority.'

'Well, then, even if everything had worked out according to

Thompson's plan, surely Atkinson couldn't have accomplished very much.'

Christopher smiled a little. 'Dorothy, did you ever involve yourself in American politics?'

'Very little. I always voted, of course.'

'And did you view your elected representatives as models of virtue, immune to any form of corruption?'

'Of course not – at least not in latter years. I lost my dewy innocence about American politicians a long time ago.'

Christopher nodded. 'And ours are no different. The influences corrupting our legislators are different to yours – we don't have the gun lobbies to contend with, for example – but they are no less toxic. They'll find the vulnerable spot in an MP and push that button in every possible way. As for minorities – they can form coalitions, you know.'

'So you're saying Atkinson had a vulnerability that could be exploited. What was it?'

He shook his head. 'I don't know. Yet. But I think Thompson knew, and that's why he was hell-bent on getting him elected.'

'Was there someone else in the picture, someone who didn't want Donald to get into Parliament? There were so many people who disliked him.'

'And not a few who downright hated him.'

I took a deep breath before broaching a subject I hated. 'Including, perhaps, his mistress's husband?'

'Brian? I feel truly sorry for Brian. Donald wasn't his wife's first lover, and he probably won't be her last. She's— Well, you've seen her. Even Brian's own son has his eye on her.'

'Yes, I noticed at the party. Christopher, how can people live like that? If what's-her-name—'

'Lilian.'

'If Lilian isn't interested in her husband, why on earth doesn't she divorce him? Or he, her? Surely he could prove cause.'

'That isn't necessary anymore. A few years ago, a new law was passed that makes divorce much simpler than it used to be. No cause need be proven, only that the marriage has "irretriev-ably broken down". But the answer to your question, I suppose, is that at some level Brian still loves his wife, no matter what. As for her – maybe there's a sense of security with Brian. As you know, I never attempted marriage, so I don't really understand how it works.'

'Or doesn't, in this case. But I have to say, the marriage that really boggled the mind was Donald's. He didn't bother to hide his contempt for poor Sarah. His affair with Lilian was known to everyone, and Ruth says he was verbally and psychologically abusive, and yet she was devoted to him. And she's not a stupid woman!'

'No. She's been efficiently brainwashed. That man married a beautiful, intelligent woman and reduced her to a quivering jelly in just a few years.' He pounded his fist on the table, making the tea things rattle and startling me considerably. 'I hope the cops never find out who killed him! I, for one, would like to shake the murderer's hand!'

'I've sometimes felt that way about murderers, but I've learned to try to suppress the feeling. I think it's okay to be glad that the victim, nasty as he was, is no longer around to make other people miserable. But the murderer – no, he must be caught and punished. For his own sake, actually, as well as for the sake of society. I don't mean to preach a sermon, but just think how awful it would be to go around with that on your conscience, always afraid that somebody would find out.'

'Do murderers have a conscience? I've known some hard cases, men who bragged about what they'd done, all the way to prison.'

'I suppose. At least it isn't all the way to the gallows anymore, at least in the UK.'

'Yes, thank God. Not that hanging wasn't sometimes preferable to languishing in prison for the rest of one's life. But you're right about the murderer, drat it. We've got to track him down.'

I thought for a moment. 'You know, we both keep saying "him". I don't have anyone specific in mind. Do you know something I don't?'

'I have some ideas, but no, no one in particular. And of course it could be a woman. Almost as many women as men hated him. And that's just including the people I know, who live here in Grasmere. The field is wider than that. Donald worked in Carlisle, and I can't imagine everyone in his office loved him. Certainly Brian didn't.'

'Brian? Lilian's husband? Is that how she met Donald?'

'It happened before I moved here, but I'm told Sarah invited Brian and Lilian to a meal.'

'At Donald's instigation, of course.'

'Of course. I think the idea was to make points with Brian, who at the time held a higher position in the firm. Of course, one look at Lilian, and the focus changed.'

'What kind of business is the firm? Lawyers? Solicitors, I mean?'

Christopher laughed. 'It's okay. We call them lawyers, too. No, Donald was an accountant.'

I eagerly grabbed that piece of information, remembering Alan had mentioned it the night of the party. 'Oh?'

'Maybe, to what you're thinking. He had certainly been throwing money around lately.'

'Ruth thinks it was Sarah's money.'

Christopher shrugged. 'I'm sure the police will be looking into that, though I have some sort of idea that Sarah's father tied up the money pretty carefully, in a trust or something like that.'

'But Donald was an accountant. And his political buddy's a lawyer. Trusts have been broken before.'

My phone rang. It would be Alan wondering where I'd gone. 'Hello, love.'

'Um – Mrs Martin?'

'Oh, sorry. I thought you'd be my husband.'

'No, this is The Inn. Mr Nesbitt came and picked up Mrs Atkinson and wanted you to know he may be late getting back. And you're not to worry.'

Was there ever a phrase that more surely engendered worry? I clicked off without even thanking the clerk. 'Christopher, I must go. Something has happened. I don't know what, but I must get back.'

'I'll drive you.'

Bless the man, no questions, just action. There are things to be said about police training.

# EIGHT

Ruth was waiting for me in the lobby.

'What happened?'

She steered me into the lounge, which for a wonder was almost deserted. 'I don't really know. Alan came to our door, said he'd been up to the room and you weren't there. Well, I had to say I didn't know where you were.'

'No, you were asleep when I left, and I didn't think I'd be gone very long. And I didn't want to bother him while he was . . . doing whatever it was. But what did he want?'

'He just said he needed to talk to Sarah, and he'd maybe be late getting back.'

'Why in the world didn't he just call me?'

'I think he didn't want to say much in front of Sarah. Or me, for that matter. He took her with him. Dorothy, what's going on?'

I had been sitting on the edge of my chair. Now I collapsed back into the cushions. 'I don't know, but I can think of some possibilities I don't like at all.'

'For instance?'

I didn't want to even say it – the old superstition that if you say something out loud, it somehow makes it more likely to come true. 'Do you think we could have some tea or something?'

'Or something, I'd say. It's bourbon, isn't it?'

She came back very quickly with two glasses, and a glass of water to add if we wanted. At that moment, I didn't, but I added a bit anyway and then downed a good stiff pull.

Ruth waited.

I took a deep breath. 'Alan went out to see if they could find some ointment for a rash in Atkinson's pockets. I think he, or someone, found it.'

'And?'

'And sent it off to be analysed.'

'I thought that took a long time.'

'Usually. Not always, if it might be a vital clue in a murder

case. So if that's it, and there's something in the ointment that
– that shouldn't have been there—'

'Then they'd obviously have to talk to Sarah about it. But they
wouldn't have sent Alan to get her if they were going to arrest
her, right?'

'Honestly, I don't know. The rules about arrest are so complicated, and they've changed recently, too, and Alan doesn't have
to keep up with them, since he's no longer an active cop. But I
should think, if they were really planning to take her into custody,
they'd have sent the real police.' I took another swig of the
bourbon, which was beginning to calm me down. 'And I don't
know why I'm dithering when we don't actually know anything.
Theorizing ahead of the data, as Sherlock Holmes always warned
against.'

'And you're going to tell me not to worry, I suppose.'

I snorted. 'No point. We'll worry, anyway. I think what we'd
better do is have something to eat to soak up the alcohol, and
then watch some TV to try to take our minds off the whole
mess.'

'Hah! Find me a television show that requires the attention of
more than three brain cells. I thought things might be better in
England, but not so.'

'I had the same hope when I first moved here, but you're right.
Maybe there's a copy of *The Times* around somewhere. War,
pestilence and famine might distract from our problems here at
home.'

We lingered over our dinner until the serving staff began to
give us meaningful looks and then retired to the lounge with a
day-old *Times*. I had to restrain myself from pacing, and Ruth
was looking at her watch every five minutes, when Alan finally
showed up.

Ruth sprang up when he entered the room. 'Where's Sarah?'

'Don't worry. She went upstairs to pack. She's going home.'

'I'm going with her!'

'Yes, she wants you to do that. Ruth, don't ask her a lot of
questions. She's a bit fragile right now.'

The English pronunciation of the word, with a long I, makes
it sound more so, I always think.

Ruth bounded out of the room as Alan sank into a chair.

I wanted to ask a hundred questions, but Alan looked so near the end of his rope that I desisted. 'Whisky?' I asked.

'Please.'

I went to the bar, got him a glass of Glenfiddich, his favourite single malt, and waited until he'd sipped a bit before I said, 'Well?'

'Fairly well,' he replied with a sigh. 'It's been quite a day.'

'They found the ointment.' It was not a question.

'Yes, a tube of Anthisan, an effective treatment for an allergic rash. It was in the pocket of the pants he wore to the sports day, not in the shorts he'd changed into, so it wasn't found at first.' He took another sip. 'Thanks for this, love.'

I waited.

'It was an almost-new tube, which was a bit surprising, because Sarah had said he'd had the rash for some time. This tube was almost full, so one of the things we wanted to ask Sarah was whether he'd used up one and bought another. But the thing that put us on full alert was fingerprints. Of course it was dusted, just as a matter of routine.'

'No! You're not saying they found Sarah's prints! But even if they did, she could have handed it to Donald at some point.'

'No. That would have made sense, but no. The shocker was that they found no prints at all. That tube was as clean as a just-bathed baby's bum.'

'But it had been used. So – so Donald's fingerprints should have been on it.'

'Right.'

'So it had been wiped clean.'

'Right.'

'Which means— What does it mean?'

'What we think it means is that something has been added to that tube, added by someone who knew enough to clean up after himself. Or herself.'

I let that one lie there. 'It's being analysed, of course.'

'Yes. But they had to send it to Carlisle, to the nearest big forensic lab. And it'll take a while, because they don't know what they're looking for.'

I knew you couldn't just test for 'poison'. There are tests for arsenic and cyanide and strychnine and almost any substance you care to name, but there are thousands of poisons, and a test for one won't discover another. Then there are the ordinary substances, often used medically, that are deadly in some circumstances. In fact, as a friend who was a poison expert once pointed out to me, anything can be toxic, even water. It all depends on the dosage.

'Of course it would take forever for them to do a complete qualitative analysis,' I agreed, 'so what are they going to try?'

'They'll have to go by symptoms, and the trouble is, we don't really know the symptoms. All we know is that Atkinson somehow wandered off the path the race was supposed to take and ended up in the tarn.'

'They'll have to talk to all the other racers and see if they saw anything.'

'Indeed. They'll have to try, at least. And, Dorothy, they live all over England. The fell race isn't just a local event, you know.'

'Oh, right, Christopher told us that, didn't he? Good grief, he said they sometimes even come from other countries. But, Alan, it'll take forever to track them all down! I suppose the organizers have their names and addresses, but it's summer. Some of them won't be home yet.'

'In any case, as you well know, the prime suspect in any murder . . .'

'Is the spouse. I know. And especially in a case like this, where the victim was such a louse. But I refuse to believe it!'

'The police don't, either. Quite. Or not yet. That's why they're allowing her to go home.'

'So tell me everything. What did they do to her, keeping her all that time?'

'They asked her about the ointment, of course. She never wavered from her story that she got it from Boots and gave it to Donald about a week ago. He used it, reluctantly, and let her put it on his back, snarling the whole time. He had used up about half the tube, and no, she didn't buy him another one, and no, he certainly would never have gone to buy one for himself, and no, she had no idea where the new one came from. Of course, they'd searched her house thoroughly and found nothing in the way of poison or even medicines, except a couple of standard pain relievers. A healthy couple, apparently. Well, you know all

that. And she kept saying that she would never have done anything
to harm Donald, that he was the most wonderful man on earth,
and so on. So eventually they decided she could go home. Not
that they've given her a clean bill of health.'

'Poor thing. She must be utterly exhausted.'

'She is, but not quite as bad as you might expect. I imagine
she endured enough mental torture at her husband's hands to
build up a tolerance. Dorothy, it's a shame! Even with the man
dead, she's still having to put up with harassment.'

'Yes. We've got to find out who really did it.'

Alan was so tired he didn't even object to the 'we'.

# NINE

That night I fell asleep like one who had been hit on the head, and didn't wake properly until Alan held a cup of coffee under my nose. My dear husband can make even brewed-in-the-room coffee tempting, and one of his most lovable qualities is that he never expects me to act human until I've had at least one cup.

He handed me that cup and went off to the shower, leaving me to come alive in my own time. By the time he came back, trailing steam, I was awake enough to see that it was a lovely day. I also saw the clock.

'Good heavens, I didn't mean to sleep the day away.'

'Yesterday was hard on all of us. I only woke up a bit ago myself. We needed the rest.'

And at that the anxieties were back. 'I sure hope poor Sarah got some sleep,' I said. 'She had the worst day of any of us.'

'Ruth told me the doctor left a couple of sedative pills with her, just in case. So I'm sure Sarah was well looked-after.'

'Good. I'm a little afraid Ruth will wrap her in cotton wool, though.'

'I don't think Sarah will allow that,' Alan said gently. 'She's stronger than you might think.'

'The good Lord knows she's had to be. Alan, what are we going to do about this?'

'Today I'm going to go to the police and offer my help in tracking down all the runners in the senior guides race.'

'And I'm going along with you, whether they want me or not.'

Alan grinned. 'Yes, dear.'

Before we took off, I called Ruth. 'How's Sarah doing?'

'She's not saying much. Not doing much, either. Just sits around looking lost.'

'Is there some church activity she could get involved in? She's spent a lot of time at the church, and doing something for other people could do worlds for her state of mind.'

'You're right. Thinking about people who are in worse trouble is the sure cure for the blues, every time. Thanks, Dorothy!'

So with that off my mind for the time being, Alan and I headed to the temporary police headquarters.

A small police force can be prickly, determined to defend their territory, eager to prove that they're just as competent and efficient as the big-city guys, thank you very much.

Or they can be friendly, open to suggestions, and eager to accept any help that's offered. Fortunately, the police from Carlisle, now working in Grasmere (which is too small to have its own force) were of the latter variety. They were happy to give us a copy of the list of race participants, together with contact information. Their people would be pursuing the same avenue, but they couldn't devote every minute of their time to it. We could.

'So what's the approach?' I asked when we got back in the car. 'Call, email, or go see them?'

'Text or email, I'd say. That could reach them almost anyplace.'

'Hmm. Except for the foreigners, maybe. If they're still in the UK, their phones might not work. I had a friend visit from America, and her phone was useless the whole time she was here. Couldn't get a signal.'

Alan sighed. 'Possible, I suppose. But most of the addresses are UK, by far the biggest number of them near here. We can but try.'

'Right. Now, look. I'm in favour of sending the messages individually instead of setting up some kind of group. A group message, unless I know the sender, always looks to me like spam.'

'Agreed. And because there are so many, perhaps we should split up the list. You send some; I send some.'

Between us, we worked out a brief message. It wasn't easy. We wanted to convey some urgency but not sound severe or demanding. 'We're not the KGB,' I commented, when one version came out sounding like it ought to be accompanied by a klaxon.

Finally, I read our joint effort aloud: '"One of the runners in Sunday's fell race has died unexpectedly, and we need to learn all we can about his actions during the race. If you saw anything unusual on that day, please respond as soon as possible to this text."

'Not wonderful,' I said with a sigh, 'but I don't see how we can say much more without raising an alarm. Even as bland as this is, I suppose we'll get the usual crop of imagined omens and reports of peculiar behaviour.'

'Probably. Most of them won't respond at all, and then they'll have to be chased down in person. And there aren't the personnel to do that, even with volunteers like us.'

'Even if the police wanted to do it, and they don't much, do they?'

It was Alan's turn to sigh. 'I think you're right. If I'm reading the situation right, those who don't think Atkinson died a natural death think his wife murdered him. They're not even pushing the forensics people to do much more than a cursory analysis of the ointment.'

'Then it's up to us, isn't it?'

'Dorothy, I'm not sure anything can be done. If we had a large police force, if they could be convinced that a thorough investigation is necessary, yes, we might be able to help. As it is . . .' He spread his hands in the classic gesture of hopelessness.

'Well, I'm not giving up. I'm sending this message to half the people on the list, and then I'm going to go back and get Christopher to tell me how to find all the people he knows who hated Donald Atkinson. There's more than one way to skin a cat.'

Alan began to laugh. 'I never thought I'd hear you use that expression! All right, my love, we'll do what we can. And if we come up with nothing, I promise not to say I told you so.'

We went back to the hotel and set to work. Copy and paste. Type in new phone number. Paste. New number. Paste. Over and over until my index finger was numb. I was about to send one more when my phone made a noise I hadn't been expecting.

'Hey! I got a reply!'

'No! Let me see.'

Alan hovered over my phone. The message said only, 'Call me.'

'Who's it from?'

I checked my list. It was one of the first names on it, one

Robert Smith. I shook my head. 'Never heard of him. Not one of the people Christopher told me about.'

'And where does he live?'

I looked at the list again. 'Keswick. Is that very far away?'

'It's pronounced Kezzick, love. I don't know the area well, as you know, but I think it's just the next town north. Small, though bigger than Grasmere. Used to be famous for pencil manufacturing, if I remember correctly.'

'Write his number down. I'm going to call Christopher and see what he knows about Robert Smith.'

Christopher answered immediately. 'Hello! I was just about to call you and Alan to see if there were any developments.'

'Nothing much yet, but something might be in the works. Have you ever heard of someone named Robert Smith? He lives in Keswick.'

'Oh, does he? I'd have thought he'd live nearer his work. At least if it's Bob Smith the newsman you're talking about. Border TV has its studios in Carlisle.'

'Whoa! Slow down. This guy is a television personality?'

'You might say that. He's the anchor of a local news show. Quite a popular newsman, seems to be a nice gent. What's your interest in him?'

'Wait. Did he by any chance know Atkinson?'

'You might say so.' Christopher chuckled. 'If Bob Smith ever hated anybody, he hated Donald Atkinson.'

'Oh, gosh! Why? The abridged version, please.'

'Well, it is actually a long story, but the core of it is that Atkinson insulted Smith, on the air, in a virulent string of lies.'

'Wow! Okay, Christopher, I've got to go. I may soon have a story or two for you.'

I clicked off and relayed the conversation to Alan. 'He hated Donald and he was there, one of the runners. What shall I do? Hand over to you?'

Alan didn't even take time to consider. 'No. You call him, but turn on the speaker. You've always been good at dealing with difficult people.'

'Comes of teaching for forty years.' I placed the call.

Mr Smith answered immediately. He had the sort of voice I expected, warm, perfectly modulated, no particular accent, not even the 'Oxbridge' that used to be standard for radio and television announcers. 'Hello, Mr Smith. My name is Dorothy Martin. I'm the one who sent the text about the fell race.'

'Yes, I recognized the number. Are you a police officer, may I ask?'

'No, I'm nobody official at all. I'm simply helping track down everyone who ran the senior guides race on Sunday.'

'And you're looking for people who saw another racer behaving oddly. May I ask who you think might have been acting a bit off?'

'I'd rather you told me,' I answered cautiously. Alan gave me a thumbs up.

'I see. Does that mean I'm under some sort of suspicion?'

'Not so far as I am aware.' Another thumbs up.

'Not giving anything away, are you? Very well. I knew a few of the men in the race. None of the women. Among those I knew, one was running only a few feet ahead of me. I nearly caught up with him, because he suddenly slowed down and began to run erratically, stumbling off the path. He veered into the woods, and I lost sight of him.'

'You say you knew him.'

A long sigh. 'Yes, his name was Donald Atkinson. And before you ask if I tried to check on him, make sure he was okay, the answer is no. I'm not proud of it, but Atkinson was, in my opinion, a wart on the face of this beautiful planet, and at that moment, I actually hoped that he had a cramp or something – anything that would keep him out of the honours.'

'Mr Smith, I assume you have heard the news that Donald Atkinson is dead.'

'You said as much in your text, but yes, I did already know. I'm in the news business.'

'My husband's friend, Christopher Prideaux, told me about you. My husband and I live down in Belleshire, way out of your territory, so we weren't familiar with you. I gather you're a household name around here.'

Silence for a couple of slow beats. Then: 'If he told you that, he probably also told you about my humiliation at the hands of Donald Atkinson.'

'Yes, in general terms.'

'Mrs Martin, where are you? At home in Belleshire, or in these parts?'

'My husband and I are staying in a hotel in Grasmere.'

'Would you allow me to come and see you? This is all somewhat painful for me, and I would much rather talk in person.'

Alan gestured a 'Why not?'

'We would like that, Mr Smith. We're at The Inn.'

'Half an hour?'

'We'll be in the lobby.'

Alan and I looked at each other after we'd clicked off. 'What does he want to tell us?'

Alan shrugged. 'We'll know that when he gets here, won't we?'

We didn't know how we'd recognize him, but we'd forgotten that he was instantly recognizable to anyone in the county who watched television.

'Bob!' someone cried as a tall, nice-looking man walked through the door. There were choruses of greeting. Subdued choruses – this was England, after all – but we were left in no doubt as to the identity of the newcomer.

Nor of his popularity. He'd brought smiles to every face in the room.

Alan stood and extended a hand. 'Mr Smith, I believe?'

'Bob, please. And you'd be Mr Martin?'

I laughed. 'I'm Mrs Martin, and yes, this is my husband, but we don't use the same surname.'

'Alan Nesbitt.' Alan shook hands again. 'It's a bit public here for you, isn't it? Would you prefer to talk somewhere else? We could go up to our room, if you prefer.'

The poor man looked relieved. 'If you don't mind. You see,' he went on as we got in the elevator, 'all these people know me, and they forget that I don't know any of them. I've been in their homes every night for years, but the screen doesn't work both ways. We had to wait for Zoom for that.'

I smiled. 'I remember once, years ago in my home town in Indiana, waving and smiling to the local TV weatherman. He was kind, and waved and smiled back. I was halfway down the street before it hit me.'

Our room was a nice size, but cramped for three people. We insisted that our guest take the easy chair, while Alan and I tried to make ourselves comfortable in the straight chair and on the side of the bed. I made tea and put it on the inadequate table, and then we sat back and waited for Bob Smith to talk.

He tried to take a sip of the tea, which was too hot to drink, and put the cup down. 'This is awkward.' He laughed a little. 'I usually have a script of some sort.' He pushed his cup away.

'Maybe I can help.' I took a sip of my own tea, still uncomfortably hot. 'As I said earlier, I talked to our friend Christopher about you.'

'And he told you why I had good reason to dislike Atkinson.'

'He put it a bit more strongly than that.'

'If he said I hated the man, he overstated. Certainly I hated what he did to me.' He turned to Alan. 'Has your wife shared the ugly little story?'

'Only the bare bones.'

'Well, then.' He moistened his lips, cleared his throat, took a sip of tea. 'As you will clearly see, this is not a story I enjoy telling. But I must, and I must make you understand.' He paused. 'It began when my producer told me to interview Atkinson on my Friday show. At the end of the news every Friday, I had a live three-minute slot for a feature. A school story, a special charity effort, a local hero – you know the sort of thing, human interest. It was very popular.'

'You're speaking in the past tense,' said Alan.

'Yes.' He took a sip of his tea and cleared his throat again. 'That show with Atkinson was the last Friday feature I did.'

'What happened, for Pete's sake? Oh, and can I get you anything else?'

He waved away the offer. 'Thank you, but no. I just have to get through this.'

# TEN

'The only way is to just tell it all. I didn't want to interview Atkinson. I couldn't see a story there. But my producer insisted that he was a rising figure in the county, that he was likely to be our next MP, that he had any number of friends in high places, it would be good for the network, he was an interesting man, blah, blah. I know now that he, the producer, was being pressured by Atkinson's bear-leader, Thompson.'

'Harold Thompson? The one who's been grooming him for politics?' I was trying to keep all the characters straight.

'That's the one. As aggressive a promoter as you'll ever find, and not an attractive individual. At any rate, I finally gave in. I thought I could survive three minutes. How wrong I was!'

He shifted in his seat. 'We had a preliminary meeting the week before, and I was confirmed in my opinion that the guy was a handsome shell with nothing inside. We talked for perhaps half an hour, and he gave me nothing to use on the air, nothing. All Atkinson could talk about was himself, how wonderful he was, that he was a self-made man, that he knew everybody important who'd ever set foot in the county, and a good many who hadn't, on and on and on. I decided that my only option for the show was to ask him an opening question and let him blether on. If he ran out of steam before the three minutes were up, I could simply ask for more information about some of the VIPs he'd mention. Super boring, but since my producer had insisted, he could hardly complain.

'It didn't go quite that way. All was well for the first thirty seconds or so. I introduced him, we sat down, I asked that first question about his life and waited for him to take it from there. Instead he smiled, a really nasty smile, and said, "Oh, but, Bob, I'd much rather talk about you. You're such a celebrity, after all! And so modest about it all, too. Just plain old Bob Smith, right? Nothing posh about you. Just like everybody else – or so you say, anyway." He laughed, an ugly laugh, and shook his finger in my face. "Even got a commonplace name. How many million Smiths are there in the UK, do you think? Maybe that's why you chose it, eh?"

'I opened my mouth to say something, but he wouldn't let me. The show was live, so I couldn't even stop the cameras.

'"Oh, Bob, what do you think your audience would say if they knew you were really from a really upscale family? Educated at Oxford – or no, maybe it was Cambridge. I wouldn't even like to guess at how much money you've got stashed away in Swiss banks, or would it be in the Caymans? No taxes to pay, eh, Bob?" He slapped me on the shoulder and never drew breath.

'He went on and on in the same vein, never giving me an opportunity to answer, and when he stopped, I didn't even have time to sign off. The cameras stopped, the lights dimmed, and Atkinson bounced out of his chair with another smile and a wave. And I was toast.

'Of course nothing that he implied was true. My name is Bob Smith, and I was born on a farm a few miles from Penrith. I went to a good grammar school and high school, and that's the extent of my education, and I've never been wealthy. But since he never stated all the slanderous filth as truth, merely as speculation, he couldn't be sued. The network lawyers were quite firm about that, but my reputation was ruined, all the same. It's true that I've cultivated my image as an ordinary sort of guy, and that it's been the basis of my success, such as it's been. The great thing was, it was all true, and somehow it appealed to the audience. And now it's gone. My producer commiserated with me after the show, just before he said he thought it would be best to discontinue the slot for a while. In the media world, "a while" means forever.'

He sat back, drained.

I was appalled. 'And there was nothing you could do? Surely your boss, or someone, would have given you some air time to refute the slander?'

'No. The station felt that denying the remarks would just cement them in people's minds and further damage my reputation, and therefore the show. They're allowing me to continue as the anchor. For now. But if the ratings go down, as they might if people believe I'm a phony, then I'll be out of there.'

'Why? Why would Atkinson do such a thing to you? I mean, what had you ever done to him?' I sounded belligerent. As I was.

'I can only think that he was deliberately trying to destroy me. I'm a popular figure around here, or I was. He was not; a lot of people disliked him. He did not have an . . . endearing personality. My guess is that he thought if I was out of the picture, so to speak, people would flock to him instead.'

'Unsound thinking,' Alan commented.

'Of course. But it was the only way he was capable of thinking. He was an utter egotist. Life, for him, was a zero-sum game. All attention, all admiration, in fact every good thing, was supposed to be lavished on him. Anything that went to anyone else was a theft from him, and had somehow to be wrested back.'

'And yet,' Alan pursued, 'you say you didn't hate him.'

'I was furiously angry with him, of course. He cost me the part of my job that I enjoyed most and may yet take away the rest. But no, I didn't hate him. How can you hate someone so pathetic? And no, before you ask, I didn't kill him. Oh, don't bother to protest! It's quite obvious that you have put two and two together. I ran the race just behind him. I had been badly damaged by him. Was I the one who caused his death? Because you believe his death was not due to natural causes, don't you?'

Alan and I looked at each other and made up our minds. 'The police aren't quite sure yet,' I said, 'but yes, Alan and I believe that he was murdered. In a very clever way that will be hard to trace to the murderer.'

'I didn't kill him. What I tell you three times is true!'

We all laughed a little at that.

'I told you I saw him acting erratically during the race. I said I didn't try to help him. So in fact I might have contributed to his death. If I'd gone to his aid, maybe he wouldn't have died. I'll have to live with that on my conscience, but I don't think that counts as murder.'

'Legally, it does not,' Alan pronounced in his most official voice. 'But in any case, you can wipe your conscience clean. If what we believe is true, he was so near death at that point that no intervention could have saved him.'

'I could have kept him from falling in the tarn and drowning.'

'He didn't drown. There was no water in his lungs. He was

dead when he went into the water.' Alan turned to me. 'I think I forgot to tell you that, but it was easy to determine at the autopsy. What actually caused his death is harder to work out.'

'You're sure of that?' Smith was unconvinced.

'Certain sure.'

'Whew! So I can go to church on Sunday without feeling like a hypocrite.'

He sounded like a new man, and I hated having to say, 'You know you're not free and clear as far as the police are concerned. We'll have to tell them about this conversation, and they'll want to talk to you. And to anyone else who saw him during the race.'

'You won't get any more replies to your texts, is my guess. No one else was near us when he began to stumble about. We were nearly at the head of the pack, only one or two ahead of us, and then a pretty good gap before the rest came along. I think I'm the only one. And I know I'm innocent, so I'm not worried.

'Now I have to get to the studio. I'm grateful to you for setting my mind at ease.' He stood and shook hands with both of us and walked out the door.

'But of course he's not in the clear,' I said when he was out of earshot. 'Because if someone tampered with that ointment, they could have done it at almost any time.'

'Yes,' said Alan simply, and we were quiet in our dejection.

True to Bob's prediction, there were no more texts that day, so the next morning Alan called the officer in charge of the investigation, gave him a summary of our conversation with Bob, and turned back to me. 'That's all we can do for now,' he said. 'Perhaps the lab will find something in the ointment sometime before the end of the century. Meanwhile, we're in a perfectly beautiful part of the country. Let's explore it.'

We called Christopher, who was devastated that he had plans for the day and couldn't go with us. He gave Alan directions to a destination he wouldn't divulge while I was listening. 'Be prepared for something incredible' was all he would say.

So we set out. I would not like to do that journey ever again. If there are roads that are narrower, or steeper, or twistier, anywhere in the world, I can't imagine where, and I never want to see them.

Alan is an excellent driver, and our car is a small sedan, but I was still near screaming point on a good many curves. And the road was *all* curves. It was so narrow that when we met another car, one of us had to find a place to pull off the road. Some of the places Alan found looked just about big enough for a bicycle, but somehow there were no collisions. I was in charge of reading Christopher's directions, but since I kept my eyes closed most of the way, Alan had to rely on the satnav.

After several hours of terror, probably really less than an hour, the car stopped and Alan turned off the engine. I opened my eyes.

We were at the top of a very high hill, in a small parking area. On the other side of the road there was a low hedge with a gap in it just about big enough for a person to slip through, and a sign saying 'Castlerigg'. We crossed the road and—

'Alan! What *is* this place?'

Before me was the most amazing, the most awe-inspiring sight I'd ever seen. There was a grassy plateau, dropping sharply at the far end to a valley. Beyond that, gorgeous mountains receded, one behind another, shading from green into blue against a picture-perfect sky with clouds rolling lazily by.

And on the grass stood enormous boulders arranged in a rough circle. Some were much bigger than others. Some were close together, others widely spaced. None appeared to have been shaped by the hand of man, simply dug into the ground. No 'lintels' topped the stones, which in any case weren't flat on top. Many were covered with lichens, showing they had been there for a very long time.

To the left of where we stood, there were other stones placed in a different pattern. We walked that way, slowly, silently. It was somehow a place where one didn't speak.

These stones formed a rough rectangle, plainly an enclosure of some sort, its farthest 'wall' the boundary of the huge circle. 'A chapel?' I whispered, and Alan nodded.

We stood gazing into the distance, over the mountains. At the edge of the plateau, a few sheep grazed placidly. The wind blew through our hair. I felt the most perfect peace I had ever known.

We might have stayed there until we turned to stone ourselves had not a group of twenty or so people arrived, chattering and laughing, breaking the spell. I tried hard not to hate them as they moved about and we headed for our car.

When we sat down in the car, Alan reached over and took my hand. 'Don't fret, love. They don't understand.'

'It's a temple. They shouldn't—' I couldn't think what, exactly, they shouldn't do.

'We felt that, but they didn't. Yet. If they stay long enough, perhaps they will.'

'It's like shouting in a cathedral!'

'Yes.' He pulled a brochure out of his pocket. 'Christopher texted me after his call to tell me where we were going, and I found this at the hotel before we left. I didn't want to show it to you earlier, because I wanted you to be surprised.'

'Gobsmacked is the word!'

'Indeed. This says Castlerigg is one of the oldest stone circles in Britain, dating back to around 3200 BC. That makes it far older than most of Stonehenge, and older even than the Ring of Brodgar in Orkney. No one knows its purpose, though it's speculated that it had to do with, quote, "ceremonial or religious purposes".'

'Religious,' I stated firmly. 'No question about it. That was a place of worship. To gods with different names from the one we worship, of course, but it was a holy place.'

'"Put off thy shoes from off thy feet",' he quoted softly. 'And it is still holy.'

# ELEVEN

We stopped at a café in Keswick on the way back and had a lavish tea, including scones with clotted cream, an all-in-one meal for our schedule-free day. We took our time getting back to the hotel, using roads that were much easier on poor Alan – and me!

We had turned off our phones while at Castlerigg, but when we reached our hotel room turned them back on. We were both reluctant to come back to the real world after our hallowed experience, and sure enough, we had an influx of text messages and voicemails.

We each had a few answers to our text message of the day before, all saying versions of the same thing: no one had seen anything peculiar during the race. Almost everyone expressed sorrow about the death of a fellow runner.

Alan and I wondered if any of those writers knew who had died.

The voicemails were all for Alan. We listened to them together.

'Alan, Davies here.' George Davies was in charge of the murder investigation. 'The lab is still working on analysis of the ointment. They've found a substantial portion of a drug they cannot yet identify. Will pursue it.'

'Alan, Christopher. Call me.'

'Alan, Davies. The drug has been identified. Call me.'

'Alan, this is important! Call me at once!' That was Christopher again.

And several more of the same.

Alan looked at me.

'Christopher first,' I pronounced. 'He's your friend, and he sounds frantic.'

'Where have you *been*?' was Christopher's greeting. 'Things are moving!'

'We went to Castlerigg, remember?'

'Oh. Yes. And it blew you away, I suppose.'

'Completely into the firmament.'

'It does that, to people with any imagination at all. But it's time to come down to earth, old chap. Have you talked to Davies yet?'

'No, he left several messages, but Dorothy thought I should talk to you first, as you sounded agitated.'

'I'm not sure I want to talk on a mobile. They're about as private as a billboard. I'll be there in ten minutes.'

He clicked off without saying goodbye.

Immediately, the phone rang. Alan sighed and looked at me. 'The police.'

'Mr Nesbitt, Mr Davies has been trying to reach you. I'll put him through.'

A series of clicks.

'Alan, I'd like to talk to you. It's urgent. Where will you be for the next few minutes?'

'At The Inn, but—'

'Good. I'm on my way.'

'This could be interesting,' I commented.

'In the sense of the old curse? "May you live in interesting times"?'

I shrugged. 'Shall I make some tea?'

'Couldn't hurt.'

'They'd maybe rather have a drink.'

'No Englishman ever turned down a cup of tea.'

Not true, I thought. I'd known a couple, good friends years ago, who didn't care at all for tea and had given me and Frank their Brown Betty teapot. I didn't mention it.

The tea was just ready to pour when Christopher knocked on the door, and Davies was right behind him. Each was somewhat taken aback to see the other there, I thought, but they were civil enough.

I poured tea and effaced myself as much as was possible, given the size of the room. All the men were or had been police officers. I was strictly unofficial, and a woman to boot. Let them pretend I wasn't there, the poor dears.

Christopher was obviously dying to tell Alan the news but deferred to Davies as the only truly official investigator.

He cleared his throat. 'Well, you were right, Alan, and most of us were wrong. You know we were inclined to treat Atkinson's death as accidental or medical. Stroke, heart attack, seizure, whatever. You pointed out enough anomalies that I agreed to investigate, but the cost was mounting, what with the extended autopsy and the forensics costs, and I was about to call a halt when the lab called.'

'You said on the phone that they had found something in the ointment that shouldn't be there.'

'When I called you that first time, the lab techs still weren't certain what it was, only that it wasn't any of the listed ingredients, that in fact the ointment was mostly the something else. But when I told them the symptoms you described, they were able to narrow it down. Turns out the ointment was almost pure nitroglycerine.'

Christopher couldn't wait any longer. 'That means someone squeezed out almost all the real ointment and substituted Nitro-Bid.'

'But – I'm confused.' I frowned. 'I thought that nitroglycerine was used to control angina and came in tiny tablets that you put under the tongue to deal with an attack.'

'That's one form of it,' said Davies. 'After what the lab boys said, I talked to our medical consultant. As an ointment, Nitro-Bid is apparently used for all kinds of things, including the prevention of angina attacks. But there are several side effects. The most important one, the one we may be dealing with here, is that it can lower blood pressure to a dangerous degree. That's just with the recommended dose, which is about two centimetres.' He measured it along the first joint of his little finger. 'Not very much. If it was slathered all over Atkinson's neck and back, over open sores, the doc said his BP would drop to almost nothing as soon as the stuff was absorbed into his bloodstream.'

'And that would have taken about how long?' Alan asked.

Christopher jumped in again. 'He was running, his heart pumping fast. It would probably have been circulating in his blood within twenty minutes.'

'Just about long enough for him to get into his running clothes, wait for the race to start, and get to the top of the fell and into the woods, right?' Alan raised his eyebrows.

'Right,' said Christopher. 'So we need to know who helped

him with the ointment just before the race. He couldn't have put it on his own back.'

'Yes,' said Alan heavily. 'We do need to know that, because if that person had any cuts or abrasions on his fingers, he could be in some danger. But it won't help us identify a murderer. That tube of ointment could have been prepared at almost any time. We need to know who slipped it into Atkinson's pants pocket. Which could also have been done at almost any time.'

I groaned. 'And that puts Sarah right back in the crosshairs. Who better to put something in Donald's pocket than his wife?'

'True,' said Christopher. 'But she says she never saw that tube, only the one he'd been using for days. You'll say, of course she'd say that, no matter what. But would she be able to figure out how to make the substitution? It's child's play to squeeze some-thing out of a tube, but no easy matter to get something back in. And where would she get hold of the nitro ointment? It's avail-able only by prescription, and not, I believe, in this country.'

'Good points, all of them,' said Alan. 'The fact remains that a spouse—'

'Is always the first suspect. We know all that!' I was getting annoyed. 'I know I brought this up, and I regret it. I raised it only so it could be knocked down. To add to your objections, Christopher, here's one of my own. All indications point to this being a premeditated act. A lot of dots had to be connected, starting with someone who hated Donald Atkinson. Well, no shortage of candidates there. Then that person had to have access to the nitro ointment, along with enough specialized medical knowledge to know its possible dire effects. He or she had to know about Donald's rash, and how he was treating it. Had to know he was running in the race, and where the route went into the woods where Donald could fall into the tarn.'

'That might not have been part of the plan,' Alan objected. 'And in fact it didn't turn out to be critical, because Donald didn't drown.'

'No, but the fact that he was found there sure confused the issue for a little while, didn't it? Delayed the search for what might really have killed him. If you're a murderer, delay is good.'

The policeman and the two ex-policemen grunted.

'So where are we even going to start looking? A foreigner?

A chemist? Who among Donald's many enemies falls into those categories?'

'You forget, Mrs Martin, about community. People talk to each other. They borrow from each other. The murderer could be a Grasmere native who knows a chemist from Carlisle, who has a good friend from America.'

'All of whom can be counted upon to keep their mouths shut?' I countered sceptically. 'And my name is Dorothy. Anyway, maybe the best way is to start at the beginning. With Donald's enemies. Christopher?'

'Their name is Legion,' he replied. 'I told you about some of them yesterday. Brian Sullivan, Lilian's husband. You remember Lilian?'

'No one,' said Alan fervently, 'could ever forget Lilian.'

I glared at him. 'Okay, Brian, the cuckolded husband.' I found my purse and pulled out the notebook I always carry. 'Looked to me like a wimp who wouldn't have the brains to plan something this elaborate, or the guts to carry it out, but his name goes down. Who's next?'

'I'm sorry to say it, but it has to be Bob Smith.' Alan gave me an apologetic look. 'He had excellent reason to view Donald with enmity. His media contacts could include almost anybody, including foreigners and chemists or doctors.'

Tight-lipped, I wrote down his name. I didn't believe a word of it, but I wasn't going to argue right now.

'And Harold Thompson.' Christopher turned to me. 'His political sponsor, or whatever you want to call him.'

'Goad. Urger-on. Self-interested pusher.'

'You don't seem fond of the man, Mrs— Dorothy,' said Davies mildly, giving us all a much-needed laugh.

'No. In fact I'm writing his name down with a good deal of satisfaction. Only did he hate Donald? I thought he was supporting him all the way.'

'He was in constant contact with him,' said Christopher drily. 'And with Atkinson, familiarity could certainly breed loathing.'

'I like it,' I said, nodding with satisfaction. 'That makes him my favourite suspect so far.'

'Not a suspect,' said all three men together, and laughed. 'A suspect, my dear,' said my loving husband, 'is a person who is of interest to the police because of solid evidence. Those people on your list are simply possibilities.'

'Well, some are more possible than others! And Mr Political Influencer is the most possible of all, in my book. Okay, who else?'

'After those three,' said Christopher, 'the list is almost endless. Donald Atkinson's utter self-interest created enemies everywhere he went. I've honestly never heard anyone say anything good about him.'

'Except his wife,' said Alan in an odd tone of voice. 'She does nothing but praise him.'

'That is often the case with an abused wife,' said Davies, 'as of course you well know. We've all dealt with them so often. They will be brought to hospital with their injuries, will tell us it was their husband who beat them up, and then in the end will refuse to let him be charged with a crime. He's a good man, really, it's all her fault, he's sworn never to do it again. And she goes back to him, and he does it again.'

'It happens that way in the States, too,' I said sadly. 'The explanation from the counsellors is that the woman has such low self-esteem that the man has convinced her she deserves such treatment. And I think that's the case here, too. You said it yourself, Christopher. He brainwashed her, hypnotized her into believing she was of no value and deserved the treatment he was meting out. Oh, his abuse wasn't physical, but it came near to destroying her all the same. She may need a lot of therapy to break away from the chains he forged.' I took a deep breath. 'Somewhere inside the cowering rabbit, though, I believe there's a strong woman. Surely it isn't too late. Miracles do happen. She's young yet, and she has Ruth's support, and her church's.'

None of the men said anything, but I could clearly hear what they were thinking, something along the lines of a worm turning.

'Christopher.' Alan spoke. 'I want to talk to you later about other "possibilities" among Atkinson's friends. Make that acquaintances, since I don't think he had actual friends. Meanwhile, Davies, what can any of us do to help?'

That was a bold step, making an assumption that he would allow me, a total amateur, to have any part in the investigation.

Alan looked amused. Christopher and Davies were taken aback. Davies, however, recovered quickly.

'I understand, Mrs— Dorothy, that you have been of considerable help to your husband in a number of investigations in the past.'

'To me, both before and after my retirement, and to many official investigators,' said Alan warmly. 'If she had been born thirty years later, she would certainly have been recruited by the police wherever she lived. She has natural talent for nosing out the truth.'

Davies gave me a little half bow. 'Then I'd be very happy for you to talk to anyone you think might be able to give us any information about the matter. We, of course, will be trying to trace the source of the nitroglycerine, as well as the movements of everyone on our current list of possibilities.'

'Thank you.' I bowed in the same way. 'That sort of painstaking search is the kind of thing the police do really well. I should tell you that I'll mostly be trying to unearth motives.' I held up my hands. 'Yes, I do know that's the least important of the pegs an investigation hangs on. But it isn't totally irrelevant, and it doesn't involve any expert criminological knowledge, just a little understanding of the way people's minds work. And I've acquired quite a lot of that over the years.'

'Then you have my blessing.' He stood. 'I'll leave you to it, and I'll try to keep you informed.'

When he was gone, I took a deep breath. 'That went better than I could have hoped. I wasn't sure he'd be wild about the idea of interference from an amateur, and an American at that.'

Alan aimed a mock punch at me. 'You are not an American anymore, my dear wife, remember?'

'Not to you. But I still have the accent, to English ears anyway, and at least half the time I speak American instead of English, and I certainly still have the uppity American attitude that a woman can do anything. So he gets lots of points for letting me butt in. And speaking of which, I was thinking of going to Donald's old place of business to see what I could find out. I don't know much about it; only what Christopher told me: that he was an accountant and Brian worked with him.'

'I've done a little digging since we last spoke,' Christopher said. 'It turns out that they were partners, as of two or three years ago. Brian had been working for a big firm for quite a while, but when Donald joined the firm, he somehow persuaded Brian that there would be more opportunities if they worked directly for their own clients. Brian had a lot more money than Donald, so he was the one who got stuck with setting up the partnership, all the legalities and fees to pay and that. And then Donald saw to it that he himself was the one who got the lucrative clients. He was the handsome, charismatic one, the fox in the henhouse.'

'And then he stole Brian's wife, as well,' I said with a snarl. 'So lots of reasons there for hatred and resentment. The thing is, though, did they have an office off somewhere by themselves, or in an office building with other people around?'

'They stayed in the building where Brian had worked but in a different area, on the first floor.'

*Second*, I mentally translated.

'Brian wasn't in favour of that, but of course Donald prevailed.'

'Good. So that means there will be people there who knew both of them.'

'They may not be eager to talk to you. In fact, they may not have much to say. Of course they all knew Brian – and Donald a bit. But office culture is different in England, Dorothy. Not as chatty as in America.'

I smiled. 'I'll get them to talk, never fear.'

# TWELVE

'And just how do you propose to do that?' asked my husband as we finished dinner. We'd chosen to eat at the hotel, as it was pretty late by the time our guests departed, and had enjoyed an excellent shepherd's pie, full of chunks of tender lamb. I should, I suppose, have felt guilty about eating one of the sweet little creatures I loved to see gambolling on the hillsides with their mothers. I didn't, not a bit.

I downed a last bite of crème brûlée and smiled at my husband. 'I'm going to try one of my best acts: the dumb American. I'll stroll into the building and up to wherever the accounting firm's office is, and start being stupid in the broadest American accent I can produce. As long as most of the employees are men, I'll be fine. Men love to believe that the ladies, God bless 'em, haven't a single brain cell. They'll thoroughly enjoy setting me straight, and I'll steer the conversation so they'll tell me all kinds of things.'

'You are an unprincipled woman.'

'True, in a good cause. The act has never worked with you, though.'

'Because I learned, early on, that you possessed quite a number of brain cells. Are we going to have coffee?'

'If accompanied by brandy, yes. The one may cancel out the other when it comes to getting some sleep.'

So we had some lovely espresso and some lovely B & B and went up to bed nicely drowsy.

Unfortunately, in my case the espresso won out. I was tired. I wanted to sleep, but the caffeine kept jumping around in my brain. What was I actually going to say to those men? What if they were mostly women? Lots of women go into accounting these days. They wouldn't buy the silly Yank routine, and direct questioning wouldn't work. It never did, when the questioner was totally unofficial, with no right to ask anything at all. I'd be out the door and back down the elevator in no time.

Drat! Why had I had that espresso? It was having another predictable effect, as well. Resignedly, I got out of bed with as little fuss as possible, used the loo, and went not back to bed, but to the easy chair by the window. No need to wake Alan.

Why had I gotten myself into this anyway? I hadn't liked Donald Atkinson one bit. Why did I care who killed him? It was none of my affair.

*Any man's death diminishes me,* said a voice in my head. *Send not to know for whom the bell tolls . . .*

Having a lot of quotations stored in one's brain has its downside. I tried hard to shut up old John Donne, but he persisted in reminding me that no man was an island, and so on and so on.

Okay, okay. I was in this whether I liked it or not. And I would, I promised John, do my best to track this murderer to his lair. However insufficient my best might be.

The promise apparently satisfied the antsy gremlins in my head. I crawled back in with Alan and was asleep in five minutes.


As I've already mentioned, I usually surface slowly in the morning. At least one cup of coffee is necessary to bring me to full consciousness, and a second to restore a decent attitude to life in general, let alone a new day. That day I surprised Alan, and indeed myself, by bouncing out before he was awake and making the coffee, always his job.

'Are you well?' he asked, when one open eye observed me busying myself with the coffee.

'C'mon! Do I usually get up at the crack of dawn when I'm sick? I'm perfectly well, just felt like getting a head start on the day.'

'Is this my wife I'm talking to, or has some beautiful stranger stolen in while I was asleep?'

'Okay, enough! Come and drink your coffee. It may not be as good as yours, but at least you didn't have to make it. And for your information, I made a promise last night to get on with this investigation and give it all I've got.'

He struggled into his bathrobe and took a sip of coffee. 'Mmm. Not bad at all. I may let you make it from now on. A promise to whom?'

'John Donne.'

My husband seldom disappoints. It took another sip or two, but he got it. 'Ah. Been thinking about bells and islands?'

'And why I should care who killed a man I couldn't stand. The Dean of St Paul's was a pretty good preacher, and he answered my question for me. So when do offices in England open for business? At home it was usually eight—'

'Nine here, most usually. Which means we have plenty of time for breakfast before you grab your lance and go tilting at windmills. Are you headed for the shower?'

'Already did that. It's all yours.'

He finished his coffee and plodded to the bathroom.

I called Christopher as soon as I could. When I was growing up, one didn't make a phone call before nine except in case of dire emergency. This was an emergency. I waited until eight thirty, fidgeting every minute.

'Christopher, I need to know how to get to Donald's office. His old office, I mean. The big accounting firm.'

'I won't tell you; I'll take you. Carlisle can be tricky, and it's hard to park.'

'Carlisle?'

'That's where the offices are. When do you want to go?'

'Oh, good heavens, if it's in Carlisle, we should have left before now! How long does it take to get there?'

'Nearly an hour at this time of day.'

'Oh, and I wanted to be there first thing! How soon can you be here?'

'Five minutes.'

The drive to Carlisle was beautiful, but I was in no mood to appreciate it. I was trying out various approaches in my head, writing a script, as it were. Of course my lines depended on the responses I got from the other actors, and I had no way of predicting that.

Christopher cleared his throat. I came back to the present and saw that we were in a city. 'Didn't want to interrupt your train of thought, but do you want me to go in with you? I know a few of those people; I could introduce you, grease the wheels a bit.'

'No! I mean no, thank you, it's very kind of you, but I want to go in as an American woman who don't know nothin' from nothin', if you understand what I mean.'

He shook his head. 'I don't, but if you do, that's fine with me. And here we are.'

He pointed to a two-storey building on our left; it looked like another shop in what was obviously a shopping area. 'Oh. I was picturing a modern high-rise.'

'Not in Carlisle, m'dear. I'll be across the way having tea if you want me. Good luck.'

I took a deep breath, got out of the car, and entered the building. I was immensely relieved that the receptionist was a man. He'd be easier to bluff. I hoped.

'May I help you, madam?'

I had an insane impulse to say 'I ain't the madam, I'm the con-see-urge', quoting from *The Producers*. I restrained myself. 'Oh! Are you an accountant?' American as all get-out.

'No, madam.'

'But there are accountants here? Because I need one.'

'This is indeed an accounting firm, but we work with companies, not individuals.'

'Oh. But all these people' – I gestured vaguely toward the sea of desks behind him – 'are accountants?'

'Yes, madam, but I'm afraid—'

'Oh, good. I'm looking for somebody to help me figure out my taxes. It's all so different here from back home, I can't make head nor tail of it all.' I gave him a megawatt smile and strode past him.

'But, madam, you can't—'

Ignoring him, I moved quickly to a desk near the back of the room, which was occupied by a fatherly-looking man working away at his computer. He looked up in surprise, and I pulled over a nearby chair.

'Hi! I suppose I should have made an appointment, but I don't always know how you do things over here, so I just came in, and you looked like such a nice, approachable man, I picked you to talk to about my taxes. Have you worked here a long time? You look – I don't know – really settled and comfortable with your work.'

'Thank you. And yes, I have been here for quite a time. I'm afraid, though, that none of us in this firm work for individual clients. You want a private accountant.'

'Oh dear, is that what that nice young man up front was trying to tell me? Your British accent is so sweet, but half the time I can't understand a word. So you can't help me?' I contrived to sound distraught, very near the end of my rope. 'I was really hoping . . . you see, I'm all alone over here, with nobody to show me how to do things, and everything is so different . . .' I sniffed, pulling a tissue from my purse. 'Can't you recommend somebody anyway?'

A man stopped by the desk. He looked very official. 'Burke, is there some problem?'

'No, no,' said the kind man. 'This lady is an American seeking help with the Inland Revenue. She drifted in here by mistake and is asking if we can recommend someone who works with private clients.'

'Hmm,' said Mr Official. 'There's always Sullivan, although . . .'

'Exactly.' Mr Burke sighed. 'There is one very competent man, Brian Sullivan, who used to work here, but set up his own private business with a partner. I'm not sure . . .'

He let the sentence die away, just like Mr Official. Bingo!

'Oh, do you think he could take a look at my problem? You say he's very competent. Does he do things like taxes?'

'Of course.' The two men exchanged glances. Finally Mr Burke cleared his throat. 'He doesn't actually work for this firm anymore but has his own independent firm in this building. The only trouble is – well, his partner just died, and he's somewhat distressed right now – making some mistakes, as I understand, that sort of thing – I'm sure he'll get it all straightened around in time, but if you need help now—'

When people leave things out, it's usually because there are things they don't want to say. I decided it was time to probe a little. 'Oh dear, mistakes? What kind of mistakes? I can't afford to get into trouble with the government. Oh, please tell me what I should do! This man sounds ideal, but of course if he's an Irishman . . .' I was hoping to play on the instinctive English distrust of the Irish, and it worked.

'The fact is, Mrs—'

'Martin.' I crossed my fingers, hoping they'd never heard of me.

'Mrs Martin, the unhappy fact is, there are rumours that Mr Sullivan might not be quite honest,' said Mr Official.

'Now, Henry, you know it was probably Atkinson who led him astray. I've always thought Brian was a good man.' Mr Burke wore a worried frown.

'Heavens! Dishonest? Goodness, in what way?'

But there I'd gone a step too far. Neither of them was willing to go into details. 'Oh, this and that, you know,' said Mr Burke. 'And it's only a rumour. But there are certainly other good accountants in Carlisle. If you'll ask Rupert, at the front desk, he can give you some names.'

'Oh, thank you! You've been so nice to help me like this! And I'm so sorry to interrupt your work. Bye!'

The office was open plan, with here and there a cubicle, but mostly just desks out in the open. I hadn't been shouting, or at least I hoped not, but apparently my voice, with its strident, nasal American accent, had carried. As I made my way back to the front, a plain little man at a desk way over to the side beckoned me over.

'I couldn't help overhearing,' he said, very quietly. 'I wanted to tell you to stay far away from Brian Sullivan. The stories about him and Atkinson are more than rumour. It's a fact that they stole from their clients, big time. Maybe Burke is right that it was mostly Atkinson's doing, and maybe now that he's out of the way, Sullivan has turned over a new leaf. But in your position, I wouldn't take the chance. Call me later, and we can talk.'

He handed me a card and turned back to his computer, and I high-tailed it out, avoiding the front desk, and sought out Christopher.

I found Alan instead. He sat peacefully in front of tea and scones in a pleasant little café across the street.

'Me, too,' I said, gesturing to Alan's plate as the waitress passed by. 'Alan, what are you doing here? Not that I'm not delighted.'

He chuckled. 'Christopher phoned me, said he had some errands to run and told me where to come. I was headed here anyway, wanting to talk to Christopher, so I didn't have far to drive. So did you have any luck?'

'I hit the jackpot, Alan! The first person I talked to – well, the second, counting the guy at the front desk – as much as told me that both Brian and Donald are – were – whatever – crooks.

And a guy I talked to on the way out confirmed it and gave me his card so I can talk to him later. How's that for a first attempt?'

He grinned. 'I had a bet with myself that you'd have a boat-load of information before you'd spent an hour in the place. Of course you have an advantage over the police. They have to tell the truth when they're conducting an investigation. Whereas your ability to tell a convincing lie is one of your best assets.'

'I didn't— Oh, thank you.' The waitress put down a fresh pot of tea, along with another cup and a plate of pastries, and went away. 'I didn't lie a lot, really, except for saying I needed help with my taxes. Played the helpless, not-too-bright American for all I was worth, and they either felt sorry for me or talked to me to get rid of a nuisance. I don't know which, and I don't care.' I poured myself some tea, refilled Alan's cup, and took a long, reviving drink.

'All right, details, please.'

Between sips of tea and bites of a lovely pastry I couldn't identify, I told him everything that had happened from the moment I entered the office. 'The best thing,' I concluded, popping the last of the pastry into my mouth, 'was that accidental encounter at the end. This' – I picked up the card – 'this Roger Taylor had eavesdropped, and stopped me to warn me against Brian Sullivan. He said quite firmly that both he and Atkinson had stolen from their clients, and invited me to call him for more.'

'Hmm. One man's opinion . . .'

'He stated it as fact. He didn't seem the sort to make up stuff. Not overly imaginative, I'd have thought. Of course, he couldn't offer proof in the moment or two at his disposal.'

'But you're going to call him and check.'

'Of course I am. This very evening, as soon as he gets home. Most businesses close at six, right?'

'Right. But this is the man's business card. Presumably the number is his business phone.'

I pointed out the small 'm' by the number. 'I'm betting this is his mobile. Anyway, I can but try.'

'Right. What are your plans for the rest of the day? It's barely mid-morning.'

'I don't have any. What about you?'

'Davies needs to know about this accusation of theft, but it would be better to wait until we have some facts to present to him. The police mind, you know.'

I grinned. 'I ought to know by now, my dear. Evidence! Proof! Facts! No room for speculation or opinions, much less impressions and hunches. Whereas I specialize in all those vague beliefs. And I remind you that they often lead to cold, hard facts.'

Alan grinned back. 'You're preaching to the choir, you know. I learned long ago not to dismiss your hunches. But we're dealing with a senior policeman who doesn't know you or your remarkable history of being right, and to talk him around, we'll need facts – which probably means waiting until you've talked to Mr Taylor. So meanwhile, have you planned any devious tactics for worming some information out of your favourite in the suspect stakes, Mr Thompson?'

'Ugh! *How* I dislike that man, and I don't even really know him. I forget – did Christopher ever tell us where he works? I mean, I know he's a lawyer – solicitor – but he must have an office somewhere.'

Alan had his phone in hand. 'Christopher? Nesbitt here. My good wife is wondering if Harold Thompson has an office anywhere near here?' Pause. 'I see. But you say he's seldom there. Where does he conduct his business, then?' A longer pause. 'Ah. You see, Dorothy would like to speak with him. Do you have any suggestions?' Pause. 'Yes, please do. And yes, we'd love to. See you then.'

He clicked off. 'Slippery as an eel, our friend. That isn't exactly what Christopher said, but that's the gist of it. Thompson has an office, nominally, but he's almost never in it. He's the club/pub/ football match sort of lawyer, meets his clients on the cricket pitch or at lunch, or anywhere he can sweet-talk them into paying him a great deal more than his services are worth.'

'I take it that's also a free interpretation.'

'Almost the exact words, actually. So Christopher said he'd ask around and see if anyone knows where the bloke might turn up in the next day or two. We're going to meet him – Christopher, not Thompson – for a drink at The Inn at five to collect his gleanings. And if something definite comes up before then, he'll call.'

'Right. That gives us most of the day to kill somehow. Any ideas?'

'We could go sightseeing. It's a fine day, and there's a great deal of the Lake District we haven't surveyed yet.'

'Yes, but from the maps I've seen, most of the glorious views involve hiking up a hill, and I'm not great at that anymore. Besides, I'm not ready yet to abandon my quest to find out as much as I can about Atkinson, and I've had a sudden thought about that. What would you think about going to talk to Lilian?' I studied his broad smile. 'Or maybe it would be better for me to go alone!'

'Oh, no you don't! You don't snatch away the piece of candy when you're just offered it!'

'You,' I said, 'are a fraud. Masquerading as a happily married man and ready to drool over the first siren to come along.'

'Mixed metaphor, my love. I don't think one drools over a siren.'

At that we both broke up. People in the tea shop were beginning to stare. 'Let's get out of here before they throw us out. Then you can call Christopher again and get the siren's address.'

Christopher showed some inclination to want to go with us ('The siren call again,' I commented), but we persuaded him that a delegation wasn't a good idea. So after we'd finished our tea and pastries, Alan entered the Sullivan address into the satnav, and we started out. 'Is Windermere far from here?' I asked. 'Because we need to be back by five.'

'A little over an hour – unless I get lost. And Sallie here won't let me do that.' He patted the screen.

I held my tongue, remembering the story I'd heard in America in the early days of GPS, when someone looking for a hotel had been directed straight into an old cemetery. That was years ago, though. Probably the technology had improved since.

Probably.

# THIRTEEN

I knew enough to keep still while Alan negotiated the narrow road and heavy traffic. The Carlisle–Windermere route seemed to be a popular one on a lovely late-summer day, and once we got into the town, the traffic was worse. Tourists were making the most of the weather, and at one point, Alan had to turn aside from the way Sallie wanted him to go because a large delivery van was blocking the way and creating a major tie-up.

However, Sallie (grudgingly, after several reproofs) redirected us, and we lost only a few minutes getting to the house, which was actually a little way out of the town proper. It didn't matter when we got there, of course, since Lilian wasn't expecting us.

And we weren't expecting what awaited us at the end of the drive up to the house.

I gasped. 'Alan! Sallie made a mistake! This is a palace!'

It was an old stone house. Huge didn't begin to describe it. Slate roof, mullioned windows – dozens of them. Wings added on everywhere you looked. A massive double front door with the kind of iron hinges I associated with fairy-tale castles.

Alan's only response was a low whistle. There were no words. We sat in the car, stunned, and might have turned around and given up if that amazing front door hadn't opened. Lilian stepped out and came over to us.

'Were you looking for something?' Her voice was crisp, her meaning clearly 'You're trespassing, you know'. Then she looked in Alan's window. 'Wait – do I know you? You look familiar.'

Alan recovered his equanimity. 'Mrs Sullivan? Yes, we met at a party the other day. I'm Alan Nesbitt, and this is my wife Dorothy Martin. I hope you don't mind an unannounced visit.'

'Mind! I'm so bored I was ready to invite the postman in for a drink. You're a godsend. Do come in, please. No, don't worry about the car; it's fine where it is.'

In a daze, I took Alan's arm as we followed Lilian into the house.

The living room was just as amazing as the outside of the place had promised, light and spacious with two big windows, and a fireplace not quite big enough to roast an ox, but a good-sized calf at least. The furniture was modern, brightly upholstered and comfortable, not the period pieces I had expected. The whole room, in fact, had the look of recent remodelling.

And it was a mess. Magazines were strewn everywhere. Glasses had been left to make rings on the lovely light oak tables. A pair of sneakers, along with socks, lay carelessly by one window. A bowl of chrysanthemums drooped for lack of water, dropping petals on the mantel.

Lilian matched the room. Beautiful in herself, but uncared for. Her hair needed a good washing and a fresh cut. She was dressed in jeans that looked frayed by age, not intent, and a tattered man's shirt. She wore dirty scuffs, and kicked them off the moment she stepped into the room.

The really annoying thing was that she still looked gorgeous.

She gestured toward one of the couches and said, 'Now, what would you like to drink? Wine? Beer? Whisky?'

She had made it difficult to request tea, and it was early in the day for anything else. 'A dry sherry, please, if you have any. Or I'd be perfectly happy with tonic.'

'Gin and tonic?'

'Actually, tonic and tonic.' I said it with a laugh, and she laughed in reply.

'Got it. With ice, I suppose.'

She'd picked up on the accent I hadn't, this time, tried to exaggerate. 'You've found me out. Yes, please, with ice.'

Alan asked for beer. When we were settled – Lilian with a tumbler of something dark amber – she said, 'All right. As I don't know you, really, and you don't know me, I can only suppose you came with an agenda.'

Her stiff drink wasn't affecting her perceptions. 'You're quite right,' I said somewhat apologetically. 'Alan and I are both uneasy about Donald Atkinson's death. Alan is a retired policeman, and he isn't satisfied that the death was accidental.'

'And you want to know who might have wanted him dead.'

That was alarmingly on the button.

'Exactly.' I began to wish there was something in my glass besides tonic.

She gulped some of her drink, which looked like neat whisky. 'Actually, almost anyone who knew him. Not excluding me.'

She enjoyed our reaction to that.

'Oh, I'm sure you know about Donald and me. We never made a secret of it. What you don't know is that I never liked him much. And I was getting really bored with him.' Another taste of her drink. 'At first it was kind of exciting. Brian is— Well, I won't go into details, but he isn't very imaginative. Donald was. But he was so completely in love with himself. Not with me, never with me. I don't think he had the capacity to love, actually. I was just another trophy, and frankly that gets old quite quickly. I wanted to end it, but – oh, I do hate to admit this – but I was almost scared of him.'

'In what way?' Alan put down his beer and leaned forward.

'Oh, the good old physical way. He would not have been above hurting me if I damaged his self-image. He was the great lover, you see, amongst all his other greatnesses. He left women; they didn't leave him. I actually thought about going away for a while, to France or Spain or even farther. I didn't want to. I love living here. I love this house.'

'The house is yours?' I interrupted.

'Yes. I bought it a few years ago. Do you like it?'

'It's splendid.' I looked around. 'I wouldn't want to live here, though. I prefer my own house. It's old, early seventeenth century, and cosy.'

'And the very devil to maintain,' added Alan. 'I too love the place, but there's never a time when something doesn't need repair or replacement.'

'And that's one reason I'm so attached to this place. It was one of the first fine houses built in Windermere, but it was completely renovated some years ago. Old on the outside, new on the inside.'

She finished her drink. 'Well, you didn't come here to talk about houses but to learn about Donald's enemies, and I'm afraid I haven't been much help. Brian hated him, of course, but Brian's not the murderous kind.'

'Forgive me for asking, but were Brian's feelings based only on your relationship with Donald?'

'Oh, no. He didn't like it, of course, but he's devoted to me, in his peculiar way, and he could tell the affair was nearly at an end. No, there was something else, something to do with the business, but I don't know exactly what. Neither of them would ever talk about it. Donald always pretended things were as smooth as cream, and Brian simply wouldn't say a word about it.'

She picked up her empty glass and put it down again. 'Then of course there's Harold, but I'm sure you know about him. Pretended to be grooming Donald to stand for Parliament, but he'd backed off of late. I think he began to see that Donald had cheesed off too many people to make him electable. And Harold is not the type to tolerate losers. Then – let's see. Oh, there are, of course, all the people Donald and Brian defrauded.'

She let the remark lie there in the sudden silence while she left the room and came back with a fresh drink.

Alan cleared his throat. 'Defrauded?' he asked.

'Oh, yes, didn't you know about that? I suppose it isn't exactly common knowledge yet, but it soon will be. Mind you, I don't actually know what's been going on, not in the sense of having evidence, but I can draw conclusions just as well as anybody. Brian has been increasingly uneasy about something to do with the business. So was Donald, though he brazened it out, denied anything was wrong. But Donald had been throwing money around.'

'Brian has not?' Alan asked.

'No. Brian's the cautious type. If he lays hands on any extra money, he puts it straight in the bank.'

'And has he been doing that of late?'

Lilian gave him an icy look. 'We don't share an account, so I have no idea.'

'Sorry to interrupt. Do go on. Donald was spending a lot.'

'Yes. He bought me some expensive jewellery. Hideous, but expensive. Not my style at all.'

She saw my look. 'I don't always dress like a chimney sweep, you know. I can look very nice when I choose, but always understated. Pearls in my ears and at my throat, that sort of thing. Never big clunky brooches or huge heavy earrings. Yes, I know I wore some of it to that party, but it isn't me. No. I had planned to wear what he gave me once or twice and then quietly sell it, perhaps in London so he wouldn't know. Now it doesn't have to be quiet.'

'Right. Expensive gifts. What else?'

'Bespoke suits. New golf clubs. He showed them to me, and I laughed, because I'd never known him to play a decent game. A new car, a new wallet, shirts – everything to make him look important.'

'And you wondered where the money was coming from,' I said. It wasn't a question.

'You bet I did. I knew he didn't earn that kind of money, and I was bloody well sure he wasn't getting it from Sarah. She may have had a big blind spot where Donald was concerned, but it didn't extend to financial dealings. Her father had taught her to be careful with money, and her inheritance was tied up in a trust or something. Anyway, she wouldn't or couldn't give any to Donald. She met almost all the household expenses, but his personal expenses were his responsibility. It made him furious. He'd married her for her money, of course, and then to find out it was indeed hers and not his set off his fuse. Not that it took much to set him off.'

'And did he hit you up for money, too?' I looked around. 'Plainly you have a bit here and there.'

I wondered if that was way too rude, but she laughed with genuine amusement. 'You could say that. I have more money than I'll ever need, and yes, dear Donald thought it would be nice if I shared, and no, I didn't. Donald was getting what he really wanted from me, and that was enough. More than enough, toward the end.'

'So you think the money he was flashing about was . . . not on the up and up?' asked my husband.

Lilian laughed. 'Alan, you are fond of euphemisms, aren't you? Yes, I think it was stolen from his clients. I know a little about accounting. There are dozens of ways to pocket money without anyone being any the wiser, for quite a time. In the end, of course, it always comes out, and then there's hell to pay.'

Alan and I had both finished our drinks, and Lilian didn't seem inclined to offer us another. In any case, we'd been there longer than we'd intended.

I stood. 'Mrs Sullivan, you've been more than helpful. I'm sorry if we've had to bring up some painful memories.'

She stood, too, and held out her hand. 'In the first place, my name is Lilian. In the second, nothing about this afternoon has been painful. More cathartic. Donald Atkinson was a right bastard, and it's been a relief to finally let myself say so. Come again, any time you like. I get very tired of my own company.'

I had turned toward the door, but I turned back. 'Lilian, what do you do with your time?'

She shrugged. 'Read. Watch the telly. Climb the walls.'

'Okay, it's none of my business, but you're an intelligent and honest woman. Just because you don't need to earn a living is no reason for you to let your mind turn to cream cheese. Find yourself a charity that interests you and go to work. Or found one! You have the money and the time and the ability to do a lot of good in the world. Then maybe you won't need to turn to another toy boy to keep from dying of boredom.'

She was so astonished by that presumptuous speech that she let Alan and me leave without a word of farewell. When I turned to look back, the front door was still standing wide open.

# FOURTEEN

We were a little late meeting Christopher, but he was happily occupied with a gin and tonic in the lounge. When Alan had provided us with happy-hour libations, we settled down to tell him about our afternoon.

'And she was drinking at a great rate, and it didn't seem to affect her at all,' I complained when we had finished the story. 'I get a little muzzy after one of these, and it isn't nearly as large or as dark as her drink was.'

Alan chuckled. 'You thought she was drinking whisky, didn't you?'

'Well, it certainly wasn't gin!'

'It was tea. I caught a whiff as she passed by. Strong cold tea.'

'But why . . .?'

'Just playing a game, I suspect. I'm-smarter-than-these-snoops, or something like that. I'm sure she hoped at least one of us would drink enough for indiscretion, but it didn't work. That really was straight tonic she gave you, love?'

'It was. Certainly no gin, and no vodka, either, unless they've come up with a totally tasteless one. But no, I would have felt it after a while. It was tonic, and very nice, too. Schweppes Bitter Lemon.'

'So you were stone-cold sober, and irritated enough to make that remarkable speech at the end. Well done, my dear!'

So then we had to give Christopher the gist of what I'd said.

'I meant it, too. I couldn't stand it any longer. Here she is, a perfectly capable woman doing nothing at all with her life, so bored she was ready to fall into bed with a man she despised, just for something to do. I couldn't keep still. And I've probably made an enemy for life – and a wealthy, influential one at that. Will I ever learn to keep my mouth shut, I wonder?'

'Probably not, my dear.' My beloved husband laughed again. 'But you said what needed saying, and probably no one but you could get away with it.'

'It remains to be seen whether I'll get away with it. That clever mind may be thinking up some retribution at this very moment. But, Christopher, did you have any luck tracking down the elusive Mr Thompson?'

'Elusive, Dorothy, is the *mot juste*. Nobody seems to have seen him for a day or two. He hasn't been to his office, nor has he called in for messages. He hasn't been to his London club or his favourite golf course. He hasn't been occupied with any court proceedings. None of his friends, at least the ones I know, have heard from him. No one answers at his house here in Grasmere or his flat in Carlisle, and none of his neighbours have seen him lately. He seems to have vanished into thin air.' Christopher took a pull at his drink.

I looked at Alan. Alan looked at Christopher.

Alan spoke first. 'I trust you're not suggesting . . .'

'Not suggesting a thing. But you have to admit it's interesting. First his promising puppet begins to look less promising. Then he gets himself killed, and dear old Harold disappears. Make anything you want of that.'

'I suppose you've thought of all the possibilities. Does he have family out of town, or out of the country, even?'

'I talked to Davies about that, just in a general way, you know. The answer is, the man seems to have no family at all. And no one named Harold Thompson has left the country in the past three days.'

I swallowed. 'I'm sure you've tried to reach him by phone, text, email—'

'Everything but carrier pigeon.' Christopher was trying to keep it light, but his worry showed in his tense neck and shoulders. 'The phone goes to voicemail. No answer to any other message.'

'His house— Oh, no, you said he isn't there. Why does he have both a house and a flat? Is he married, by the way?'

'Divorced. A long time ago, from what I hear. And no, I've heard no rumours that his flat is some sort of love nest. His office is in Carlisle, so sometimes it's convenient not to have to drive home to Grasmere.'

Hmm. Grasmere wasn't all that far from Carlisle, and Harold didn't have a name for keeping his nose to the grindstone and working late at the office. I filed that Carlisle flat away under 'needs investigation' and opened my mouth to ask Christopher another question.

Alan beat me to it. 'Does he drink heavily?'

Aha! Maybe Alan had hit on the explanation.

'I've never seen him anything close to drunk. And I *have* seen him turn down a second round in a pub, though he'd often offer one himself, and make his what looked like plain sparkling water.'

So there went that idea. 'Does he make a lot of money? Houses and flats aren't cheap in this neck of the woods.'

'Well.' Christopher hesitated. 'I believe his law practice wasn't enormously lucrative.' He had put a slight emphasis on the words *law practice*.

I'd had it. 'Oh, for heaven's sake! This is just us, Christopher! If you're trying to tell us something, come right out with it.'

'There are laws about slander.'

'Right. Take it as read. So if you won't say it, let me. You're implying that here's yet another guy in this nasty little group who's defrauding somebody. I begin to wonder if anybody in this idyllic community is playing it straight. Present company excepted, of course. Alan, you've been very quiet. What's your take on it all?'

'I think that we don't know enough. We know almost nothing, in fact. We've heard a plethora of rumours but not one solid piece of evidence. And I, for one, am hungry. As I often remind Dorothy, to her annoyance, low blood sugar hampers the efficient working of the brain. I suggest we have ourselves a meal, here or elsewhere in the village, and try to make some plans when we have a few working brain cells.'

'But not,' I put in, 'before I call that man from the accounting firm. He might just give us some hard facts.'

'Love, I hate to rain on your parade, but chances are the chap will be at his dinner, and won't be too pleased to be called away. Meal first, detection later is my advice.'

I hated to admit that he was probably right.

Christopher said he needed to get home, so Alan and I had a meal at the hotel. I imagine it was good; all the food we'd had there so far was fine, but I was in such a hurry to get on with our search that I didn't really notice what I was putting in my mouth.

We went straight up to our room after dinner, wanting privacy for the phone call. I took a deep breath, picked up my mobile and the man's card, and punched in the number.

He answered promptly. 'Taylor here.'

I turned on the phone's speaker. 'Mr Taylor, my name is Dorothy Martin. You gave me your card this morning at your office. I had been inquiring about finding a personal accountant.' I'd allowed some of the American to drop from my accent.

'Ah, yes. I'm very happy you called. I had feared you might go ahead and do business with Mr Sullivan, which I assure you would be a terrible mistake.'

'You did say that he and his partner had – um – dealt improperly with some of their clients.'

'No. I said that Sullivan and Atkinson had stolen from their clients. I don't pussyfoot, Mrs . . . Martin, was it?'

'Yes, and I'm very glad to hear it. I don't care for euphemism, either. But I have to ask – have you proof of what you're saying? There are laws about slander—'

There was a silence at the other end.

'Mr Taylor, are you there?'

'I am. Mrs Martin, what is this really all about? You're not looking for an accountant, are you?'

'No, sir, I am not, and I'm glad to drop the playacting.' I looked at Alan, who shrugged. 'The fact is, I'm looking into Mr Atkinson's death. I'm visiting in Grasmere with my husband, and we happened to attend the games last Sunday, when Mr Atkinson died. My husband is a retired policeman – a chief constable, in fact – and several things about the death seemed to him, and to me, to be questionable.'

'I see. And you have taken it upon yourself to investigate what you perceive to be a crime. You obviously have no official standing, or you wouldn't have gone to the trouble to weave that elaborate web of deception.'

'You're quite right. We – that is, my husband and I and our friend Christopher Prideaux – are working with the police on the case, but—'

'Christopher. You're a friend of Christopher's?'

'He and my husband go way back. They worked together in Cornwall.'

'Well, why didn't you say so! I know Christopher. He helped untangle a nasty mess for me once years ago. I'll tell you about it someday, but for now – where can we meet, so I can give you chapter and verse?'

Alan shrugged again.

'Is there a good pub somewhere? We're at The Inn, and it's very pleasant, but I'm developing a case of cabin fever. I'd like to get out.'

'Lots of good pubs. My favourite has a quiet little corner. We're just past the worst of the tourist invasion, so we should be nicely private. It's a bit out of the way, so I'll pick you up. Ten minutes?'

The pub wasn't exactly quiet, but there was a private corner where the noise level was just high enough to mask our conversation. Mr Taylor went to the bar and got pints for himself and Alan, and tonic with ice and lime for me. I didn't even have to request the ice.

Our table wasn't very big, but Mr Taylor pushed the beer mats out of the way and pulled some papers out of his jacket. 'These are letters from some of S and A's clients. That's what they called themselves, S and A Accounting. When clients began to notice discrepancies in their accounts, first they complained to S and A, and then when that didn't go anywhere, some of them turned to us. They knew Sullivan had worked for us originally and thought we might be able to get answers from him. As soon as I get permission from the writers of the letters, I'm going to turn them over to the police. Meanwhile, I've copied the letters and removed the senders' names and the amounts of money involved, to protect their confidentiality when I show them to you.' He handed one sheaf of papers to me, another to Alan. 'I wouldn't have dreamed of doing this for people I don't know, but you're friends of Christopher's.'

That, I gathered, was sufficient guarantee of our bona fides.

'I also added up the amounts of money involved, so you'll understand the scale I'm talking about. There was never more than a few thousand from any one client, but they added up to well over two hundred thousand pounds.'

I gasped. 'That's one whole bushel load of money. In the States, grand larceny for sure.'

'The crime of larceny no longer exists in England,' said Roger. 'This would be tried as robbery and/or fraud. I'm not certain about the precise definitions which apply to individuals as opposed to businesses, but the outcome would not have been good for S and A. Now that Atkinson is dead, any legal proceedings are held up.'

I frowned. 'Will that give Brian Sullivan a chance to repay the clients? That is, would he be liable for all of it, even if Atkinson did most of the book-cooking?'

'It depends on how their partnership was drawn up,' said Roger, 'and when and where. The laws have changed over the years and are different in different parts of the UK. So the answer is, I don't know. And to tell the truth, I don't think Sullivan has anything like enough money to repay even half the debt.'

'His wife does.'

I didn't know I said it aloud until Alan replied, 'She could repay. But would she? She didn't appear to me to care two-hundred-thousand-pounds worth about her husband.'

'Hard to tell. She's not easy to read. But what I was actually getting at was this. If Brian is now in a situation of having to pay back even half of what the partnership stole, he's worse off than before. And he would surely have known that. He's a number cruncher, after all. So where's the motive for murdering Atkinson?'

The two men looked at each other. 'My dear,' said Alan at the same moment that Mr Taylor began, 'Mrs Martin—' Both gave me a pitying look.

Alan continued. 'Dorothy, love, have you forgotten that Donald hurt Brian where he was most sensitive? A man can forgive many things, but not the theft of his woman. We don't know how a rather ordinary little man like Brian managed to snare a trophy wife like Lilian, but having done so, to have her snatched away from him was the most unkindest cut of all.'

I sat back and sipped my tonic, needing the refreshment. 'I feel really sorry for him,' I said, surprising even myself. 'I mean, look at him. He's a middle-aged man watching his second marriage disintegrate. Even his son has eyes for his gorgeous wife. He got caught up in a toxic partnership with a rotten sleaze who not only involved him in fraud but started bedding his wife as well. And now that the sleaze is dead, things are even worse, because Brian's now deeply in debt and suspected of murdering Donald. All right, Alan, maybe not officially, but certainly in the world of rumour. He must be in despair.' I watched Alan's eyes echo the thoughts that were forming in my own mind.

'Call her,' he said urgently.

'I don't have her phone number!'

Mr Taylor had caught up. 'I have Brian's landline number. I don't know if they still use it.'

He picked up his mobile and placed the call. It rang and rang.

Just as he was about to give up, we could hear a loud, angry female voice saying, 'Who the hell is this?'

Taylor handed me the phone and put it on speaker. 'Lilian, this is Dorothy Martin. I didn't have your mobile number. This is urgent. Is Brian at home?'

'No. What do you mean, urgent? I can give you his mobile number if you really want to talk to him.' Her voice implied that she couldn't imagine anyone wanting to talk to him.

'Have you seen or heard from him today?'

'No, and what's that to you?'

Alan took the phone. 'Alan Nesbitt here. Mrs Sullivan, we think Brian might be in considerable danger. Not to mince words, we think he might be suicidal. He must be found.'

The silence was so long I wondered if the connection had been lost. 'Mrs Sullivan?' Alan said.

'Suicidal?' Her voice was thin and almost unrecognizable.

I stepped back into the conversation. 'He certainly has good reason for deep unhappiness, if not despair. Where might he be found? A favourite pub, perhaps?'

'He doesn't go to pubs. He doesn't go any place where he might meet people. He's a loner. He likes to walk the hills.'

My heart sank. This part of England was *all* hills.

'Is there a particular path he likes?'

'I don't know. I never go with him.' Her voice was still a thin thread.

'Try, Mrs Sullivan! This could be very serious indeed.'

'There's a path down from our terrace, very steep, that leads to a proper path along the lake. I think he went that way some-times.' Her voice was growing stronger. 'Mr Nesbitt, why do you think Brian might be suicidal?'

'I think you know why, Mrs Sullivan.' Alan sounded as grim as I've ever heard him.

Another silence. 'I'm calling him right now. He'll answer if he knows it's me. Then I'm going to look for him.'

'Wait – wait one minute. Give me his mobile number – and yours.' He wrote them down, not even having time to say goodbye before she slammed the receiver down.

'She's just discovered he's important to her after all,' I said.

'I hope it isn't too late,' Alan replied.

# FIFTEEN

'Two of them missing,' I said to no one in particular. 'Brian and Harold.'

Mr Taylor having left us, we'd gone back to The Inn, and I was in a blue funk.

'Pull yourself together, love,' said Alan. 'Lilian is out looking for her husband, and we have no reason to think Harold is in trouble, or at least not that kind of trouble. It's my belief he went to ground until all the fuss is over.'

'Then you think he's involved in Donald's murder?'

'Or at least in the cloud of scandal and fraud that seems to be engulfing everyone who had anything to do with Atkinson. What a piece of work that man was!'

'Yes, well, I've said before that Harold is my candidate for First Murderer. And no, I don't have any good reason except that he's a sleaze, like Donald, and he's disappeared. Always a suspicious act.'

'Brian has disappeared, too,' said Alan gently. 'Do you also suspect him?'

'No. Call me inconsistent, but no, I don't. He's pathetic, Alan. I'll bet that once, before Donald got hold of him, he was an ordinary, honest, hard-working man. But he was manipulated into a cringing puppet. Like Sarah. I'm not so worried about Sarah. She has people to help her – Ruth, the church. She'll be all right once she regains some confidence. But Brian is out there on his own. The puppet strings have been cut, and he's collapsed. At this point, I don't think he has the guts to pick himself up, and he certainly never had the sly cleverness to plan an elaborate murder. I can see him pushing Donald off a cliff in sudden desperation, but this kind of murder – no. Alan, should we get a search party together? That thought of a cliff—' I shuddered.

'Don't forget, even suicide takes a kind of courage. Of course we don't know the man at all, but if we're correct in our reading of him, he's more apt to curl up in a ball somewhere and wait for fate to overtake him. I had some experience with his sort when I was a working policeman. Often they won't make up their mind to take the final step until they see someone coming after them. I think the best plan, for now, is to let Lilian search. She won't alarm him.'

'If she finds him. She didn't sound any too certain about where to look.'

'No, but she might know more than she admitted to us. She's a lady who likes to play her cards close to the chest. And think, Dorothy. If she isn't able to find Brian, the alternative is to call out a whole rescue squad. This is not at all an easy area to search, and I doubt we could convince the authorities to issue a call based simply on our feelings of unease.'

I sighed. 'I suppose you're right. So is there anything we can do about Harold?'

'I don't see what. The police are looking for him, and that's the sort of job they're very good at. They have the resources and the authority.'

'So we're dead in the water.' I said it before I heard myself, and cringed.

'Not quite that. We've got off on a tangent. Our original intent was to investigate a murder, not track down missing persons. Do you have your notebook handy?'

I excavated. Eventually I had to turn the purse upside down and dump everything on the bed. Once I got rid of the used tissues and the grocery receipts and a three-week-old church bulletin and a slip of paper with a couple of unidentified phone numbers on it, there was the small book, the cover dog-eared and a couple of pages missing – blank ones from the back, fortunately.

I held it up, a pen in the other hand.

'Right. What do you have so far?'

'Almost nothing. Just names. Brian and Harold. Oh, and Bob Smith,' I added reluctantly.

'I know how you feel about him, but he was grossly insulted on the air, in front of his fans,' said Alan. 'We do have to follow him up. Now, we had suggested some questions that needed to be answered about each of our possibilities. We've worked motive to death, but have done almost nothing about means or opportunity.'

'That's because the cops can do that much better. Just as they can search for missing persons. Lots of contacts, lots of people to follow up hints, lots of authority to ask questions.'

Alan nodded. 'Yes to all that. Still, we can ask some questions, too. Let's look at means.'

'Nitroglycerine in the ointment. We know that.'

'But we don't know who put it there,' said Alan patiently, 'or who made sure it was applied to Donald's rash. He couldn't possibly have done it himself. His arms certainly, but how many times have you asked me to put lotion on your back because you can't possibly reach that spot between your shoulder blades? Someone had to help.'

'Bob!' I said triumphantly.

'But you thought he was innocent.' Alan looked puzzled.

'I do. No, I don't mean he did it. But he was there. He was right behind Donald in the race. I have no idea where they all dressed, but there must have been something like a locker room somewhere. Bob might have seen what happened with the ointment.'

'But if he did—'

Alan and I exchanged horrified looks. I looked for my phone, which I'd misplaced as usual, and finally spotted it on a chair under my spare sweater. Then there was the search for Bob Smith's number. Voicemail.

'Mr Smith, it's Dorothy Martin. Please call me as soon as possible. It's urgent.'

'Don't get in a swivet, darling. He's probably at the studio. I'm not sure when that channel airs the news, but it ought to be right around now.'

I paid no attention to him. 'Call Christopher,' I ordered. 'He'll know. He might even know where Bob is if he isn't working tonight.'

But Christopher's phone went to voicemail, too. Alan left a message and turned back to me.

'We have to go to the studio,' I told him. 'I don't know where it is, but somebody will. If Bob saw anything, or even if the murderer thinks he did, he could be in the most terrible danger!'

'Dorothy. Calm down and think about this. Even if Bob did see someone applying ointment to Donald's rash, it is most unlikely to have been the murderer. We have agreed that the murderer is an extremely clever and careful person, who planned this out every step of the way. Would he have taken such a risk? In a setting with so many people milling about? I hardly think so.' He ruffled my hair. 'Yes, we need to talk to him, find out what he might have noticed, find out who else was on the scene, all that. But it's not an immediate matter of life and death.'

I let out the breath I hadn't known I'd been holding and took Alan's hand. 'You are so good for me. I was hunting windmills to tilt again, wasn't I?'

'As fast as your horse would take you. Now let's get ourselves a bedtime snack to keep busy until someone calls back.'

I was getting frantic when Bob Smith returned my call. 'Sorry, I was on the air. Urgent, you said.'

'Yes, but I was wrong. Important, yes, but not all that urgent, as Alan made me understand. Anyway, could you join us for coffee or a drink? We've thought of a few more things we'd like to ask you about – well, I'm sure you know about what.'

'Ah, yes, the well-known privacy of the mobile. You're at The Inn? I can be there in about half an hour, and coffee would be perfect.'

Alan went out and bought a small bottle of brandy and then ordered decaf for three in our room. 'And could you bring us an extra chair, please?'

The tray, the chair, and Bob arrived together, perfect timing. Bob and Alan added a little nip to their coffee, and we settled down to business.

'My wife's had some interesting ideas about the murder case,' Alan said, 'so I'll defer to her.'

'You were in the locker room, or wherever the guys were changing into their running gear, getting ready for the fell race, right?'

'Right. It was just a tent with a bench or two and a coat rack where we could leave our other clothes. It was small and we were a bit cramped, so we got out of there as soon as we were decent.'

'Were you in there at the same time as Donald Atkinson?'

'Not longer than I could help! Donald in business clothes was quite offensive enough. In the buff, or nearly, he was utterly disgusting. He fancied himself, you know. He posed. Wanted to make sure everyone saw how fit and trim he was.'

'Did you notice his back particularly?' That from Alan.

'I was trying not to look at him at all, which wasn't hard in that scrum. But I did catch a glimpse of his back in the mirror. It looked like he had a nasty rash, and I was delighted, I'm sorry to say. The perfect specimen had a flaw after all. And from the look of it, a most annoying one. He'd smeared some sort of white stuff all over it, but it still looked blistery and itchy, though I didn't notice him scratching at it.'

'You didn't see him applying the ointment?'

'No. Actually I don't think he could have done it himself. Devilish hard to reach your own back. I thought his wife must have done it, poor thing.'

But we knew she hadn't. Or said she hadn't. So we were no further forward.

'Was anyone else there, anyone who was a particular friend of Atkinson?' asked Alan.

'The man had no particular friends. I don't doubt there were a good many acquaintances in the tent. Certainly he chatted to nearly everyone. I knew very few of the men there. You remember I don't live in Grasmere, and in any case, there were racers from all over the UK. If I had known Atkinson was running, I would not have entered. Though I should have guessed. Any opportunity to show off—' He cut himself off short. 'I beg your pardon. I'm being insufferable. It's true I had no time for Atkinson, but the man is dead. No need to dance on the corpse. Forgive me.'

'You have,' said Alan, 'if you'll allow me to say so, been most moderate in your comments. Considering the way Atkinson treated you, you're a model of forbearance.'

'Stop beating yourself up,' I chimed in. 'The man was a thoroughly nasty type, and the world is better off without him.'

'I doubt his wife thinks so,' murmured Bob.

'At the moment, she doesn't,' I agreed. 'She's too close to the situation to see clearly how badly he treated her. But I have high hopes for her, especially with Ruth Williams by her side. Ruth is an outspoken woman who won't let Sarah wallow in sentimental despair.'

'A bit domineering, perhaps,' Alan commented.

I chuckled. 'She's American. Most of us grew up being a bit pushy, by English standards. But she's what Sarah Atkinson needs right now, someone to help her stand upright until she can do it by herself. But we digress. The topic was Donald Atkinson in the locker room, and who else was there. Any more ideas, Bob?'

'I wasn't paying close attention. Once I saw Atkinson, my one thought was to get out of there as fast as I could. There were, I think, two or three men I recognized, but only with the vague idea that I'd seen them somewhere. I couldn't put a name to them.'

Alan leaned forward. 'If you saw the list of the men signed up to run that day, do you think you could pick out a few that you know?'

'Probably not. I never knew their names.' He sounded very tired and not a little fed up. 'I'd help if I could, but I honestly have no idea who was there with Atkinson. I don't even know why it matters.'

'I'm not sure it does, actually.' I stood. 'Alan, I think we should let this tired man go home. Bob, if you think of anything that might be at all relevant, I'm sure you'll let us know.'

'How long do you think you'll be here in Grasmere?'

Alan raised his hands in the 'who knows?' gesture. 'As long as we can be of any use in the investigation, I suppose, though we're both getting tired of hotel living. The food here is excellent, but we've nearly run through the menu.'

I nodded. 'And I hate having to keep out of the room part of the day so the staff can clean it. I suppose it's living in luxury, but home is better, even if we do have to clean up after ourselves.'

'You know,' said Bob, 'there might be a chance, this late in the season, of getting a holiday cottage. They're not cheap, but they do give you more freedom. And they're self-catering.'

I looked at Alan. 'Maybe, if we find we have to stay for a while—'

'It's certainly an idea,' said Alan tactfully. 'Thanks for the suggestion, though we'll hope we don't need to act on it.'

'I hope so, too.' Bob ran a hand through his hair. 'I want to get this miserable thing behind me, so I can get on with whatever life Atkinson has left me. Goodnight, and thank you for the coffee.'

# SIXTEEN

B oth of us slept late the next morning. There didn't seem anything pressing to get up for. The police were looking for Harold Thompson. Lilian Sullivan was looking for Brian, or perhaps (I hoped) had found him, safe and sound. We could do nothing to help in either case.

We opted for a light breakfast of coffee and buns in our room. Alan knew better than to talk about anything serious until I'd downed my second cup of coffee and showered. He observed my choice of clothes for the day, the jeans and tee that I'd travelled in from Sherebury, and said, 'You don't plan to go out today, I see.'

'Not to any place where I have to look put together, anyway. Comfort first. We've been running around far too much. Anyway, where would we go? We need to get ourselves organized, figure out if there's anything productive we can do here. And if not, I vote we head for home.'

'Agreed. I've been thinking about it and come up with a few ideas. You may not like one of them.'

'Oh? What do you want me to do that I won't want to?'

'I want you to spend some time with Ruth Williams. We've had some male viewpoints about the late unlamented. I'd like you to get the prevailing women's perspective. I'll bet Ruth could tell you plenty, and didn't you say she'd asked you out to lunch? But you'll probably have to change your clothes.'

'Oh, well, if that's all! We've been here more than a week, though, and I don't know if I have any clean tops.'

'Ask Ruth where you can buy something pretty. And you'd best get a move on, love. Morning is racing by.'

I got lucky. Ruth answered right away. She was still playing nanny, but Sarah was going out for a haircut and then some church work and wouldn't need watching over for a while.

'She's doing better, anyway. Donald's funeral will probably be sometime next week, when the police have finally finished with his body, and that may set her back, but so far she's handling everything well. So why don't I pick you up and take you to my favourite dress shop and then to lunch.'

'Oh, and while we're at it, is there a launderette someplace? We have no clean clothes anymore.'

'I'll show you. Fifteen minutes?'

'Can Sarah get herself to the hairdresser and so on?'

'She can drive Donald's car. It's big, but she surprised me yesterday by handling it very well.'

'I suspect we've been taking her at Donald's estimation instead of looking at the real Sarah. She may surprise us all in time. I'll see you at the front door in fifteen minutes.'

Ruth took me first to a little shop where I found an attractive shirt, pointing out a launderette on the way. Then we went to a small café with simple but adequate food. I was content. Food was not the point of this luncheon.

She came straight to the point. 'Have you learned any more about Donald's death?'

'Not much. Quite a number of people had good reason to hate and/or fear him. We're discovering that he not only had an unpleasant personality, because of his rampant egomania, but he was involved in various criminal activities as well, and so were some of the people around him.'

'Spell it out.'

'He and Brian Sullivan, his associate accountant, stole a great deal of money from their clients. This is not just rumour. An accountant from a big firm who knew them both has documented the fraud and plans to turn the evidence over to the police. Alan and I are very worried about Brian, who may have to pay it all back and certainly hasn't the money to do so. Added to his position as a person of interest in the murder, and his anguish over Atkinson's affair with his, Brian's, wife, we fear Brian may be suicidal. And he's gone missing.'

Ruth swallowed hard. 'Is there more?'

'Quite a lot, I'm afraid. Donald's political crony, Harold Thompson, is a lawyer under suspicion of having blackmailed his clients. There's no proof of that as yet. Blackmail victims are understandably reluctant to come forward. It is a fact, however, that Thompson has a good deal more money than can reasonably be derived from his law practice. And Thompson has also quite thoroughly disappeared. The police are looking for him, but with no luck so far, and it's been a couple of days now.' I played with my sandwich. 'The truth is, I find Thompson to be an odious man, and that may be one reason he's my pick for the murderer. And that's truly unfair. I've met him only once, briefly at Christopher's party, but I didn't like him then, and everything I've heard about him has reinforced my opinion. A slick wheeler-dealer.'

Ruth waited.

'Oh, and then there's poor Bob Smith.'

'The news man? Why "poor"?'

'Donald destroyed him, on the air. You must have missed it. You've seen Bob's Friday interviews?'

'Yes, and enjoyed them. Very refreshing.'

'Well, this one wasn't. Somehow Thompson talked the station into featuring Donald in one of those interviews, and it was a total disaster. They're broadcast live, so once Donald began to assassinate Bob's character, there was nothing he could do. Donald never gave him a chance to get a word in edgewise, and by the time it was over, Bob's well-earned reputation as a nice guy was trashed. And done in such a careful way that there was no grounds for a libel action.'

I pushed my plate away. 'So you see, we've learned a lot about Donald, but without getting any closer to identifying his murderer. Which is why I came to you to get a perspective on the whole mess from the point of view of the women of Grasmere.'

'Well.' She sipped her lemonade. 'As I said, the women in the church groups and the WI and so on never talked about Donald when Sarah was around. But when she wasn't, they said plenty. The younger ones had been all dewy-eyed about him when they first encountered him. Even I have to admit that he was incredibly good-looking, and he came on to some of them, the prettiest ones. But then the others told them about his affairs, and how he preferred women with lots of money, and they occasionally saw how he treated Sarah. So I think it's safe to say he had very few if any friends among Grasmere women. When they started snubbing him, the ones who'd been all over him at first, he reacted exactly as you can imagine. Started making snide remarks, calling them by insulting nicknames, that sort of thing.' She stopped to think, chin on hand. 'I can't think, though, of anyone in particular who actually hated him.'

'How did they react when he died?'

'Mostly they just shut up about him, I think on the principle of not speaking ill of the dead. But Dorothy, you have to understand that if they knew anything about his death, they wouldn't tell me. They've accepted me up to a point, and I've made several good friends among the church women, especially, but I'm still an outsider.'

I thought about that. 'When I first came to Sherebury, after Frank died, I mean, I looked into the death of one of the canons at the Cathedral. I found a lot of people were willing to talk to me just *because* I was an outsider. I didn't matter. I wouldn't tell anybody what I was told because I didn't know much of anybody. Of course that advantage is long gone, but now through marriage to Alan I'm almost a native, and the whole town knows I'm a nosy parker and tolerates me. At this point, I suspect you're sort of in between those two categories. But who's your best friend here? Isn't there someone who would trust you enough to tell you things, if she knew you were trying to help catch a murderer?'

'My best friend is Sarah,' she said flatly.

There was nothing I could say to that.

Back at the hotel, I bundled up our laundry, took it and a book to the launderette, and prepared to sit and wait for a while. However, the attendant assured me that for a small extra fee, she would move it from washer to dryer and fold it when it was done. Amazing!

I went back to the hotel, wanting to tell Alan what little I'd gleaned from Ruth, but he was full of news of his own. 'Brian is back home!' he said triumphantly the moment I walked into the room. 'Lilian found him.'

'Where? And when?'

'Asleep in the woods, in the middle of the night. She told me he had taken the path she mentioned, and when there was too little light to see properly, he veered into the woods and took shelter under a tree. Fortunately the fallen leaves were thick, so he was able to scoop out a sort of nest against the tree trunk and curl up. When she found him, he was, she said, in a tight foetal position but very cold, anyway. She had a hard time waking him.' He paused. 'She didn't say so, but I got the impression she was terrified he was dead.'

'It got cold last night. If she hadn't found him, he might well have been dead by morning.'

'Not of exposure, love. It wasn't all that cold. But we both know that a person can sometimes will his own death.'

'And we thought his mind was tending that way.'

Alan shook himself like a wet dog, ridding himself of that thought. 'Yes. Well. At any rate, she did find him, and did manage to wake him, and then called his son to come help her get him home.'

'She called Kevin. Who is in love with her himself.'

'No. In thrall to her beauty, perhaps. I imagine last night's episode might have put paid to that complication. So they got Brian home, and Lilian plied him with brandy to warm him up and also ensure a sound sleep, which he was just coming out of when you left for lunch.'

'How did she sound? Irritated about all the trouble? Angry? Relieved?'

'She seemed to me to be feeling exactly the way Helen and I used to, years ago when one of our kids came back after being gone long enough to send us into a frenzy of worry. A mixture of profound relief, recognition of how much the miscreant meant to us and sheer blazing anger that we'd been let in for so much anxiety.'

'So you think there was love in Lilian's reaction?'

'No question about it. Sometimes it takes a knock on the head, but I believe that part of Brian's trouble may be on the mend.'

'There are still large chunks left.'

'Indeed. Now, you were wanting to tell me what you learned from Ruth.'

'Not much.' I gave him the gist of the conversation. 'I'd been hoping to get some ideas about the murderer from the woman, but Ruth was no help.'

'Hmm.' Alan ran a hand down the back of his neck, his usual gesture when he was thinking something out. 'I wonder. You were able to talk to almost everyone in Sherebury about the canon's death.'

'Yes, that was back when I was a safe stranger, and American at that.'

'You're a stranger in Grasmere now. And American. You played the American card very successfully with the accountants. Why couldn't you try your luck with the WI, or the altar guild, or some other women's group?'

I tried to think of a tactful way to tell him women are much less naïve about other women than men are, but before I could frame the thought, he read my mind. As he so often (irritatingly) does.

'I know, I know. You could fool the men, but the women will see through you. I agree. That's why I'm suggesting you play it straight with them. You're an American somewhat lost in the convolutions of English mores, and especially English politics, and you can't quite see how Donald could hope to be elected, since it seemed that a lot of people disliked him. And so on. You can do that, and it might just turn up something useful. What do you think?'

'You know, you could just have something there. Anyway, what have I got to lose?'

Alan's expression changed. 'I hadn't thought of that.' He frowned. 'I wonder if we've been unwise to get involved in this matter. We, or at least I, have been thinking of it principally as a puzzle to be solved, a chase of a sort. But the person we're trying to hunt down has already murdered one man. What's to stop him, or her, from doing it again? The old saying used to be "you can't be hanged twice".'

'And now not even once. But unless I'm wrong, the prison sentence can be a lot longer for multiple murders. So I'd think the killer would give some serious thought to whether killing again is worth it.'

'It would certainly be worth it if the second murder kept the authorities from solving either crime. Dorothy, we need to rethink this.'

'No,' I said firmly. 'You're just trying to protect me again. If I weren't involved, you would go full steam ahead until the villain was behind bars. We've settled this before, my love. Neither of us will take foolish chances, but I refuse to be sidelined while the game is afoot. Nor will I allow you to come with me as I try to talk to some of these women. They wouldn't say a word to me if you were there. For one thing, Donald Atkinson wasn't the only very attractive man around!' I batted my eyelashes at him, and he laughed.

'All right, woman, you win. Am I allowed to worry about you?'

'Worry all you like, so long as you don't interfere. Seriously, though, we're both in an age group that any of our "persons of interest" consider to be negligible. One foot in the grave, probably afflicted with at least mild dementia, along with fading eyesight and impaired hearing and virtually no reasoning capabilities. Add in the fact that we're both strangers around here and I'm American, and I can't think anyone would find either of us dangerous. I may go out and buy a cane just to reinforce the dotty old lady image. Now let's have some tea before I call Ruth to get some introductions.'

# SEVENTEEN

Leaving Alan to pick up our clean clothes, I called Ruth, and was disappointed and a little annoyed to find that she shared Alan's notion about the hazards I might encounter. 'This might not be a such a great idea, Dorothy,' she said doubtfully. 'You could find yourself in a sticky situation.'

'Oh, I don't think so,' I said lightly. 'But if I do, I've been in sticky situations before. I'm sure I'll be fine. My dear, I've been in a classroom with forty-two sixth-graders! Life can hold no more terror for me.'

That brought the laughter I'd hoped for, and she arranged for us to meet in the morning at the church. 'Saturday's the regular day for the altar guild. They call it something else here, but they have all the same duties as back home. As you can imagine, Saturday's the busy day, getting ready for the Sunday services. We take the time to plan ahead, too, for the next week, and work out a schedule if someone has to miss her regular duty.

'And then a lot of them are members of the WI, too, so you might get tips from them if they know someone in that group who might be able to tell you something.'

'That all sounds good, only . . . will Sarah be there, do you think?'

'I doubt it. It's been less than a week, after all. If she is, of course, I'll just take a couple of the women aside and ask if we could go out for tea afterward. I just hope you know what you're doing!'

I didn't, of course, but I tried to sound confident. 'I'm sure I'll be fine,' I repeated, and clicked off.

'So that's a start at least,' I said to Alan with a sigh after he'd returned from the launderette and I'd brought him up to speed. 'Who knows if I'll get anywhere, but women know a lot that men never know they know. If you follow me.'

Alan made an ambiguous noise.

'Okay. Skip it. What are we going to do with the rest of today?'

'Your wish is my command, my dear,' replied Alan, 'so long as it doesn't involve anything too strenuous. My mind and body are both set at dead slow after all we've been doing of late.'

'Would it be too strenuous to go visit Brian and Lilian? Not to ask questions or anything, but just as a gesture of kindness.'

'If they want us, I think that would indeed be a kind thing to do. Shall I call, or will you?'

Lilian sounded very subdued on the phone with me, as if some of the hard edges had been rubbed off, and she was pleased at the idea of a visit. 'Of course we'd like to see you. I'm planning Brian's favourite meal; why don't you join us?'

I hadn't realized it was getting on toward dinner time. 'Oh, we wouldn't want to intrude. We could come later—'

'No, now, if you will. It will be a pleasure. Please come!'

She sounded almost pleading. Which was absurd. I decided I was misinterpreting. 'Well, in that case, thank you. We'd love to. An hour or so?'

'Or sooner.'

I clicked off and told Alan about the rather odd conversation. 'She sounded almost desperate. And eager for us to get there as soon as possible. I don't understand.'

'Nor do I, but there's only one way to learn what's going on. Do you need to change clothes?'

I decided I didn't, and we were off.

There was a different feeling at the Sullivan house when Lilian showed us in. For one thing, the living room or front room or whatever you wanted to call it was in immaculate order, a fire in the vast fireplace combatting the late-summer chill. For another, Lilian herself was in immaculate order, neatly if casually dressed, hair and make-up perfect. Her face, though, was almost haggard.

She astonished me by giving me a hug as we came in. 'I am *so* glad to see you. Please do sit down and have a drink. Straight tonic again, Dorothy?'

'Actually I'd like a little bourbon, if you have any. With water, please.'

'And ice?'

I laughed at that. 'No, I've learned to prefer bourbon without ice. Positively un-American, I know.'

She gave me a smile that was just a stretching of her lips and turned to Alan for his drink order.

Brian was nowhere to be seen.

When Lilian returned with a tray, she put a tall glass down for herself, containing something clear and sparkling, and another just like it in front of an empty chair. 'Brian will be down in a minute, after he gets cleaned up,' she said. 'He slept most of the day.'

I couldn't stand it any longer. 'Lilian, this is all very awkward for you, isn't it? Honestly, wouldn't you rather we left the two of you to—'

'No!' She took a sip of her drink. 'No, don't go. Yes, the situation is awkward, but that's why I need you. Brian is so upset about last night that he won't say a word to me. I want you – I *need* you – to start a conversation. He's embarrassed and depressed and ashamed, and he can't find the right words to talk about it. I want you, both of you, to get him started.'

Oh, help. I've sat at some uncomfortable dinner tables, but this one promised to set a Guinness record. I sipped my drink, hoping a little nip would liven up my mind, which at the moment was a total blank.

To make matters worse, the moment Brian entered the room, Lilian stood. 'Brian, you've met these nice people. I have to see to a few details in the kitchen.'

She disappeared, and Brian was left standing in the middle of the room looking as though he'd like to disappear, too.

Alan, bless him, was up to the challenge. He had stood when Lilian did, and now walked over to Brian and shook his hand. 'We met briefly at Christopher's party, but you probably don't remember. My name is Alan Nesbitt, and the lovely lady over by the fireplace is my wife, Dorothy Martin. We've been told that you've been having a terrible time of it, and we're both so sorry.'

'I— How do you do? No, I'm sorry, I didn't remember your names.'

'Small wonder,' I chimed in. 'You've been living through seven different kinds of hell. Sorry doesn't begin to say it. But do sit down. Lilian brought you a drink, and she told us she's preparing your favourite dinner.' I nodded towards the chair Lilian had indicated was his. He sat, ignoring the glass on the coffee table in front of him.

If there was to be any social interaction, it was plainly up to Alan and me to initiate it. I picked up my own drink and moved nearer to Brian. 'Look here, my friend. You need to know that I'm quite sure you had nothing to do with Mr Atkinson's death. My husband feels the same way. *Think*, Brian! Have you been contacted by anyone official since you got home?'

He swallowed hard. 'They don't know I'm here yet.'

'Oh, don't be silly! Of course they know. This is a village. When someone goes missing, someone who's in the middle of a drama, the police will find out. And I'm sure your wife called to tell them you were home safe.' I wasn't sure at all, but it seemed like a reasonable assumption. 'Now have something to drink and relax a notch or two. Lilian's knocking herself out cooking a fabulous dinner for you, and she'll be terribly disappointed if you don't enjoy it.'

'I disappoint her all the time.'

'Right,' said Alan. 'That's why she took off last night to search for you, and kept at it in the dark and cold until she found you. Man, if that's the action of a woman who's disappointed in her man, I've learned nothing about psychology in my long life as a policeman.'

Brian winced. 'You're a policeman?'

'Long retired. That's not why I'm here. I came as a friend. Chill, man!'

That bit of jargon from my usually formal English husband startled me into laughter, and Alan joined me – and after a moment, Brian gave in and smiled.

That was when Lilian rejoined us. She glanced at me with what looked like gratitude and said, 'Well, this is a merry crowd! Drink up; dinner will be on the table in five minutes. Dorothy, would you mind helping me for a moment? My daily doesn't work on Fridays.'

'So she's your almost-daily,' I commented as I followed her to the kitchen.

'Yes, and soon she won't be that. We're selling this house and moving to a smaller place I can manage by myself.'

'Selling this house! But it's so beautiful—'

'Shh. Brian doesn't know yet. I haven't told him I'm paying off his debts. Here, would you put this trivet on the table?' She handed me a lovely piece of iron filigree that held a decorative tile, probably Italian or Spanish in origin, and turned to lift a large pot off the Aga. 'And if you could reach down that bowl . . .'

Lilian had prepared a coq au vin that smelled like heaven. With a crisp salad for contrast and crusty baguettes to sop up the sauce, it was not an elaborate meal, just a perfect one. We sat down to a table set with fine linen and lovely heirloom china. The wine glasses were certainly Waterford.

Lilian raised her glass. 'Before we begin, I want to make a toast to the man I love, the wonderful man I promise to cherish all my life – to Brian!'

As glasses clinked, I think it was only astonishment that kept Brian from dissolving in tears. Fortunately, Alan, seated next to him, managed to knock one of the baguettes to the floor as he set his glass back on the table, and the resulting flurry of activity saved the day.

'Well done,' I murmured while Brian was rummaging for more bread in the kitchen.

'I can't imagine what you're talking about,' Alan murmured back.

I wanted to ask about the gorgeous china we were eating from – I suspected it was Spode and was almost crass enough to turn over my bread and butter plate to find out – but any reference to Lilian's wealth was probably off limits just now. There seemed, however, to be no reason not to comment on her skill as a cook. 'Brian, I don't wonder that this is your favourite meal. I've never tasted such wonderful coq au vin. What's your secret, Lilian?'

'No secret. I just followed the recipe, one from a famous American.'

'American? But this is so very— Oh, I get it! Julia Child, right?'

'Indeed. I've tried a lot of French cookbooks, but some of them are deliberately obscure, it seems to me. Child may not have won the approval of Le Cordon Bleu, but any of her recipes that I've tried have been easy to follow and virtually foolproof.'

'This is perfect, my love,' said Brian, the first words he'd uttered at the table.

'Oh, I'm glad you think so!' Lilian blushed like a teenager at the compliment. 'I haven't done any real cooking for such a long time, I feared I'd lost my touch.'

She turned to Alan and me. 'We'd formed the habit of eating out most of the time. Or when Brian wasn't home for a meal, I turned into a sloth and just snacked on whatever was in the fridge. But that's going to change, as of now. Brian, I haven't had a chance to talk to you about this, but please listen to what I have to say.'

He looked apprehensive.

'No, it's nothing frightful.' She smiled her million-dollar smile. 'I'm just hoping that we can work out a different way of life. You've always been working so hard, and such long hours, that we scarcely had any time together. Meanwhile I've done nothing at all, at least nothing useful. Dorothy, you pointed that out to me the other day. I was furious at you for a little while, until I realized that you were absolutely right. So I've had an idea, Brian, and I'd like to tell you about it while Dorothy and Alan are with us, so they can add their suggestions.'

She sipped a little of her wine. 'My idea is this. Brian, you may not know that I've had some experience with office work, before we were married. My father went through some hard times when he was young, so even though money wasn't a problem, by the time I left school, he wanted me to be able to earn my living, just in case. He made me take a secretarial course and work for a bit in, believe it or not, an accounting firm. That's why I went to that party where we met.' She unleashed the thousand-watt smile again.

'What I'm proposing is that we, you and I, go into business together. We'll start fresh, with new clients. You'll do all the number crunching, of course, and I'll handle the correspondence, keep the appointment book, all the boring details. We'll pay ourselves some reasonable salary. Best of all, we'll be together. What do you think?'

Though a turn of her head included us in the question, it was obviously aimed at Brian, who looked glum. 'I would like working with you, my dear, but I'm afraid it's impossible. My debts – my reputation—'

'You will have no debts.' A deep breath. 'We still don't know exactly what the courts will decide you owe, but whatever it is, we can settle it. You've never liked this house, and I agree it's far too big for us. I'm putting it on the market tomorrow.'

'But – but – you're so proud of the house. You love it!'

'Not as much as I love you. Not as proud as I am of you. Who was that old Greek who was always looking for an honest man? He could have stopped looking when he found you.'

'But I – we—'

'You fell into bad company,' said Alan. 'Donald Atkinson was certainly not an honest man. He defrauded clients and pulled you into the scheme. Now you and your wife are having to pay, literally, for his crimes. You're not trying to weasel out of it. You're stepping up to your responsibilities. And you, Lilian, are sticking by him and making the ordeal a chance to bond firmly. I congratulate you both.'

Lilian looked straight at her husband. 'Brian, I've been an appalling wife to you. I'm saying now, in front of our friends, that I'm truly sorry, and I promise to do better.'

She had tears in her eyes, and so did Brian. When they fell into each other's arms, Alan and I, seeing that our presence was no longer necessary, fled for home.

# EIGHTEEN

'What do you think?' Alan asked on the way back to the hotel. 'Will it work out?'

I hope so, but it's far from a sure thing. Lilian's wallowing in guilt right now. She knows how close she came to losing him, and sees herself as the sweet, brave wife who's going to spend her own money to bail him out. And he's wallowing in guilt, too, for getting taken in by Atkinson and then giving up on life. So for a while they'll probably go on cooing over each other.

'But guilt isn't the same as love. Lilian will begin to resent having to give up her house, and will lose patience again with Brian's weaknesses. If they do set up that business together, I can see disaster looming. When two people have very little in common, being in each other's pockets all day long can drive them both mad. I can see little annoyances becoming big issues, Lilian raging and Brian cowering. Her heart is certainly in the right place, but her mind . . .' I sighed.

'I agree. I doubt she sees that she's stage-managing the whole enterprise. This is all her idea, developed without consulting him at all. He may be a weakling, but few men want to submit to a nose ring.'

'Especially English men,' I jibed, 'who want to be in charge at all times.'

'Right,' he said, 'and don't you forget it! And what are your plans for the rest of the evening?'

'Whatever you say, dear,' I deadpanned. 'You always know best.'

We chuckled all the way back.

A pair of sweet Yorkshire terriers were sitting with their owners in the lounge when we went in. I regretted not having treats for them; Alan always carries some in his pockets when we're at home. They came over anyway to sniff at proffered hands and accept pats on the head.

'Oh, Alan, I completely forgot—'

'To check on the menagerie. I was going to remind you. Of course you know Jane is spoiling them rotten, but it isn't too late to call her.'

We hadn't seen our beloved beasts for over a week, and our other worries had driven them right out of our heads, or mine at least. I placed the call.

Jane answered immediately. 'Wondered when you'd start to fret,' she said in the gruff voice that belied her marshmallow heart. 'All well and happy. Mike bosses the rest; some of mine, too.'

Mike, the rare male tortoiseshell, had come into our lives as a tiny kitten barely old enough to leave his mother, having been found and adopted by our dog Watson, who seemed to think he was the kitten's mother. The two senior cats, Esmeralda and Samantha, had hated Mike on sight, but they soon learned to tolerate him. As he grew, fawned over by Watson and Alan and me, he gradually assumed command of the household and was now the acknowledged king.

'Even your dogs?' I said, somewhat sceptical. Jane owns a flock of bulldogs that look just like her.

'Not all yet. Winnie's coming around. Good scratch on the nose.'

'Oh, Jane, I'm sorry! Mike should know better.'

'Dog asked for it. Be respectful from now on. When are you coming home?'

'We're not sure. We've gotten involved in a sort of complicated mess.'

Jane hooted. 'All normal, then. Everything fine here. Don't hurry.'

I ended the call. 'They're all okay. Mike is getting Jane's dogs under control.'

'Doesn't surprise me,' said Alan. He looked at me, one eyebrow raised. 'And?'

'They don't even miss us. I think it's about time we got back, before they forget us entirely.'

'We could do that. Tomorrow, if you like.'

'And leave the investigation hanging.'

'It isn't our responsibility, you know. There don't seem to be many avenues left for us to explore. The police are working hard to locate Harold Thompson, your pick of the lot.'

'I know but— Oh, I just hate to admit failure! And think of all the people whose lives have been disrupted. They need to know what happened. In modern jargon, they need closure. And so do I. And anyway, tomorrow I'm going to talk to the altar guild.'

The lounge had emptied. Alan gave me a peck on the cheek, helped me get out of the squashy couch, and said, 'We'll give it some thought. Tomorrow. After all . . .'

'Tomorrow is another day,' we chorused.

I had agreed to meet Ruth at the church, so as soon as Alan and I finished breakfast, I headed out. The weather looked a little chancy, so I debated about an umbrella, but I could always call Alan or Uber if the heavens opened. So far, it was the kind of day I like best: pale grey sky, light wind, temperature a bit brisk – the kind of day that made walking a pleasure.

Ruth was just inside the south door. 'I've been thinking about this,' she said. 'I'm going to introduce you to the ladies and then go about my business. I think they'll talk more freely to you with me not around.'

'I agree. I know almost nobody here, so what they tell me won't go any further. If they tell me anything.'

'Exactly. The shipboard romance syndrome. Have you decided how you want to play it?'

'I thought I could say that I'd been on the altar guild at home in the States – which is true, by the way – and was thinking about joining in Sherebury, but I knew some things were done differently, so I wanted to watch and learn. It's sort of lame, but the best I could come up with.'

'It'll do. All you really need is some sort of excuse for being there. Probably someone will have seen you with Sarah and me the other day, and that will give you a chance to ask a few questions. So come on up to the front.'

Two women were busy setting up the altar for tomorrow's Eucharist, while others concentrated on polishing the candlesticks and the lectern and making sure the lectionary book was turned to the proper readings. Two more women ranged throughout the church doing the flowers.

As Ruth and I approached, one of the flower arrangers turned to us and smiled. 'Morning, Ruth. I see you've brought your friend back. Is she a new recruit?'

'No, Dorothy's just an observer today. Dorothy, you remember Ellen.'

I didn't, but I smiled and nodded and followed up. 'Not a recruit for your church, I'm afraid, but I am hoping to volunteer at my own back in Shrewbury. I was on the altar guild years ago, back home in the States, but I've noticed you do some things a bit differently here in England, so I thought I'd come and watch you for a while, if I won't be in the way.'

'Surely they'll teach you at your own church!' Ellen, up on a step stool, poked a chrysanthemum into a block of Oasis.

That was the weak spot in my excuse, of course. 'Well, the truth is, I go to the Cathedral, and their volunteers are kind of starchy, so I thought if I could go already knowing what I'm doing . . .'

She nodded and relaxed. 'Oh, yes, cathedral guilds! Holier than thou, so to speak. You won't find us like that. Watch all you want. Or I could use a little help with this job. I haven't quite enough chrysanths, and I can't decide which would be better to fill in, the dahlias or the asters.'

'I'm certainly no good at flower arranging, but those purple asters would make a nice contrast. Or perhaps . . . can those be lupines, this late in the season?'

'They are! I've learned how to protect them and keep them blooming. These are the last of them for the year, though, I fear. You're quite right. They're good colours to fit with the rest, and the shape contrasts nicely with the round blossoms. Hand me up one of them, will you, dear?'

I chose an especially lovely spike, full of deep pink florets, and decided it was time for business. I heaved a loud sigh. 'The church is looking so lovely. It's a great pity that Mrs Atkinson can't be here to help. I'm sure she'd like to be, but I guess it's too soon.'

'And what she's mourning about, I can not see!' said Ellen tartly, jabbing the lupine in viciously. 'That husband of hers was blighting her life, and she was too loyal or blind or something to see it. The day he died was the best day of her life, and I hope she figures that out soon. Maybe a white one now, or do you think the blue and white?'

'Oh, the blue and white. They're such gorgeous specimens.

Honestly, they look like they came right out of a seed catalogue. So do you have any ideas about who might have, um, helped Mr Atkinson out of this life?'

'What *do* you mean?' Ellen gaped at me.

Uh-oh. I forgot that Atkinson wasn't generally known to have been murdered. I gave Ruth a panicky look.

She glared back but undertook to rescue me. 'Dorothy reads way too much crime fiction. I suppose she thought that anyone as universally hated as Atkinson must have been, as she puts it, helped a little on his way out.' She gave me another look and melted away.

'Yes, wishful thinking, I suppose,' I said, making a face. 'Or perhaps not that, exactly— Oh, forget it. My mouth moves independently of my brain sometimes.'

Ellen wasn't stupid. 'What you really mean is that you think he was murdered. And if you're thinking that Sarah killed him, you should be in Broadmoor.'

'I assure you I have no such idea. I don't know Mrs Atkinson well, but all I've seen of her tells me she's a gentle person who was devoted to her husband. I do admit to wondering why that was so, since everything I've heard about him makes him sound like a terrible bully who wasn't very nice to her.'

'And that's throwing roses at it.' She gave one last nudge to an aster that had drooped a bit, and stepped down. 'There, that'll pass in a pinch with a push.'

'It looks lovely,' I said sincerely. 'I don't know how you create such elaborate arrangements. All I know how to do is stick a few roses in a vase, and sometimes they look fine and sometimes they look ridiculous. These creations on pedestals are so lovely, especially when there's ivy, or something, sort of flowing toward the floor. I don't even know how you can make them stay where you put them.'

'Oasis is the answer!' She held up a small piece of the green foam. 'I don't know how they ever managed before this stuff came along. Don't they have it in the States?'

'Oh, yes, but I've never used it. My flowers tend to have floppy stems that would never poke into that stuff. In face, they remind me a little of Sarah Atkinson. Sweet, but with no strength.'

'That's exactly why Sarah needs friends like us. Some flowers need a little wire to help them stand up straight.' Ellen showed me an unused dahlia that had green tape wound around its stem. 'That's to hold the wire on, and the tape provides some stability, too. That's what we've tried to do for Sarah. Wrap her around with our confidence in her. You know she's very capable when she's out from under that monster she married?'

'I do know a little about her capabilities. She showed me around the church the other day, and her descriptions were so vivid and interesting. Much better than the official brochures. But then after her husband died, and she and Ruth came to the hotel and spent a little time with my husband and me, she could only talk about how wonderful he was and how lost she'd be without him. Honestly, I began to feel that if he weren't already dead, I'd be very tempted to— Well, no, not that, but to do something drastic.'

'You're not the only one. Sarah is very much a part of this church community, and we try to look after her. Ruth is her closest friend, of course.' Ellen looked around as if to make sure Ruth was out of earshot. 'She's a trifle smothering, actually. I suppose because she's American.' Then she put her hand to her mouth. 'Oh, I didn't mean— I'm sorry—'

'It's all right. I've lived in England for quite a while and am actually a citizen here now. But I know what you mean. I think many Americans tend to wear our feelings on our sleeves more than the English do, and may perhaps act more forcefully in some situations. Some English people I know have tiptoed around subjects so much they drove me bananas. I've had to restrain myself on more than one occasion when I thought I knew exactly what needed to be done, and my neighbours, even my husband, seemed to be taking far too much time to do it. So I can understand Ruth's approach.' I paused. 'But what I'm wondering – what if someone else decided he or she knew exactly what needed to be done to deal with Donald Atkinson – and did it?'

'To protect Sarah, you mean?'

'Or for some other reason. I'll be candid with you. I've been learning a good deal about the animosities Atkinson created with almost everyone he knew, in all his activities.'

'Why?' Ellen began gathering up her tools and tossing debris into a plastic bag. 'Why do you care? Even if he was murdered, finding out who killed him won't be of any help to Sarah. And frankly, it seems to me to be none of your business.'

Wow. This Englishwoman certainly didn't tiptoe. After the first shock, I was pleased. This was someone I could get to like. 'You're quite right. It would be none of my business except for one thing. Well, one main thing: my husband, who is English, is a retired chief constable. We attended the sports day, and when Atkinson didn't come down after the last race, he and a friend, also a retired policeman, became concerned. They alerted the race officials and then sent me and Ruth and Sarah back to our hotel to await news.

'So that involved Alan, my husband, from the very beginning. He and Christopher, his friend—'

'Wait. Christopher who?'

'Prideaux. He's from Cornwall, and—'

'And a good person. I know Christopher. Everybody knows Christopher. He does a lot for this village, even though he's not lived here long.' She sounded friendlier.

'Yes, I just met him, though he's a friend of Alan's from way back when they both lived and worked near Penzance. I've learned to like and respect him even in such a short time. Anyway, he and Alan discovered a few things that led them to believe the death wasn't accidental, so they've been unofficially deputized by the investigating team to help. And as I have worked with my husband over the years in several puzzling matters, the officials have allowed me to do what I can, as well. So there you have it. I've talked to a number of the men who were involved in Donald's life, and now I'm hoping to get the point of view of the women in the village. Because I think women are more observant than men about certain things, like relationships.'

'Got it. You're Miss Marple.'

'Or a geriatric Nancy Drew. Take your pick.'

That actually got me a laugh. She took a look around the church. 'Most of us are about finished for the day. Would you like to have a coffee with me and two or three others? I think we need to talk.'

# NINETEEN

'I'd be so grateful. Should we ask Ruth to come along?'

Ellen hesitated. 'I'd rather not. We'll all talk more freely without her. I suppose she'll be offended.'

'I don't think so. I already told her I thought that might be the case. She may even have left us already.'

Neither of us could spot her, so that little awkwardness was staved off. Ellen spoke quietly to two of the other ladies, and the four of us walked to a nearby café.

Morning coffee is one of those delightful English customs that have nearly died out in many places. In the cities, life has become rushed and crowded, leaving people no time for a leisurely mid-morning break. Fortunately, villages tend to maintain the tradition, especially villages like Grasmere, where tourism rules.

Even though high tourist season was winding down, the shop was busy enough that a quiet conversation would be masked by other chit-chat.

We sat down with our coffee and pastries, and Ellen assumed the role of mistress of ceremonies. 'This is Dorothy Martin, all. Originally American, now a British subject living in Sherebury and visiting here with her husband Alan, who is a retired chief constable. Remember that; it matters. Dorothy, my friends Sue and Margaret. Now, you two, Dorothy is looking into the way Donald Atkinson died. Her husband doesn't think it was an accident, and neither does Christopher Prideaux, Alan's old and dear friend. The investigators, the official ones, are from Carlisle and don't really know people from around here, so they're allowing Alan and Christopher to help.'

'And me,' I added. 'Strictly ex-officio, but I have some experience in solving difficult puzzles. That's why I wanted to talk to some of the women of the village. I was sure you'd know lots of things that escape the notice of the men, even men like Christopher who are trained to observe.'

The women's faces looked neutral. I forged ahead.

'So I'm asking you three: do you know of anyone who might have had strong feelings about Atkinson, feelings that might have led to murder?'

They exchanged glances. 'It would help if we knew how you think he was murdered,' said Sue. 'We understood he fell in the tarn and drowned.'

'I'm afraid I'm not at liberty to say very much, except that he did not drown. There was no water in his lungs.'

'That means he was dead before he went in. So he could have had a heart attack, stroke, some kind of seizure – lots of things.'

'Yes, of course. The medical examiner doesn't think it was any of those things, though.' I shut my mouth firmly.

'That doesn't leave too many possibilities, does it?' Ellen was thinking. 'Obviously he wasn't shot or hit on the head. Those violent methods of killing leave signs.'

'What that leaves,' said Margaret impatiently, 'is poison. Some slow-acting poison that would make him stumble and die, conveniently just as he was at the summit of the run. That means premeditation.'

'It also,' said Ellen, 'means great difficulty in proving anything. If it was some sort of pill he took, anyone could have put that pill in with the rest at any time. One of the most effective ways of killing and getting away with it. Whoever did it could have been well away from here last Sunday. Out of the country, even.'

'You're a mystery reader like me, I surmise,' I said, trying to laugh.

'I am. Which brings me to one of the first principles of detection. Miss Marple and Hercule said it all the time: don't believe all you're told. Most people lie about all sorts of things that have nothing to do with crime, but a murderer has the best reasons to lie. You told me you and your husband have talked to a number of men involved with Atkinson in one way or another. I urge you to consider which ones might have been lying to you.'

'Alan and I have thought about that, of course. Oddly enough, the two we are inclined to believe most fully are the two that have the best reasons to hate him. I'm sure most of you saw the occasion when he humiliated Bob Smith on the air, with a load of innuendo. Mr Smith says none of it was true, but because it was phrased as a string of ifs and maybes, he can't sue for libel.'

'Oh, yes! It was that little hatchet job that solidified my hatred of Donald Atkinson. I happen to have known Bob for a long time, and a more honest, reliable man never lived.' Margaret wadded up her napkin in a ferocious fist. 'You're right. If anyone had cause to murder the rat, it was Bob. But he wouldn't, no matter what.'

I nodded. 'That was our impression. And then there's the man whom Donald injured maybe more than anyone else.'

I didn't have to name him. All three women nodded. 'Brian Sullivan,' said Ellen, 'is a wimp. A Sad Sack. The whole village knew about the affair, of course, and everyone was aching for Brian to grow some backbone and put a stop to it, but he just drooped more and more and said less and less. We almost expected him to put a stop to himself instead.'

I didn't respond to that. If the village found out about his near-suicide, it wasn't going to be from me. Nor did I think I should mention Lilian's new attitude, which might not last very long. I just nodded sympathetically. 'He's had a lot to put up with, including being a prime suspect for the murder. At least, I suppose he is.'

'And so, of course, would Sarah be, ordinarily,' said Ellen, and the others nodded. 'At least in novels, the spouse is always the first one the police go after.'

'I think in real life, too. It makes sense, actually. Marriage is the closest relationship there is, and if the mates are compatible, it can be lovely, but if there are problems, they can grow like mushrooms. When you're with someone day after day, an irritation can chafe until it becomes intolerable. However, the little I've seen of Sarah Atkinson makes me quite sure she isn't a murderess. Not only did she adore her husband, however mistakenly, she's a gentle, timid soul. I can barely imagine her killing a spider.'

All three women nodded. 'She's not the sort of worm that turns,' said Margaret. 'She'd be more likely to apologize for getting stepped on. Her fault for being in the way sort of thing.'

'So we've eliminated most of the best candidates. I haven't yet had a chance to talk to his . . . I don't know what to call him. Political groomer? Harold Whatshisname.'

'Thompson,' supplied Ellen. There was an unmistakable sneer

in her voice. 'He's a manipulator, a genuine puppet master. We all think he was losing interest in Donald, who'd quit dancing when Thompson pulled the strings. Or at least wasn't dancing the right way.'

'What was Thompson's interest anyway? What did he have to gain if Atkinson did make it to Parliament?' I had been told the answer, but I wanted to hear what the women had to say.

'Money, of course.' This time it was Sue's scornful voice. 'Men like him never do anything except for money. He has a finger in lots of pies around here, and influence in the House could make some investments far more profitable. There are rumours, for example, of a proposed rerouting of one of the major roads through Cumbria. If it were to go through land Thompson owns, he could make a huge profit in all sorts of ways. The purchase price of the right of way, the new businesses he could build along the way, contracts for the road itself – lots of lovely lolly. So when Donald started demonstrating some independence from his puppeteer, Thompson wasn't a bit pleased.'

I didn't ask how they knew. Village gossip isn't always right, but I've found that the rate of accuracy works out to about ninety per cent. 'I wonder how I might get to talk to him. I met him only once, at a party Christopher gave when we first came to town last week. I have to say I didn't take to him much, but maybe I was being unfair.'

'You got it right,' said Sue with a shake of her head. 'He's a despicable man, almost as bad as Atkinson. Not quite, because he doesn't even pretend to be pleasant. Like Donald, though, he has no time at all for anyone who can't be useful to him.'

'I've forgotten what he does for a living, if I ever knew,' I said ingenuously. 'I've been told his main interest is politics.'

'Yes, because the political life provides marvellous opportunity for graft. He is nominally a solicitor.'

Time for the dumb American again. 'I'm never sure what that means. Some kind of lawyer, I know, but what does a solicitor actually do?'

'Almost everything one of your lawyers can do, except court-room work. The people who plead cases are barristers. They are briefed by solicitors, but most solicitors have little to do with criminal law. They do all the rest: prepare wills, deal with property

transfers, any questions about inheritance, sometimes lawsuits
– essentially anything to do with money.'

'Ah.' I left the comment there, but Sue picked up on it.

'Yes, indeed. It can be a lucrative field, and I don't mean just
exorbitant fees, though our Harold certainly charges through the
nose. But it's also easy to pick up a little on the side. A pound
here, a guinea there, it all adds up. Not that he's ever been caught,
mind you, so everything I'm saying is slander.'

'Good heavens! Now I want to talk to him more than ever.
Where would be the best place to find him? At his office,
probably?'

'He isn't there,' said Margaret. 'He isn't anywhere. He's
completely disappeared, leaving his clients in the lurch.'

Well, of course I knew that, but I was interested that these
women knew it, too. Which probably meant that the whole village
knew.

'That doesn't sound good. Do you suppose he's running away
from a victim, a client who found out he'd been defrauded?'

'Or from the law,' said Sue grimly. 'Any odds on him being
the murderer?'

'Why?' asked Ellen pointedly. 'All right, Donald wasn't
behaving the way Harold wanted him to. That's no reason to kill
him. Harold could just drop him, find some other likely puppet.
Donald was well known in the constituency, but so are a lot of
other people, people who are hungry for attention, for power.
Though the power of one man from one small area, and in a
very small Parliamentary minority – well, it's pretty limited to
say the least. Honestly, I can't think of a single reason to murder
Donald Atkinson, aside from his truly repellent character.'

'Money, sex, and power are the big three. And sheer hatred,
of course,' I added. The women looked a little startled. 'The
mystery books have taught me a lot. There really aren't too many
motives for murder.'

'You forgot revenge,' said Ellen. 'Or the ever-popular killing
to silence someone who knows too much.'

I sighed. 'And in America, all too often, mass killings for
apparently no reason at all. We say those killers have some form
of mental illness. I think, myself, that they act partly from sheer
rage at the world, and partly for thrills. However, that sort of

thing doesn't apply to this matter. I can't go into the details, because only the police know most of them, but I understand that this was a long-premeditated, very carefully planned murder, committed by someone with both brains and nerve – no half-crazy idiot with a grudge.'

'All of that would apply to Harold Thompson,' Sue insisted. 'I admit I can't think of a motive, but give me a while and I'll come up with one. I would so like to see that creep in the hands of the law!'

The other women nodded agreement. 'But first catch your hare,' quoted Margaret to general laughter.

# TWENTY

Well, so that was interesting and pleasant, and I felt I'd made some new friends, but I didn't see that I'd made any progress at all toward finding the murderer. I wished I could have asked them who might have travelled to a place where the nitro ointment was available, but the police were keeping that part of the plot up their sleeves for now. I did give the women my mobile number and asked them to call if they got any bright ideas, but I didn't expect much.

I paid our bill for the coffee and was just leaving the café when my phone rang. It was Alan, wondering if I had any ideas about lunch.

'I'm not actually hungry right now. I've been having coffee and goodies with some of the women from church. But a little later I could really go for – don't laugh – a nice gooey pizza, if such a thing is to be found in these parts.'

He laughed. 'I'll do some research while you walk back. Did you accomplish anything?'

'Not much. I'll tell you about it when I get there.'

When I got back to the hotel, I related the little I'd learned. 'Nothing new, really. Apparently the prevailing opinion about Harold Thompson is much the same as mine: sleaze. They'd love to cast him as the murderer, especially since flight is a strong indication of guilt, but they couldn't come up with a convincing motive any more than we could. So how did you spend the morning?'

'As unproductively as you did, essentially. Christopher and I got together and hashed out the whole thing, all the suspects—'

'Persons of interest.'

He laughed. 'Okay, I stand corrected. Persons of interest. We discarded everyone except Harold, and kept him in only because he's disappeared, and it must be for a reason. We're sure of that. We just don't know what the reason is.'

'I suppose the police haven't had any luck finding him.'

Alan sighed. 'They now know a great many places where he isn't. But given the size of the planet, that doesn't narrow the problem down much.'

'No.' I sighed, too. 'Have you heard from Lilian and/or Brian?'

'I phoned Lilian. All is still for the best in the best of all possible worlds.'

'Hmph! I give it a week at most.'

'Cynic! You're probably right. But regardless of how that marriage works out, it seems to have little to do with this little matter of murder. Are you hungry yet? Shall I order that pizza?'

'You found a place.'

'Several. I'm calling the one that comes most highly recommended.'

'I don't suppose they deliver.'

'No, but it's only five minutes away. Perhaps you could fetch us some beer from the bar, meanwhile.'

The pizza was good. Not quite what I could have found back home in Indiana, where thick Chicago-style was the norm, but good.

'We should have invited someone to share,' I commented as I regretfully turned down a third piece. 'This is way too much for the two of us.'

'Yes. A shame we didn't think of it. Now, if this were an American hotel, there might well be a small fridge in the room, and a microwave.'

'Right. With all the atmosphere of a hospital, and just as sterile.' I shuddered. 'I'll take this place over an American chain any time. I know what we'll do, though. I'll call Ruth and see if she can use the leftovers. I want to talk to her, anyway.'

I ended up inviting her to join us, either to partake of lukewarm pizza or take it home. She opted to pick up a sandwich at her favourite pub on the way, along with a beer from the hotel bar. So we arranged ourselves in our room as best we could, given our limited seating, for a talk about our problem.

'I ran into Ellen at the church after you had your little kaffee-klatsch,' Ruth commented. 'I'm afraid she found you a bit too trusting and reminded me that people lie a lot.'

'She said that to me, too. "Don't believe all you're told." It's a sound principle, and I'm afraid I do tend to trust people, unless they're obvious twisters like Donald and Harold. If they told me the sun was going to rise tomorrow, I'd instantly seek someone to give me last rites to prepare for the Apocalypse. But the other people we've talked to seem utterly believable. Christopher – well, that goes without saying. I have only pity for Bob Smith, and believe every word he's said. Brian is too downtrodden to come up with a lie. Lilian would lie about anything and do it well, too, but I can't see she had any reason to in this case. Anyway, unless she hired someone to do the job, she couldn't have managed the logistics. So I can't think who might have been lying to us.'

Alan considered the question. 'We've never talked to the appalling Harold, or not since Donald's death, anyway. I certainly wish he could be found, so we, and the police, could do that. Or failing that, discover and chat with Donald's alleged victims.'

'Oh, that reminds me. I wonder if our informant from the accounting firm— What was his name?'

'Taylor. Roger Taylor.' Alan looked a trifle smug.

'Okay, so your memory's better than mine. Good thing one of us can remember stuff. Anyway, did he ever give the police that list of the people Donald and Brian supposedly rooked? He gave us the letters but with the names removed. A conversation with them might be enlightening.'

'I don't know that he did, but I'll find out.' He picked up his phone and punched in a number while I tried to remember the name of the officer in charge of the case.

'DCI Davies, please.' A pause. 'Ah, George. Alan Nesbitt here. I hope I'm not calling you away from something vital.' Pause. Laugh. 'No, I'm afraid we've made no progress, either. I'm wondering, though . . . We'd like to talk to some of the people defrauded by the Atkinson/Sullivan firm. Did Mr Taylor turn those names over to you?' Pause. 'Oh, really? When he talked to us, I had the impression he intended to give them to you immediately.' Pause. 'I see. Yes, I'm happy to do that. I'll stay in touch.'

'So Taylor didn't give him the list,' I said when Alan had ended the call.

'No. Hasn't even mentioned it. In fact, Davies didn't know anything about Taylor.'

'Nor do I,' Ruth put in, 'but he sounds iffy to me.'

I explained about Taylor warning me about Brian and providing documentation. 'We really do need to talk to those people. Not that I think any of them are murderers, but just to cover all the bases. Alan, I'd better call him, hadn't I?'

Alan frowned. 'Yes. And find out why he hasn't told Davies about them.'

'I don't suppose he'd be working on a Saturday afternoon, so it's probably okay to call him now.' I found the number after a little searching on my phone, but there was no answer, not even voicemail. 'That's odd. People these days are glued to their phones.'

'Unless they forget to charge them, or misplace them somewhere. Mobiles aren't the answer to all the world's communication problems.'

'So we're stuck.' Ruth flopped back in her chair, discouraged.

'No, we're not!' I proclaimed. 'We haven't asked the person most closely involved. I'm going to call Brian. If I know anything about his character, he's been poring over the company's books and working out to the penny what is owed. He may be a wimp, but he's a conscientious wimp.'

I placed the call. Brian answered on the first ring, sounding – what? Harassed? Distracted? Not eager to take a phone call, anyway.

'Brian, it's Dorothy Martin. I'm sorry to bother you, but I have sort of an important question. Do you have a minute?'

'I'm very busy. Could it wait a day or two?'

'I'll only take a few minutes of your time, and it truly is important. I'm just wanting to know if you have a financial record of your dealings with your clients.'

'I'm an accountant. Records are what I do. And they are, of course, confidential.'

Brian sounded as if he'd begun to grow a spine. If that was Lilian's doing, I took my hat off to her. 'Of course they are. But – forgive me, Brian – but there are stories that perhaps your partner – um – took a little more out of the business than was strictly his due.'

'If you're saying that he stole from me, that's true. If you're saying that he stole from our clients, that's probably also true. He was clever about it. I'm working night and day trying to reconcile the books, trying to figure out how he did it. Then I'm going to pay it all back, no matter what it takes.'

'With Lilian's help, of course.'

'She's said that. I don't want her to. It's my problem, and I intend to solve it myself.'

'But if it's a great deal of money—'

'I don't know yet how much it might be. Donald was taking home good-sized cheques. I was not, although he kept urging me to do so. I couldn't see how our fees could generate that kind of money. It seems I was right. Now if you'll excuse me, I really must get back to—'

'But, Brian, you might not have to do that. Your old friend Roger Taylor talked to us about Donald, and said he had some information about the – er – fraudulent activities. I do really hate to say this, but he has letters from some of your clients complaining about money they think your firm stole from them. I tell you only because those letters might save you a great deal of work with—'

'Who,' said Brian, 'is Roger Taylor? I know no one by that name.'

Oh, dear. Had stress caused Brian to start losing it? 'He worked with you at that big firm in Carlisle, the one you left when you and Donald went into partnership.'

'Oh. Well, there were so many men there. I knew very few of them, and made almost no friends among them. If this person says he was a friend of mine—'

I tried to think back. 'No, maybe he didn't say that, exactly. Just that he knew you, and – um – that he had his doubts about Donald's honesty, and hoped it hadn't rubbed off on you. Something like that.'

'But why would our clients write to him? Surely if they had a complaint, they should have taken it up with us.'

'I don't know. Maybe they did, and Donald brushed it off somehow.'

'In any case,' said Brian firmly, 'I have no need to deal with the man. Our books may be in some disorder, but I can straighten them out. Given time to work on them.'

I can be thick-skinned when necessary, but I couldn't ignore so obvious a dismissal. 'Well, I'll leave you to it, then. Good luck.'

He ended the call before I got the last words out.

Alan, having heard only my side of the call, said, 'You're usually better than that at making up a story.'

'I know. He caught me off guard. I hadn't really thought out what I wanted to say to him, and when he claimed he had never heard of Roger Taylor, I was taken aback.'

'He said that?'

'In so many words.' I relayed the rest of the conversation.

'I can believe that he didn't make friends at his old firm. He doesn't seem to make friends easily. But to claim he didn't know him at all seems a stretch.'

'Do you suppose Taylor is the one who's been lying to us? I think maybe I'd better talk to him again. But I can't if he doesn't answer his phone.'

'You could go see him on Monday.'

'But that's two days away! I want to get this business over and done with and go back home to our family.'

'We can go home any time. You know that.'

'Yes.' But we both knew we wouldn't leave something this important unsettled. Too many people's happiness depended on the answers we were trying to help find. 'How do we get ourselves into these sorts of messes, anyway?'

'I get dragged in because I'm an ex-cop and I'm supposed to have some answers, or some ways of getting answers. You jump in because you care about people and about justice. And I wouldn't have it any other way.'

Ruth stood, looking embarrassed. 'If you two are going to start billing and cooing, I'm outta here. I won't claim I'm not jealous! Dorothy, I'm going to keep talking to the ladies at church and the book group and the WI – everyone I know, in fact. Or maybe just listening. Now that you've planted the idea that the sleaze was murdered, you can be sure it'll be the only topic of discussion. If there are any straws in the wind, these women will catch them and weave them into a net to catch a villain.'

'Ruth, that's positively poetic! Here's hoping you come up with something. So far we've drawn a total blank.'

'Maybe your Roger person will turn up and give you some ideas. Or just possibly the disgusting Harold will come galumphing home and confess. See you!' She left with the rest of the pizza, and I collapsed onto the bed.

'I think I'm burned out. I want to go to sleep and wake up on another planet.'

'Somewhere over the rainbow? Tell you what, love. Let's order room service, a salad or something to balance the pizza, and some nice wine, go to bed whenever we feel sleepy, and go to the early service tomorrow. A little divine inspiration wouldn't hurt.'

'And might help quite a lot. You're on.'

We were just finishing our meal when Alan's phone tootled. He swallowed his wine and answered, immediately turning on the speaker. 'Good to hear from you, Christopher. You have news?'

'Yes, though it's very sketchy. I just heard from Davies that they spotted Harold Thompson.'

'That's good news indeed! Where is he, and what's he up to?'

'I said the news was sketchy. I know only that they saw him at St Pancras this morning about to board the Eurostar. Unfortunately he also saw them and melted into the crowd. They searched, of course, but you know what the London stations are like. And it was during the morning rush hour. They searched the train, but he wasn't aboard, and they made an attempt to search the station, but it was hopeless. I thought you'd want to know straight away, even though it's almost nothing.'

'It's not a lot, but at least he's still in England. Thanks for the call, and let me know when you hear anything further.'

'What do you think that means?' I asked Alan.

'Don't know. He could be fleeing a murder charge, or running away from business problems, or not fleeing at all, just planning a nice holiday in Paris.'

'Which he didn't mention to anyone around here.'

'Indeed. At any rate, he probably won't try the Eurostar again.

And he knows now that the police are on his tail. Let's hope that provokes him into doing something stupid. In fact, I think that's worth a toast.'

We refilled our glasses and solemnly clinked them as Alan pronounced, 'To a stupid move, and a resolution.'

That was, I thought, a little premature, but it was a fine goal.

# TWENTY-ONE

I woke early to a beautiful day. Even in early September, the sun in England rises far earlier than it used to back home in Indiana. Years ago, when I first moved to Sherebury, it took me some time to get used to the differences in the light, very early sunrise and late sunset in summer, very late sunrise and early sunset in winter. I had to look at a globe to realize that all of England lies north of all our lower forty-eight. I've seen kids playing soccer near York at ten thirty in the evening in midsummer.

At any rate, the sky this morning was a lovely pale blue at six thirteen, and the breeze coming in the window was sweet and fresh and joyful with birdsong. I couldn't think for a moment why I was in such a good mood, and then I remembered. Horrible Harold was, perhaps, close to being caught, and would, I hoped, soon sing like those delightful birds out there.

I stretched, accidentally kicking Alan. Well, almost accidentally. He grunted, turned over, and fixed me with a bleak eye.

'Early church, remember?'

Another grunt. 'Not this early.' He turned over again and pulled up the covers.

Well, I was going to get up, anyway. Life felt good, and I didn't want to waste the lovely morning. I made coffee and sat down to think about what lay ahead.

We didn't know when, or even if, Harold Thompson could be tracked down and brought back to Grasmere for questioning. If he did arrive, probably Alan and I would be excluded from the interview. No matter. I would like to be there, but an ex-officio, especially one as very ex as I, could hardly expect to be in on the act. I could give whoever would be there a list of things I wanted to know. This afternoon was plenty of time to compile that list, which in any case would almost certainly duplicate a lot of the official questions.

All right. The other person I was truly eager to question was

Roger Taylor. I sure hoped he had charged his phone, or found it, or remedied whatever problem had caused him not to answer yesterday. I wanted a lot of answers from him, and I wanted that list of Donald and Brian's disgruntled customers. Surely on a Sunday I'd be able to find him.

I had a moment's qualm. Were inquiries about a murder a proper way to spend a Sunday afternoon? Oh, why not? I didn't expect to be having a good time, and anyway, trying to serve the cause of justice was God's work.

Wasn't it?

I was getting hungry, and we'd eaten all the biscuits that had been provided by the management. By now it was past seven, and there wasn't time for a real breakfast, but maybe I could run downstairs and pick up a pastry or two. I nudged Alan, purposefully this time.

'Mmm?'

'Rise and shine, my dear. I'm going to shower and dress and get us some breakfast goodies. And we have to get out of here in about half an hour.'

We made it, but only just. We walked into the church just as the priest entered the chancel to begin the service.

I love all the bells and whistles of a full High Church Eucharist – the procession, the hymns, the chanted liturgy, the anthems, the works. But there was something very moving about the quiet, simple Communion service that morning. One thought about Jesus sharing a meal with his friends. No pomp, no fancy touches. Just bread and wine and love.

Alan and I didn't speak until we had nearly arrived back at the hotel. 'Happy?' he said, taking my hand.

'Very,' I replied.

We were ready by then for a leisurely breakfast, which I ate with gusto and the usual guilt about all the cholesterol, and then glanced at the Sunday papers before repairing to the lounge to plan our day. 'Do you suppose Mr Taylor is a churchgoer?' I asked tentatively.

'Most people aren't these days, more's the pity. They don't know what they're missing. Since we're just guessing, I'd say he's more likely to spend Sundays on a golf course.'

'Is there one here?'

'Bound to be. I'm not an avid golfer, as you know, but I'll bet there are several courses nearby. We're too close to Scotland, where the game was invented and is pursued fanatically, not to have courses all over the map. Great heavens, woman, we're not all that far away from St Andrews. You have heard of St Andrews?'

'Not living on another planet,' I said with dignity, 'yes, I've heard of the most famous golf course in the world. But what makes you think Taylor is a golfer?'

'No reason, except he just looks like that sort of man. We could check with his friends.'

'If we knew who his friends were. Don't forget Brian claims not to know him.'

'Which gets us right back where we started, needing to talk to him about Brian's supposed fraudulent activity.'

'I think we should stop calling it Brian's,' I objected. 'I'd stake quite a lot on the thefts, if indeed there were thefts, being Donald's idea. He was so twisted a corkscrew would have looked arrow-straight by comparison. And I've just had an idea. Is Christopher a golfer?'

'In a mild sort of way. Socially, like me.'

'Then why don't you call him and see if he'd take you round to nearby courses? You could ask if Taylor is a member. And you might even play a round with Christopher.'

'No clubs. No shoes.'

'Surely you could rent clubs, couldn't you? And if they won't let you play in trainers, maybe they rent shoes as well. Look, dear heart, you've been working and worrying the whole time we've been here on what was supposed to be a holiday. Cut yourself some slack.'

'And what do you propose to do while I'm engaged in riotous living?'

'I'm going to call Ruth and have her take me sightseeing, which is what one is supposed to do in this famous beauty spot. I know, I know, we've done a little of that, but Ruth will have a foreigner's point of view about what's not to be missed.'

So we dawdled away the rest of the morning, and then while Alan went off in search of Roger Taylor and, I hoped, a little R & R, I called Ruth, hoping that her afternoon was free.

It wasn't. She was going out with some of her painting friends to try to capture some of the beautiful hills near Grasmere. 'Come with us, why don't you?' she invited.

'Good grief, Ruth, I haven't an artistic bone in my body. I can draw one of those cartoon cats, you know, a couple of circles and some ears and whiskers and a swirly line for a tail. That's it.'

'Doesn't matter. I'm packing tea goodies, which you can share, and you can sit with us and enjoy the lovely day and the scenery, and tell everyone how talented they are. I'd ask you to bring Alan, but this is a women-only group.'

'He's going to be away for the afternoon, anyway. He's hoping to play a few holes of golf with Christopher.'

'Hmph. Golf and gossip, is my guess.' She snickered.

'And you'd be right.'

'And I'm also betting that you have some gossip in mind yourself.'

I sighed. 'I cannot tell a lie. If you think your fellow artists wouldn't find it distracting, I'd love to find out what they know or guess about the murder.'

'For heaven's sake, we're not all that serious about what we do! Nobody's trying to get into the Royal Academy, or whatever the pinnacle here is. We just paint for the fun of it, and as an excuse to get out in the fresh air. So get into something comfortable, and I'll pick you up in – what, half an hour?'

I hadn't packed the jeans which would have been best for sitting around on grass or whatever, but I put on my oldest slacks and a sweater I didn't much care about, and set out happily, taking my walking stick just in case. This was far better than my idea of sightseeing, as it would combine a beautiful view with (I hoped) lots of opportunity to learn something.

The perfectly lovely weather brought out a lot of painters. When Ruth got to a place where we could leave the car, she had a little trouble fitting into one of the few spaces left. 'We'll have to walk from here, but there's a good path. Can you manage?'

'Of course,' I said in my best Queen Mum manner. 'I may not be quite as spry as some of your friends, but I'm far from dead yet.'

I worked hard to conceal my shortness of breath when we got to the place the group had chosen. The path had been steep at the end, and I was grateful for my stick. But the view was worth it. Spread out below us were all the beauties that have made people rave about the area for generations. The hills were covered in trees just beginning to turn from green to bronze. The deep blue sky held decorative white clouds that might have been designed by Constable. The obligatory lake reflected the sky and clouds. Fields were golden with the stubble of the recent wheat harvest, and as the perfect final touch, the green pastures were dotted with sheep. As the women set up their easels, I wondered how they could possibly choose which bit to paint from such an embarrassment of riches.

Ruth found a flat spot for her easel and set it up with the ease of long practice, taping a large piece of white paper to the flat surface. I'd carried her bag of paints, brushes, a bottle of water, and a few other impedimenta, while she'd lugged the rest, including our tea.

'*And*,' she said with the air of a conjuror, 'I even brought a shooting stick for you.' She produced a peculiar-looking object that opened into a tube with a small hammock-style canvas seat at one end and a spike at the other, for driving into the ground.

'So that's what that means! I always thought it was a strange British term for some kind of gun.'

'So did I!' said Ruth with a giggle. 'When I joined this group, they told me I was going to need one, and I had to confess I hadn't the slightest idea what they were talking about. So I bought one, but I found I wasn't using it much. I paint rather quickly and I like to be close to the picture. Anyway, it gets uncomfortable after a while. You'll see. But it's better than sitting on the damp grass, and then there's the question of getting up again.'

'Always a problem,' I agreed. 'More so with every added year. It was very thoughtful of you to bring it, and I don't want you to think I'm not grateful, but I do plan to move around some, looking at everyone else's work.'

'And picking their brains.'

'That, too.'

With that, she finished setting up her supplies, a large and well-used box of colours, brushes, and a small bowl of water. She began not with paints but a pencil, roughing out her vision of the scene.

I watched for a while, leaning on the shooting stick, but without colour there wasn't much to see, so I soon moved on to the next artist.

She was a striking woman in her forties, at a guess. Her black hair was cut short and with no attempt at styling. She wore no make-up; her clothes were strictly utilitarian and somewhat spotted with paint. Yet her slim, taut figure and prominent cheekbones gave her an air of distinction. This, I felt, was a person who knew her own mind.

Her picture looked like her. She had focussed on a single tree, a venerable oak whose branches had been twisted by winds and sheer age. She, too, had begun with pencil, but was now beginning to fill in the green of the leaves and mix just the right brownish-grey for the trunk and branches.

'Do you mind if I watch while you work?' I asked diffidently. 'I'm a friend of Ruth's and just came along for the ride. She said she thought I wouldn't be bothering anybody.'

'Not at all! We're not serious painters, you know, just hobbyists. What do you think so far?' She added a touch of bronze to a section of leaves.

'You've captured the soul of that tree,' I said honestly. 'It's been here a long time and knows everything there is to know about this valley.'

She looked up in surprise. 'You know that trees have souls. Not many people do.'

'My father was a botanist, and so was my first husband. I've always loved and revered trees, especially oaks. I expect you can tell I'm American-born. Our oaks are different from yours, different species, but equally majestic and wise.'

She turned and looked at me fully. 'Now I know who you are. You're the woman who's nosing into the death of that blister.'

'My husband and I are, yes. Dorothy Martin,' I added, extending my hand.

She nodded. 'I can't shake hands. Too painty. Helen Mirren, and no, I'm not related.'

I laughed. 'You must get so tired of dealing with that question.'

'I do, and it's worse because I have more right to the name than she does. Her birth name was something slightly different, whereas mine is the name in the christening register. No matter. Why are you trying to find out who killed that disgusting man?'

'I understand how you feel about him. I've gathered most people are the same. Me, I met him only once, briefly, and I can't say I took to him. But I keep thinking of John Donne.'

'"Any man's death diminishes me" and all that. I suppose. I can't say I feel diminished because Donald Atkinson is dead.'

'Sarah does.'

'Well, she shouldn't! He bullied her unmercifully.'

'She does, though. It's partly for her sake that we're trying to find some answers. Of course you know we're strictly unofficial.'

'I thought your husband was a policeman.'

'Was once, but he's long retired. It's only because he still has some connections that he's being allowed in on the investigation. And as for me, I'm tolerated, sort of, because of Alan.'

'You said poor Sarah's one of your reasons for poking about. What's the other?'

'A respect for the law.' I looked her straight in the eye. 'Law is all that separates us from savages. It has to be upheld.' I pointed to her picture. 'You love the majesty of the oaks, and so do I. And I love the majesty of the law.'

The glazed look on Helen's face told me what she thought of my pontificating. I bit my lip. 'Sorry to sound so preachy. But I do feel strongly about it. No matter how much of a monster the man was, and I freely confess that he probably was a grade-A villain that the world is much better off without, no one had the right to murder him.'

Helen cleared her throat. 'Yes. Well. I'm sure you're right. But are you – are they – any closer to catching whoever did it?'

'Not really. They're pretty sure of several people who didn't do it, so that narrows it down.'

'Narrows it down to whom?'

'I'm sorry, I can't tell you that. I don't know what the police are thinking, actually, so Alan and I are only dealing with our own best guesses. What about you and your friends? What's the feeling in the community?'

She shrugged. 'As I said before, nobody cares very much one way or the other.'

'You're not worried about a murderer going free in this small community?'

'Oh. I hadn't thought about it that way. You're saying he might kill somebody else?'

'It's been known to happen,' I said drily. 'Killers will kill to protect themselves, if they think someone knows something compromising. Have you never read any crime novels?'

'But they're just fiction.'

'Based on solid fact, I assure you. But I'm distracting you from your painting. I should let you get on with it. It's going to be wonderful.'

'Thank you. Nice of you to say so, when I've been so rude to you.'

'You haven't. We just have differing views, that's all. It's allowed.' I smiled and turned away. 'I'd better go back and see if Ruth is ready for tea.'

'Wait. Tell me your name again and where you're staying.'

'Dorothy Martin. The Inn at Grasmere.'

'If I come across anything that might suggest who the killer is, may I phone you? I'm beginning to understand where you're coming from, and who knows? Something might turn up.'

I thanked her profusely and gave her my mobile number before moving away. I didn't really want any tea just yet, but I moved over to Ruth's pitch to see how she was doing.

'Any luck?' she asked as my shadow fell across her work.

'Not really. I've only talked to one painter, and she has no interest in figuring out whodunnit. I got the impression she'd rather give him the key to the city than see him arrested.'

'You're sure it's a man, then?'

'No. Manner of speaking. That's coming along beautifully.' I peered over her shoulder to look at the painting more closely. She had drawn in the details now and begun to wash some of the areas with colour. One grassy hillside was dotted with grey-and-white sheep, their long fluffy coats making them look a little like stuffed toys, and Ruth had painted in one alert brown dog that wasn't actually there. 'Has the dog gone away?'

'Wasn't there at all. But she often is, and she provides contrast for the green of the grass and the blue of the lake.'

There was no blue on the paper. 'Umm—'

'Blue comes next. Go away, do, and bother somebody else. I'll want a break and some tea in about half an hour.'

I did as I was bidden, using my cane to move cautiously up the hill. The path had been reasonably easy going. Off the path there were stray rocks and tussocks to trap the unwary.

My next quarry had found a flat outcropping of stone to support her easel. She was working in pastels, which I thought appropriate. Her curly grey hair, gold-rimmed glasses and comfortable bulk made her look like somebody's grandmother. Her hands, too, with their prominent veins, swollen knuckles and liver spots, spoke of age.

She looked up as I approached. 'Come to critique?' she asked with a smile. 'Have a look, dear.'

Her smile changed to a cackle as she saw my face change. 'Expected something sweet and niminy-piminy, didn't you?'

Her picture was an abstract study in broad strokes of pure colour. Sky, lake, field, meadow – all were there, but with no detail, only colour and an indication of shape and texture. And yet . . .

'I can feel the wind,' I said slowly. 'And hear it.'

'Ah! You have the imaginative eye. That's what I wanted to get down on paper. But you are surprised! Admit it.'

'I certainly am. I thought you'd paint quite differently.'

'I'm very nice to my grandchildren and bake lovely cakes for the church teas. This' – she gestured toward the picture – 'is the other side of me, the unconventional side. And that's the side that'll be useful to you, my dear. Oh, yes, I know who you are and what you're after. Ruth told me about you. Sit down on that boulder over there and let me tell you my ideas.'

# TWENTY-TWO

She took a Thermos out of her bag. 'Some tea?'

'I'd love some, but Ruth brought enough for both of us. I shouldn't take yours.'

'But I'm offering, and you wouldn't be rude enough to refuse. I have an extra cup somewhere.' She rummaged and found a glass that probably held water when she was using watercolours. The tea looked strong enough to stand by itself, and she didn't offer milk or sugar. Oh well, it probably wouldn't kill me. I took a sip and tried not to make a face.

'Another surprise, eh? You thought I'd prefer the straw-coloured stuff that little old ladies are supposed to like.'

'If you read everybody's minds that way, I'm sure you have good ideas about Atkinson's murder.'

She cackled again. 'I'm not clairvoyant, but most people make assumptions based on my appearance. It's fun to prove them wrong. You don't actually have to drink that tea, you know, and I do have some sugar somewhere. No milk; too much trouble to pack.'

'I'll drink it and risk heartburn. It's wet, and I'm thirsty.' The second sip wasn't quite as bad. 'So tell me who you think did it.'

'I haven't got that far yet. You probably know half the village is rejoicing that he's gone.'

'The male half?'

'Oh, them of course, but a good few of the women, too. His good looks soon palled as we began to find out what a bastard he was.'

She paused and eyed me for my reaction to the word. I refused to react. I think she was disappointed, but she made no comment.

'Of course you know how he treated Sarah.'

I nodded.

'Such a waste! She was a pretty girl, not beautiful but attractive, and capable. He took all that away from her.'

'I've been told that, and I can see for myself that she has no self-confidence. What I've wanted to know is why. Why would he want to do that to her?'

'He was one of those egomaniacs who can't stand to see anyone else get any praise or admiration or, God forbid, love. It all had to come to him. When she first married him, she was well loved in the community. That wouldn't do. He had to destroy her. Of course he married her for her money, and when he found out he couldn't get his mitts on any of it, he took out his fury on her.'

I took a deep breath. 'Do you think she killed him?'

She glared at me. 'Are you mental? Sarah Atkinson has trouble swatting a fly. She feels sorry for them.'

'But they don't bully and demean her. Her husband did. Everyone has a breaking point.'

'Well, if Sarah does, she hasn't reached it yet. She's *grieving* for him, poor deluded fool. And just what is your interest in this anyway? You don't live here. You're not even English.'

'American by birth. Now a citizen of the UK.' I was getting distinctly nettled. 'I don't happen to have my passport with me, but it's at my hotel, if you care to inspect it. As for my interest in the murder, my husband, though retired, was a very senior policeman indeed, and is well respected throughout the system. He has been asked to help the local police, and I'm serving as his eyes and ears.'

The woman cackled again. 'I wondered if I could get a rise out of you. You're so damn polite. I always thought Americans were rude.'

'And I always thought the English were courteous,' I retorted.

'So we're even. My name is Monahan, Patricia Monahan. Husband Irish, deceased. Me, I'm as English as they come, born in a village in Kent. Ruth told me your name, but I've forgotten it.'

'Dorothy Martin. My husband's name is Alan Nesbitt. We live in Sherebury, in Sussex.'

'Ah, yes, the smallest cathedral city in the kingdom, and not far from my old home. Which is a pretty village, but I much prefer Grasmere. I've enjoyed our little game, Dorothy, but you want to stop playing and learn what I know about the public benefactor who rid the world of Donald Atkinson. I expect our movie star over there told you she isn't interested in tracking him down.'

'She did. Do I take it you agree?'

'No, I don't. Atkinson was a— There are no polite words for him, and I won't offend you again by calling him what he should be called. But murder is murder. I would have stood on and cheered if he'd been shown up in public for what he was, and I wouldn't have pretended any sorrow if he'd died of some loath-some disease. But I do draw the line at murder.

'And now I'm going to disappoint you. I led you down a garden path. I don't know who the murderer is, but I do know something about why he was killed, and that points to one of a very small number of people.'

'And it has to do with theft.'

'Funnily enough, no. Ruth said you were clever, so I was sure you'd got on to that. Yes, of course he was a thief. He tried all sorts of ways to make off with Sarah's money, and when he couldn't, he started playing games with his clients' funds. There are any number of ways a good accountant can cook the books, and he was a very good accountant, from what I hear.'

'So his fraudulent activities were common knowledge?'

'They were widely suspected, because his lifestyle was much more lavish than seemed possible on legitimate earnings, though no one could ever prove anything. I told you he was good. The source of his wealth was actually quite different.'

I waited. She waited, applying more bright colour to her picture.

She sighed. 'You win. You're better at the silent treatment than I am. Donald Atkinson, along with all his other sins, was a blackmailer. He was bleeding his so-called friend, Harold Thompson.'

I swallowed hard. 'Over what? I've heard that Thompson isn't a very scrupulous lawyer – solicitor – but I don't know any details.'

'Nor do I. I did get the impression that whatever the trouble was, it wasn't recent. Harold is from London originally. Of course every breath he's taken since he moved to the Lakes has been observed, catalogued, and filed away in the village's collective memory, but London is different. One can hide there. People don't know each other and don't particularly care.'

I thought about the gossip I'd gleaned over the years from my American friends living in Belgravia, not far from Victoria Station and Buckingham Palace, and said only, 'And how did you pick up on this bit of information?'

'From Sarah Atkinson, believe it or not! We were arranging flowers together one Saturday, and she began to talk about how wonderful Donald was and how badly Harold was treating him. I didn't pay much attention at first. She was always blethering on about Donald the Magnificent, and I could hardly tell her what I thought of him, so the safest thing was to murmur something meaningless from time to time. But she was getting heated this time and actually raised her voice!'

'Sarah shouting? I can't imagine!'

'Of course not! She raised it almost to the level of audibility and said that Harold had actually threatened Donald.'

'Good heavens! But that's terribly important!'

'Maybe. Maybe not. It was weeks before the murder. According to what she told me, Harold said something about blackmail being dangerous, and Donald laughed it off, whereupon Harold said something about going too far one day. And then Sarah dropped a spoon or something – she was in the kitchen making tea – and the men realized she could hear them and scarpered. Now what do you think of that?'

'I think the police ought to know about it. Okay, so maybe it was a long time ago, but these things can fester. I'm going to tell Alan right away, so he can pass it on.'

'And go after Thompson? They have to find him first. If he's still in the UK, I'd plump for the far reaches of Scotland. There are some bits up there that aren't even on the map.'

'Now you're exaggerating.'

'Only a bit. Two of my friends were lost for nearly a week not far from Ben Nevis one winter. They nearly died. There was no mobile service, and their OS map was useless, they said, too much of it virtually blank except for the contour lines. And on a mountain it can be almost impossible to tell if you're going up or down. Especially in the snow.'

'Thompson wouldn't go to a place like that,' I objected. 'You only have to look at him to know he's fond of his creature comforts. But I'll get Alan to tell the police what you said. So if you'll excuse me, I need to get on it. Thanks for your help, and I hope you'll put that remarkable picture in a gallery when you've finished. People need to see it. Bye!'

I was itching now to get back to the hotel and talk over all of my new information with Alan, but as I picked my careful way down the hill to where Ruth had set up her 'studio', I remembered that Alan was probably out on a golf course somewhere. Well, I could call him, at least. I pulled my phone out of my pocket and reached voicemail. Oh, of course he would have silenced his phone. A ringing mobile was even less welcome to golfers than to concertgoers or worshippers. Drat.

Ruth looked up as I made my noisy approach, crunching small pebbles and greenery underfoot. 'I thought you'd never get back! I'm dying for my tea.'

'Me, too, or at least for the food that goes with it. I had a cup of perfectly awful tea with your friend up the hill. Or at least part of a cup. I managed to toss most of it into the bushes when her back was turned.'

'Oh, you must have been with Pat. Yes, she does make terrible tea. Get me my backpack, will you?' She rummaged in it. 'Here's a cup and a plate. The goodies are in the big plastic bag and the tea in the Thermos. Milk's in it already, so I hope you like it that way. I did bring some sugar packets; they're in there somewhere.' She sat on the grass and prodded her pack into a sort of cushion for me up against a tree since I couldn't manage to eat and drink sitting on the shooting stick.

I sat gratefully and spread my little feast on the grass. 'I'll need a crane to get up again.'

'Yes, that's the trouble with aging, isn't it? I can still almost make it up, and I can help you when the time comes. So tell me, did you learn anything interesting?'

'A lot that I'm dying to tell Alan, and I can't, because he's switched his phone off.' I devoured one small, crustless sandwich and reached for another.

Ruth nodded. 'As silent as Trappist monks, golfers are. I've always found it silly. It's a game, not a religious rite. But what did Pat tell you that's so urgent?'

Between bites, I explained about Pat's blackmail theory. 'Of course, the police will have to ask Sarah directly, but do you think she'll remember the conversation after several weeks?'

'She probably remembers every word Donald spoke from the time they first met. She was addicted to him. Or hypnotized, or something. I've never quite understood how a woman as intelligent as Sarah could fall for the line of a lying, abusive hypocrite, but she did. I wasn't here when it all began, of course, but I've heard plenty about it from her friends. They don't get it, either.'

'Sheer sex appeal?'

Ruth shrugged. 'I could never see that he had any, but as they say, diff'rent strokes. Anyway, do you think it's true? The blackmail theory, I mean.'

'I think it could be. It fits the character of both men, as far as I can tell, which isn't of course very far. All I know about either of them is based on hearsay and brief first impressions. I disliked them both at first sight, but that's not reliable.'

'Not always, but we've both met a lot of people in our long lives. I think we've learned to spot the nasties early in the game.'

'Maybe. I'd much rather Harold were the villain, because I don't like him, and I do rather like Roger.'

'From the little I know about that Roger person, I can't say I'm wild about him. But I don't like Harold Thompson, either.'

'The thing is, I just learned— No, I'd better not talk about that.'

Ruth's eyes were piercing through me. 'What aren't you telling me?'

Oh, dear. 'I'm sorry, but I think I'd better shut up. There are some things the police would rather keep quiet about at this stage.'

'I see. You're willing to use me as an intro to people who might pass on useful gossip but not to trust me with details. I thought we were friends, but I guess I was wrong.'

'No, you weren't wrong! Please don't be offended. The thing is, Alan and I have worked with the official police quite a lot, but always with the caveat that we didn't compromise the investigation. If I told you any more about anything, I know you wouldn't intentionally let it go any further, but it's easier for you if you can honestly say you have no idea. Do *please* understand! From one American to another!'

'Okay, okay! But I want you to know I expect the whole story when your tongue is unchained. Now I suppose you want to go find Alan and confer.'

'Well, but your painting—'

'It's gone all sweet and pretty, like something out of a kid's colouring book. Hopeless, beyond repair. Let's go.'

There wasn't a lot of the afternoon left, and I spent it trying to reach Alan. Voicemail every time, so I wrote down everything I could remember of what I'd been told, though I'd already forgotten the woman's name. I've become hopeless with names, one of the more irritating problems of aging. Ruth would tell me, though, when she'd gotten over her snit.

I was almost at the nail-biting stage when my phone rang. I snatched it up. 'Alan! At last! I have lots to tell you.'

'It'll have to wait, I'm afraid. I'm with Davies. Roger Taylor is in custody.'

'No! But he isn't—'

'Not on the phone, love. I'll be home for dinner, just as soon as I can, but you might want a snack meanwhile. Talk to you later.'

And he was gone, leaving me more frustrated than before. Yes, I'd go have myself a snack – and a drink to go with it.

I asked for a good deal of water in my bourbon and had munched my way through two packets of crisps by the time Alan finally showed up. He sat down next to me and eyed my empty glass. 'Still compos mentis, my love?'

'It was mostly water. I didn't know how long I'd have to wait. Alan, I have so much to tell you!'

'And I would also a tale unfold. But could we find some food first? I'm ravenous. Maybe we could have something sent up to our room?'

I was ready for another of their delectable shepherd's pies, starting with soup to offset the chill of the evening and followed by a wonderfully decadent concoction of chocolate and berries and ice cream. We took a second alcoholic libation up to our room while we waited for our food, and began to narrate our day.

'You first,' I said, beginning to relax. 'I'll make a note of all the things you got wrong and then tell you the true story.'

He grinned. 'You do give a chap confidence. Cheers.' He took a healthy swallow and sighed. 'Ahh. It's been a long day.' He set his glass down and assumed his instructing position, hands tented.

'Begin at the beginning,' I demanded.

'Yes, ma'am. That would be when I fetched Christopher. He knew of two or three nearby golf clubs and was happy to take me round, though he didn't know if Roger played.

'We struck lucky at the first one. Yes, Roger Taylor was a member, and yes, he was out on the course, and yes, I could hire clubs and could play in trainers, just this once. They weren't as busy as one would expect on a Sunday afternoon, so they would allow us non-members to play. The fee astounded me! I haven't played for a long time and didn't realize how much the cost was inflated, like everything else these days.'

'Yes, dear. Assuming you're not now bankrupt, do continue.'

'No, we can still afford this meal. On with the dance, let joy be unconfined. Christopher and I played as fast as we could, and I'm afraid we cheated on some holes so we could catch up to Taylor. He had quite a start on us and was holing out on the eighteenth before we saw him. Let me tell you, he wasn't best pleased when we came up and invited him for a drink. He fumbled with lame excuses, but Christopher and I weren't police trained for nothing; we can both recognize lies at forty paces. So we ignored his blethering and more-or-less dragged him to the clubhouse.

'When Taylor found himself shanghaied by two former policemen tangentially involved in a murder investigation, he panicked. The first thing he said when we sat down was, "All right, I forged those letters. But I never took them to the police, and I never did any real harm".'

'Wow! The guilty flee where no man pursueth.'

'And in so doing condemneth themselves. And before we could recover from our astonishment and question him further, he turned pale and clutched at his chest.'

'Oh no! Heart attack?'

'Not quite. Christopher reached for his phone to call for help, but Taylor signalled no, reached into his pocket, and pulled out a pill box. He took one tiny tablet, placed it under his tongue, and said, "I'll be all right in a minute".'

'Nitroglycerine!'

'Exactly. The classic signs and treatment for angina. It worked, by the way. In a few minutes, Taylor said his pain was gone, and he looked perfectly normal. We might have stopped questioning him at that point, worrying that we might have caused the stress that led to the attack, but he opened his mouth again and once more firmly inserted foot. He said he was sorry he had caused us anxiety, that he usually used a preparation that kept these attacks in check, but his last tube of it had been lost and he'd had no time to get to France for more.'

'France! Are you saying he used that stuff, what's it called, that was in Donald's tube of ointment for his rash?'

'Nitro-Bid. At that point we had to take him to the temporary headquarters and have him talk to Davies. The usual warning, the whole rigmarole. He would have been wise to ask for an attorney, but he said he was innocent and didn't need one. Love, he said everything he should not. One could almost feel sorry for him. He admitted that he hated Atkinson, because he, Taylor, had been in love with Sarah and had had to watch Atkinson marry her and, in his words, "destroy" her.'

'Motive,' I said with a sigh.

'And means. He swore his tube of Nitro-Bid went missing before Atkinson was murdered, but he couldn't remember exactly when or how. His theory was that it had been stolen, but he had no idea who might have taken it. So you see Davies had no choice but to hold him.'

'Means and motive. Two of the big three. What about opportunity?'

'That's the big snag in cases like these, the ones I call delayed-action murders. He could have mixed the nitro into Atkinson's ointment at virtually any time, and then substituted that tube for the innocuous one at, again, virtually any time before the sports day. If no one saw him do it, it's going to be damned hard to prove he's the one.'

'And what was his explanation for his funny business with the fake complaining letters?'

'We didn't get around to that. Nor did we ask why he had gone to ground, so to speak, what with not answering his phone. Davies will probably deal with that. I do think, though, that our search is over. The man freely admits that he hated the victim, he had ample access to the murder weapon, and he's been actively avoiding us. That makes a convincing case, don't you think?'

'Ye-es. I guess so. He just doesn't seem the type, though.'

'My dear woman, you know perfectly well there isn't a murderous "type". They don't all have piercing eyes or low growly voices. The policeman's lot would be a far less unhappy one if you could spot 'em on sight.'

'Don't patronize me! I know that as well as you do. The first murderer I ever encountered was a pillar of the Cathedral! But I've never heard of one who was ineffectual, a retiring character who wasn't up to much.'

'Is that your assessment of Roger Taylor?'

'Not quite. Ineffectual is maybe the wrong word. He's just . . . oh, very much the stereotypical accountant. Serious, rather dull, a bit pompous, neither stupid nor brilliant. Not at all the sort to dream up a complicated murder like this one. Not, I'd think, a conniver.'

'And I tend to agree with you. But our ideas about his character have no weight as evidence, and the evidence shows that he had one of the best motives, jealousy, and the very unusual means. They'll work hard on proving opportunity, and when they do, Bob's your uncle.'

I sighed. 'Is there any more wine?'

# TWENTY-THREE

Despite an early morning and a certain amount of tramping in the afternoon, even despite more alcohol with dinner than I usually allow myself, sleep didn't come easily that night. Alan, an exhausting day behind him, was out for the count within minutes. I tried to turn off the hamster wheel in my head with all my usual techniques. I recited the twenty-third Psalm, twice. I did mental arithmetic, complicated multiplication problems and some long division. I constructed the calendar for the next several months in my head, working out the day of the week for Christmas and even taking a stab at the date for next Easter, though that was impossible without knowing the phases of the moon.

Nothing worked. I would just get to the third week of November when Roger's face would pop up, looking worried as he warned me not to take my business to Brian. Why? What did he have against Brian, Donald's innocent dupe?

Okay, I was assuming Brian was innocent, even though he must have at least suspected what was going on. He should have reported the fraud, of course. Why hadn't he?

The deceptively sweet-old-lady painter, whatever her name was – Pat, that was it – was sure Donald was blackmailing Harold Thompson. That raised the question: was he also holding something on Brian? It was hard to imagine what. Innocent Brian. If he was.

I turned over for the tenth time, trying not to wake Alan (though I probably could have done calisthenics in bed without disturbing him, so sound was his slumber).

What did I actually know about Brian? Know, not surmise. He had worked with Donald Atkinson despite Donald's affair with Brian's wife. Said wife, who had oodles of lovely money, was now energetically looking after Brian, even to the extent of repaying the victims of Donald's fraud. Why? He was a loner, according to his wife. That was hearsay, but I'd seen nothing to the contrary. Certainly hail-fellow-well-met was not the description of Brian that first came to mind.

In fact, he was an accountant like many. Like Roger, come to think of it. But certainly not like Donald, who seemed to view himself as God's gift to the world, particularly the female half.

Which led to a speculation. Perhaps Brian chose his career out of a desire to do what he was good at, to deal with numbers and avoid having to deal much with people. That would imply his honesty. Whereas Donald got into accounting because he, too, was brilliant with numbers, especially with juggling them. Implying his innate dishonesty.

His whole pattern of life, indeed, clearly demonstrated that he had one goal in life: his own ascendance. His ego was so immense, there was room in his world view for no one and nothing else.

And where did Brian fit into that? I didn't even know how long he'd worked for – with – Donald. For or with? I should check on that, too. Or someone should. Tomorrow. Tomorrow the sixth of September. Or was it the seventh? Or had I missed out a week altogether? If September began on a Monday . . . but that was last year. Or maybe next year . . .

Alan was shaking my shoulder gently. I muttered something and turned my head away from the too-bright light of the rising sun.

'Sorry, love. I know it's far too early for you, but I have to leave and I didn't want you to wake up and wonder where I'd got to. Shall I pour your coffee?'

Coffee. That word got through. I rolled out of bed and stumbled to the bathroom. When I came back, Alan had a cup of steaming coffee and a pastry waiting for me on the tiny table. He waited until I'd downed half the coffee before he put on his hat.

'I must go. Davies phoned me half an hour ago and wanted me at his headquarters right then. I don't know why. Don't know anything, but I must go. Call me only in case of dire necessity, and try to stay out of trouble.' A hasty kiss on the cheek and he was out the door.

I didn't even try to speculate until I'd finished my coffee and poured another cup and the brain cells began to respond.

Something new had come up in the murder case. They hadn't told Alan what it was, but they wanted his help, or his opinion, or something.

Information, probably. They knew he and I had been talking to people, gathering snippets. Whatever new data had come their way overnight, whatever new pieces of the puzzle, they thought Alan might be able to help fit them into place, using pieces he held.

Pieces he and I held. I knew some things he didn't. I'd been so swept up in the news about Roger Taylor, I'd forgotten to tell him about the blackmail theory!

That woke me up once and for all. If it was true, it put Harold Thompson absolutely at the top of the list of murder suspects. Except at this point it sounded as if the police didn't have a list, only a single entry: Roger Taylor.

Which I just didn't believe. Okay, Roger had hated Donald. So had virtually everyone who knew the man. That seemed to me to be a weak motive, or at least not a damning one.

He used the drug that had been employed to kill Donald. It was not available in England, which cut down the number of people who might also be using it. Still, angina is a common complaint, especially among men of a certain age. And France is not all that far away. To one born and bred in Indiana, a trip to France sounded exotic, difficult, and time-consuming. To a Brit, it's hop on a train in London and get out in Paris a bit over three hours later. That's how long it used to take me to get to Chicago if I drove up to South Bend and took the South Shore. Nothing to it. If pressed for time, one could do London–Paris and back in a single day, with time for a gourmet lunch at almost any bistro.

To my mind, that did away with the 'means' argument for Roger's guilt. He had access to the drug. So did anyone who had recently visited Paris, or any other place in France where there was a pharmacy.

If the blackmail story was true, the police had to know about it and step up their search for Harold Thompson. But if it wasn't, I'd be in big trouble for wasting police time. Perhaps it was just as well I hadn't told Alan about it.

The brain was purring away smoothly now, firing on all

cylinders. The first thing I had to do was get a decent breakfast to keep those little grey cells happy and efficient. The next was to go see Sarah.

I phoned her before I even showered. There was no answer. It was still early. She might still be in bed, or doing something at the church, where she might have her mobile turned off. I tried again after a quick breakfast; still nothing. Very well. I'd try the church, which was an easy walk on the sparkling autumn day.

The weather was the sort that invites comparisons with champagne, the sort that should be spent enjoying nature, perhaps boating on the lake or picnicking in the woods. I thought ruefully of the pleasant, leisurely vacation Alan and I had envisioned when Christopher invited us to this idyllic spot. Instead, we had spent the whole time tracking down a murderer whose victim was mourned by nobody.

No, I was wrong. Donald Atkinson was mourned by one person, whom I hoped to see and talk to soon. I stepped up my pace.

I was in luck. The church door was wide open to the brisk air and beneficent sunshine, and I could hear the subdued chatter of ladies as they worked at various chores. One of them came up to me as I entered.

'May I help you? The church isn't actually open just now, but if there's something you need—?'

'Thank you, but I'm just looking for Sarah Atkinson. My name is Dorothy Martin. She and I met a few days ago.'

The woman's face lost its welcome. 'Oh, yes. I'm not sure Sarah is here today.'

I spotted her just then, rearranging brochures in the small shop. 'Oh, there she is. I'm not going to trouble her, you know. I'm actually trying to help. Excuse me.'

Sarah looked better than the last time I'd seen her. Dressed casually in corduroy pants and a wool pullover, she was visibly thinner, but she was clean and tidy and had washed her hair and applied some lipstick. One could see hints of the pretty girl she used to be. Her movements as she went about her chore were quick and decisive.

She glanced up as I approached, and dropped the brochures she was holding. 'Oh, Mrs Martin! I was hoping to see you, or anyone who could tell me anything. When are they going to let me bury my husband? Surely they don't still need his body for forensics or whatever. I don't understand why they won't let me have him back.'

I moved closer and helped her pick up the leaflets from the floor. 'I'm afraid I don't know. I do know, from past experience with Alan, that the police sometimes hold on to victims far longer than one would think they should, and especially in poisoning cases. But of course you know he's in good hands.' I looked around me at the lofty ceiling, the altar at the far end. 'The best hands, in fact.'

'He— I do know that. But Donald wasn't always a regular churchgoer. In fact, he sometimes said things that made me wonder—'

'I wouldn't worry about that if I were you. We don't know what was in your husband's heart, but God does. All shall be well.'

Her face lit up at that. 'That's Julian of Norwich, isn't it? I love her sayings, and I'm sure you're right. It's just that—'

'It's just that you've had too much on your mind lately to think straight. Look, unless you're too busy, I'd love to take you out for coffee and talk about your husband.'

'Well, I suppose the shop will do for another day or two. Yes, I'd like to talk to someone who didn't know him, who can be impartial.'

That certainly didn't apply to me, but I'd try to be a comfort rather than an irritation. The poor woman didn't need any more irritation.

I chivvied her out of the church rather quickly, fearing that Ruth might come up and ask to join us. I hadn't seen her, but if she was there and saw us, she'd surely want to watch over her protégée.

The nearest café was virtually empty at this hour of a Monday morning. It wasn't nearly time for traditional elevenses. Never mind. I'd been up early and was more than ready for another dose of caffeine, and I was sure that Sarah, disturbed as she was, could use some as well, along with a few calories and some cosseting.

I didn't want to upset her further with probing questions, but

I had to know if the allegation of blackmail had any basis in fact. Cosseting first; then I'd try to find a way to introduce the stressful subject.

When we had fragrant coffee and a plate of tempting pastries in front of us, I began. 'Sarah, I've been worried about you. How are you getting along?'

'Mrs Martin—'

'Dorothy, please.'

'Dorothy, you're obviously happily married. You can't imagine what it's like to lose a husband.'

'I can, though. Alan is my second husband. I was married before I moved to England to a perfectly wonderful man who died very suddenly of a heart attack. We had so many plans, and then suddenly he wasn't there anymore. It was as if my life had no shape, no meaning. I went about doing the ordinary things, because one does, but it was all empty.'

'That's it exactly. But at least your husband died a natural death. Mine was murdered.'

'That must make it a thousand times worse. I can't even find words to say how sorry I am that you're having to go through all this. Especially you, such a gentle person who does so much for your church.'

'I don't do much, really, just try to keep things tidy. It gives me something to do.'

'Have you thought about getting a job? I've heard you are very skilled in office work.'

'I was, long ago. I don't know if I'd fit in now. Donald never wanted me to work.'

I leaned across the table. 'Sarah, listen to me. Donald is gone. The life you lived with him is gone. You have to live with Sarah now, and the only way you're going to do that is to rediscover who Sarah is. I think your friends will tell you she's an interesting and worthwhile person.'

Drat. This conversation wasn't going at all the way I'd planned. I'd meant to ask leading questions, and instead I was playing Ann Landers.

She didn't respond, so I tried another tack. 'We spoke once about your dramatic ability. Is there a local dramatic society you might get involved in? Really, you have talent, and I'm not just saying that to make you feel better. I don't believe in comforting lies.'

'No, I think you're a very honest person. And forthright. You say what you think.'

'I hope I haven't said anything to offend you! It can be tricky for an American. I've lived in England for quite a while now, but I still trip over nuances sometimes. A word that's quite innocuous in American may be really nasty in English. It took me quite a while to understand how offensive some ordinary words are. I won't tell you which ones, because—'

'Because you don't want to sound vulgar.' She laughed a little, which was certainly a step in the right direction. 'I suspect I know some of the words you mean. And no, you haven't offended me. How could you? You've said nothing but kind things to me. I'm sorry if I haven't responded very well. I'm still not really taking anything in.'

'No, of course not. It's too soon. And you still don't know who did this terrible thing. I don't mean to cause you still more distress, but do you really have no idea . . . or no, of course you don't, or you would have told the police.'

Sarah sighed. 'Poor Donald had to deal with many unpleasant people. I understood it was necessary for someone in his position, but it wasn't always agreeable when they came to the house to see him. I didn't always understand what they were talking about. I've never been very knowledgeable about business or politics. But I could understand angry voices!'

'Did you recognize any of the angry voices?'

'Oh, I always knew who they were. Donald expected me to be their hostess, show them to the drawing room, offer them drinks, all that. Then he'd take them off to his study. I never asked questions. I didn't want to know what they were doing, and Donald didn't want me to know. He always said that his affairs were none of my business.'

She paused. 'Mrs Martin – Dorothy – I hated all of it! Those men frightened me. Donald was a good accountant, making a good living, and anyway we didn't even need his money. I told you, didn't I, that I have money of my own, and I could easily have run the household without him getting into politics. I can't explain, but I had bad feelings about those arguments. Donald would never listen to me, just told me I was being foolish and it was necessary that he get into the House, so I stopped talking about it. Except for one time when I did hear something of what was said. I asked Donald about it, but he became very angry and—'

'Sarah, you must tell me. Did he strike you?'

'No! No, he never did! He said . . . very unkind things and stormed out of the house.'

'This could be important, Sarah. I'm sorry to ask you to remember all these hateful things, but what did you hear?'

'The study door was open, just a little. I think he'd been about to leave, but he said something about blackmail! And he laughed and said something about two playing that game, and he'd be sorry he ever tried it. And then I made some noise in the kitchen, and Donald saw that the door was open and I could hear, and he slammed it shut and I didn't hear any more. I didn't want to! And then he left and that's when Donald accused me of listening on purpose and – and lost his temper and said those dreadful things. I wasn't listening on purpose. I never wanted to know anything about Donald's political dealings, truly.'

She was crying now, tears flowing silently, and I felt like sixteen kinds of bully, but I had to ask.

'Who was it, Sarah? Who said these things?'

'That dreadful Harold Thompson. I don't like him. Someone told me he's gone away, and I'm so glad. I hope he never comes back.'

Well, there was my confirmation. I had believed Pat's story, but I couldn't go to the police with a third-hand account. Now here it was from the horse's mouth.

The conversation had been conducted in Sarah's usual near whisper, and we were in a secluded corner of the café, so it was unlikely that we had been overheard. Still, I had to get her out of there before someone noticed her state of mind. 'My dear, I've upset you. I'm so sorry; I need to get you home. Is your house close enough that we can walk, or should I call Uber?'

She made an ambiguous gesture that decided me. She was in no state to walk even a short distance. I made the call, and a car was there to fetch us in minutes.

The police needed to know this immediately, but I couldn't

just abandon the woman I'd disturbed so badly. I rummaged in her cupboard, found a bottle of brandy and poured some, which I insisted that she drink while we talked about other things, anything I could think of – the house (which was lovely but entirely sterile), the church, her friends, anything.

When the brandy began to take effect, I called Ruth, glad I had her number on my phone. I admitted I was to blame for Sarah's condition, apologized, and asked her to come right away. I hung up on her diatribe, which I deserved, and waited until I heard her car stop outside before I left by the side door. I could take my scolding later. Right now, I needed to pass along some vital information.

# TWENTY-FOUR

C all only in case of dire necessity, Alan had said. He'd probably meant some emergency, possible harm to me or someone we loved, something like that. Well, I was going to call, anyway. It was *necessary* that he and the police know about Harold's whopping big motive. I did hope he wasn't so immersed in whatever he was doing that he had silenced his phone.

He hadn't, but he was very put out indeed that I was calling. 'What is it, Dorothy? I really can't talk right now.'

'You can listen, though. This is very important. I've just learned that Donald was blackmailing Harold Thompson, which gives Harold a huge motive for murder.'

'And you learned this from whom?' Scepticism dripped from his voice.

'Sarah Atkinson. Do you want me to tell you all about it?'

Pause. 'Yes, but not on the phone. I'll be there as soon as I can get away.'

I didn't actually pace the floor until he came through the door, but I was very glad to see him, all the same. He looked tired and out of sorts, and I remembered that he'd been up early and had been working ever since, and it was nearly lunchtime. 'Look, why don't we go out and have a pint and something to eat, if we can find a private corner.'

He nodded wearily and let me lead the way.

We had discovered that a nearby bar had excellent beer and good bar food. Now that high tourist season was over, they weren't crowded, so we got our beer and placed our food orders and sat down in a quiet corner.

Alan took a hefty swallow of his beer and sighed with satisfaction. 'I was dry as the Sahara. Arguing will do that.'

'So you were arguing with Davies?'

'Disagreeing, shall we say? We never quite reached the point of a row, but we came close. He's quite sure Taylor is his man.

I agree there's a good deal of evidence pointing in that direction, but Taylor kept firmly denying it, and the more he talked, the more inclined I was to believe him. Davies had taken him into custody on the basis of evidence about his whereabouts during the week before the sports day.'

'And was he anywhere out of his normal orbit?'

'No. That's part of why I tended to believe his story. Yes, he was in close-enough proximity to Atkinson that he could have found out about the ointment he was using for his rash. Yes, he could have bought an identical tube of the stuff. He would have had time to doctor it with the Nitro-Bid and could even, by moving fast, have switched the tubes on sports day.'

'He was there? Sports day, I mean?'

'He was. Told us he tried never to miss it, and had been despondent during the years it was cancelled by the pandemic. Davies and I questioned him pretty closely about the events that day, and there's no doubt that he was there and paying attention. He said he hadn't watched the early classes in the fell race, and as none of the men questioning him had watched them, either, there was no point in going into the matter.'

'So in theory he could at some point have been sneaking off to substitute tubes.'

'In theory, yes. In practice, I wonder. The race was probably the best organized of all the events that day. There were judges and timers and starters and who knows what all over the shop. I find it hard to imagine someone unauthorized getting into the area.'

'Before Donald actually went down to the dressing room? I don't know when he arrived at the games.'

'Davies checked on that. He didn't show up until the previous race was almost over, and went straight in to change into running gear.'

'Oh, I remember. Donald was out there near the starting point, showing off his perfect muscles and perfect tan. And that's when Sarah joined us – and Ruth. But enough of this futile speculation. I have to tell you what I learned today. Or actually, I learned it yesterday, but I needed to verify.'

'Dorothy, I'm a tired man who needs a nap. Tell me the story without embroidery.'

So I told him, exactly as Sarah had told me, and then reported how I'd first heard the story. 'I've read enough mystery novels to know hearsay isn't evidence, so I had to get it straight from Sarah's mouth.'

'Tell me again, in her exact words as nearly as you can remember.'

I did.

'So she said it was Harold Thompson who said the word blackmail, and later said that two could play that game. It's important, Dorothy.'

'I know it is. The whole thing depends on who was blackmailing whom. It seems clear to me that Donald was blackmailing Harold, and Harold was threatening to retaliate, perhaps to blackmail Donald in return.'

'It certainly sounds that way, although no court in the land would accept that fragment of the conversation, with its ambiguous pronouns, as proof of anything.'

'No. But put that together with what we know about the relationship between the two men. Harold had been grooming Donald for office for some time. That's a known fact. Of late, though, the idea seemed to have lost momentum. Lilian told us that, and I heard it from other sources as well, so I think we can count it as fact. Add in the fact that Harold has vanished, and I think there's ample reason for the police to go after him more energetically than they have in the past.'

Alan tented his hands. 'Motive, very strong if Harold was indeed being blackmailed. Blackmail is a notoriously risky profession. Opportunity, piece of cake. The two lived in each other's pockets. Means?'

'France is only a few hours away. A check of Harold's passport records will tell us how recently he's been there. He would have had to get a prescription, though. Or— Wait a minute! Roger's tube of Nitro-Bid was stolen!'

'If he's telling the truth. And how would Harold have got hold of it?'

'I don't know, Alan. One more thing to ask Roger. But I think you'd better get back to Davies right away and tell him about the blackmail. Then maybe he'll let Roger go home. That poor man must be frantic by now.'

'Unless he really is the murderer.'

I glared at my husband.

'My dear woman, you know we can't cross him off the list on the strength of one piece of evidence. But I'll go talk to Davies and see what he thinks.' He sighed. 'What do you propose to do for the rest of the day?'

'I'm going to call Ruth and see how Sarah's doing. She wasn't in very good shape when I left her this morning. I'd made her remember an episode she would much rather have forgotten. Ruth wasn't happy with me, but I'll just have to deal with her ire.'

'I hope I won't be long. Perhaps we could actually sit back and relax and enjoy this beautiful place for a little while?'

'We're going to need a holiday to recover from this holiday. Go, dear.'

Ruth was in a much better mood than I had anticipated. 'Sarah's recovered. I think maybe your little session with her was therapeutic. She had to admit to herself how badly Donald treated her. Anyway, she sniffled for a while and then made us some tea, instead of letting me do it. And then she made a terrific decision. She's going to get a dog! She said she always wanted one, but Donald wouldn't hear of it. Noisy, messy, needy.'

'And requiring attention that should come to him.'

'Exactly. But now she can have one. We had a little lunch together, and then she went straight off to a kennel.'

'What kind of dog? What breed, I mean? Though actually we've found our mutt to be entirely satisfactory.'

'I've heard mutts make the best pets, but Sarah's set on a King Charles spaniel.'

I couldn't help laughing, remembering our earlier conversation about them. 'Such an appropriate pet for an Englishwoman! I can't help wondering, though, if King Charles is annoyed about how cute they are – so much cuter than—'

'Indeed! They are sweet little dogs, aren't they? And for a woman with no children, a King Charles might make a great substitute.'

'I always found my cats to be almost-acceptable stand-ins. I never had a dog until our Watson came along a while back, but he's been a wonderful addition to the family. Even the cats have grown to love him. Well, I'm glad Sarah's taking positive action. It's a very good sign. I hope she finds a terrific dog right away. She needs something to love.'

Alan came back shortly after that phone call. Apparently Davies had not welcomed the information about Harold Thompson. 'He'd been so sure that the case was solved, pending some clear evidence that Taylor had given Donald the doctored ointment. Now he has to start over, collecting evidence against Thompson, and finding him, which so far has proved impossible. Of course he's not pleased with either of us.'

'No. He doesn't really want to arrest the wrong man, but he wants to be done with a confusing and irritating case. Understandable. Anyway, there's good news on the Sarah front.' I told him about her quest for a canine companion.

'Best thing for her. I hope she gets a puppy. They require constant attention, and the right one delivers constant love. Just what she needs.'

'I'm just glad she's coming out from under Donald's heavy hand and beginning to realize there's a good life waiting for her. She's developing a spine.'

'Donald's death didn't come any too soon. A few more years and there wouldn't have been any Sarah left.' He yawned widely. 'My love, would you mind terribly if I just gave it up for a little while? I hate to admit it, but I do really need a nap.'

'I wouldn't mind one myself. Let's face it, we're neither of us getting any younger, and it's been a pretty stressful couple of weeks. Turn off your phone, and I'll call down to the desk and ask them to fend off anyone who wants either of us.'

We were asleep in minutes and slept right through until our growling stomachs made us aware it was dinner time. I sat up and stretched. 'Pizza?'

'Anything quick. I just realized I'm starving.'

I found my phone and turned it on. 'Oh, dear. A lot of people have been trying to reach me. Ruth – she called three times. Other numbers I don't know. And one call from Jane. I'll call her first. It must be important; she wouldn't call just for idle talk.'

She answered on the first ring. 'Where have you *been*? I've answered calls for you all afternoon.'

'Calls for me? Who's been calling?' I was especially distressed because Jane was speaking in whole sentences, something she almost never does.

'Police. Friends. Someone from the telly. All from where you're staying. You in some trouble?'

'How on earth did they get your number? I'm so sorry they've bothered you. No, we're not in trouble, exactly. We just took a nap this afternoon and turned our phones off because we were really tired, but I can't imagine why so many people wanted to reach me.'

'Best call and find out. Then tell me.'

She ended the call. I looked at Alan. 'What's going on? I'd better call Ruth. And you call Christopher. Between the two of them, we'll find out.'

'I'm calling for pizza first,' he said in his chief-constable, he-who-must-be-obeyed voice. I didn't argue. I was famished, too. I called Ruth.

'Where have you *been*?'

This was getting tiresome. 'I've been taking a nap. Which a woman my age has every right to do without asking permission from anyone. It seems something has happened, something that required my immediate attention. It also seems that the world has gone on turning without me.'

'Well, if you're going to be snippy about it!'

'Ruth, you or someone else has even been bothering my friends at home about whatever it is, which I don't take at all kindly. Now I've got that out of my system, what's the big crisis?'

'Sarah is gone.'

# TWENTY-FIVE

'**G**one! You don't mean she's died!'

'No. At least we hope not. She left her house right after lunch without saying a word to anyone, and now we can't reach her. We're afraid she might have done something foolish.'

The mood I was in, I came very close to lambasting poor Ruth for that euphemism, one I particularly despise. I took a deep breath. 'Ruth, if you're thinking she's suicidal, I have to disagree. You said yourself she was feeling much better and was going to get a dog. She is probably having to look further afield than she thought, to find just the right pet.'

'No. She found a dog she loved at the very first shelter. Female, the right age, the right personality, beautiful.'

'Of course. King Charles spaniels are always adorable.'

'This one isn't pure bred, but that made her even better for Sarah, who hates snobbery, even with dogs. So she brought her home and called me about her, sounding happier than she has for ages. She said she'd call again when she had Charlotte all settled. That's what she named her – Charlotte, after William and Kate's daughter. That was hours ago, and when I didn't hear anything, I called her. No answer. So I went to the house. No one's home, not even the dog. The car's there. Dorothy, we're all frantic!'

'So you called the police.' I thought I sounded neutral, but Ruth heard the criticism I was trying not to voice.

'Of course we called the police. What would you do when a woman in a very fragile state of mind disappears, when she doesn't answer her phone, what would you do? Get on with your knitting?'

'I'd probably go looking for her,' I said honestly.

'We did that!' Ruth was almost spitting. 'She's nowhere to be found. But since you don't care, I'll go talk to the police again.'

A mobile phone can't be banged down like a rotary phone, but plainly Ruth would have if she could.

'I heard,' said Alan. 'I suspect the people next door heard. Ruth's tones weren't exactly dulcet, were they?'

'She was screaming like a fishwife. I do understand why she's upset, but she's making a federal case of it. Have you talked to Christopher?'

'Yes, briefly. When he refused to get the police involved, Ruth called Davies herself. He's not happy. Nobody's happy.'

'Tempest in a teapot, isn't it?' I raised my hands in the classic gesture of exasperation. 'No, I don't mean that, exactly. Sarah needs to come home. But it's only been, what, six or seven hours? If it weren't for Donald being murdered, nobody would be thinking twice about it.'

'But he was murdered. Even though there's no logical connection to Sarah's absence (I refuse to call it a disappearance, not yet), one can't help feeling an added sense of unease.'

'Do you think she might be in danger?'

'I don't think anything!' Now the exasperation was Alan's. 'How could I? I just woke up; I'm still foggy. And I know nothing about the case. No, I won't call it a case. Not yet. About the matter.' He stood up, ran a hand through his hair and stretched his shoulders. 'Make some coffee, would you, love? I got voicemail at the pizza place. Maybe a shower will help.'

He stomped to the bathroom while I looked around for coffee makings. We'd used them all up, so I sent for coffee and pastries. I thought about our hotel bill for over two weeks' stay and lots of room service, and then decided not to think about it. I yawned, went in and splashed cold water on my face, and was reasonably bright-eyed and bushy-tailed when Alan reappeared and the coffee arrived.

'Whoever figured out how to make coffee should be given the Nobel Prize,' Alan propounded.

'I agree. Unfortunately it was probably a lot of somebodies, over the years, and we'll never know who they were. I hope Saint Peter has a special niche for them. They were benefactors of mankind. Alan, what should we do about Sarah? I am actually worried about her, though not beside myself, like Ruth.'

'She's Ruth's dear friend, nearly her daughter. To you, she's a pleasant, casual acquaintance. And I hardly know her at all. Of course Ruth's distraught and we're merely worried. What I'm going to do, *after* I finish my coffee, is ask Christopher to come over and tell us everything. Then maybe we can plan a sensible course of action. So far, the Don Quixote approach seems to have been of little practical use.'

I nodded. 'I think the windmills are winning.'

Christopher, when he arrived, agreed that no coordinated effort had been made to find Sarah. 'For one thing, she hasn't been gone all that long.'

'In America, I think someone has to be gone for twenty-four hours to qualify as missing. Except for children or the elderly.'

'There's no hard and fast rule about it here. The response depends on the circumstances. Davies isn't inclined to take this too seriously, but Ruth Williams wants us to call out the army. I'm afraid there's a tendency to explain her away as a hysterical American and/or a woman of a certain age.'

'For one thing,' I said, bristling, 'she's well past the age you're carefully not specifying. Sixty if she's a day, I'd say. In any case, hysteria isn't confined to any particular age or sex or nationality. So I do agree with her that circumstances warrant some special attention. Is there any possible reason why Donald's murderer might want to go after Sarah?'

'If she knew something. Or the murderer thought she did.'

'How closely did you question her about that?'

Christopher pondered. 'The police searched the house, of course, looking for anything that might have caused her husband to collapse. That was before the autopsy revealed the nitroglycerine. After that was known, and they were virtually certain it was a case of murder, they searched more closely. At that point, they let me go with them, since I knew her and might be of some comfort. She had to be told it was officially murder, and of course that distressed her greatly. She was not able then to think clearly enough to be of much help, nor did she come up with anything useful until her mention of blackmail, just this morning.'

'A pity she didn't mention that little detail earlier,' said Alan, with a grimace. 'We could have got on to Thompson much sooner.'

'Oh, but she did!' I clasped my hand to my mouth. 'What an idiot I am! I heard about it from Ruth's painting friend yesterday, and I don't know when *she* found out. I tried to call and tell you, Alan, but you were out on the golf course and had your phone turned off. Then they arrested Roger and you were out of touch. And then I thought I should wait until I confirmed it with Sarah. I know you don't like third-hand information. But if Harold somehow found out she was talking about it, and came to get her—'

'It would be a case of locking the stable door after the horse was long gone,' said Alan comfortingly. 'No point to it. In fact, it would only have been another charge against him, and I don't think Harold Thompson is a fool.'

'Still,' I persisted. 'He might want to get rid of her so she couldn't testify against him. Only two people heard that encounter. One of them is dead.'

'You have a point,' said Christopher, stroking his chin. 'I'll see if I can ginger Davies up a bit. Of course, the search for Harold is still on, but I'll suggest it might be pumped up.'

'And I'll support you,' said Alan grimly. 'I don't have a lot of influence anymore, but I'll use what I have. This isn't a small local problem anymore.'

'Before you invoke the Met, or whoever you plan to call, there's one point we haven't considered,' I said. 'Given that the blackmail conversation happened as narrated by Sarah, what if she got it wrong? You told us stories about Harold extorting his clients, remember – what if it was the other way round, and it was Harold blackmailing Donald?'

'For what? Among all the sins we think Donald committed.'

'Does it matter?' I shrugged and spread my hands. 'And if Sarah got it right and it was Donald who was the extortioner, what was Harold's dirty little secret? Though I suppose that doesn't matter, either, or at least not at this stage. The point is, if Harold was the blackmailer, he could well have run away in case somebody else knew about it.'

'And now you've raised another issue that we, or at least I, haven't thought about,' said Alan, frowning. 'As we've interpreted her remarks until now, Sarah thought Donald was blackmailing his friend, or at least his colleague, Harold. Why didn't she react to that? She's a law-abiding citizen, or at least that's the impression I have. Why did she just let it drop? You'd think she'd have been horrified, but apparently she turned a blind eye – or deaf ear. Davies is going to find that extremely suspicious.'

I slowly shook my head. 'Yes, you're right, and I hadn't thought about it till this minute. Her reaction, at least as she described it to me, was to get furious at Harold. Not that she said or did anything, mind you, or at least if she did, she didn't tell me. My memory of the conversation is that the moment Donald realized she'd heard, he closed the office door. Then when Harold left, he unleashed his temper, accusing her of listening on purpose. She tried to defend herself, but he just got more and more abusive and finally slammed out of the house.'

'Abusive?' Both men pricked their ears.

'Not physically. I asked and she said, "He never did", which I found revealing and terribly sad. Plainly these temper tantrums were frequent, but the abuse was all verbal and psychological. But the last thing she said to me was that she hated Harold and never wanted to see him again. Or no, it was, "I don't like him. Someone told me he's gone away, and I'm so glad. I hope he never comes back". As if she blamed the whole incident on Harold. And before you say that doesn't make sense, I think it does, from her point of view.

'She was Donald's slave, hypnotized by him,' I went on, thinking aloud. 'He robbed her of her very self, but all she could see was how wonderful he was. So if something was wrong between him and Harold, of course it was Harold's fault.'

I paused to regain my composure. 'This will earn me another several thousand years in Purgatory, if there is such a thing, but I can not summon up any good feelings about Donald Atkinson. From where I stand, he was pure evil!'

# TWENTY-SIX

There was an understandable pause after that rant. Alan broke it. 'And yet you're doing all you can to bring his killer to justice.' He said it as nearly without expression as possible.

'Yes.' I had myself under control now. 'Not for his sake, but Sarah's. She needs to know, or she'll never heal. And for the community, and, well, for the sake of justice itself. Murder can't go unpunished.'

I felt my face growing hot with embarrassment and wondered, not for the first time, why it seems oddly improper to voice one's convictions. Especially in England, where feelings are supposed to be kept firmly to oneself.

Alan cleared his throat. 'Yes, you're quite right. So let's get back on track. I think it's safe enough to say that Donald was the blackmailer, Harold the blackmailee, if I may coin a word. Now we know that in most cases, it's the blackmailer who gets killed, not his victim. It's a dangerous game, as I said before. So assuming for the moment that it's Harold we're after, are there any new hints as to where he might have gone?'

'He hasn't left the country, even though he was seen at St Pancras. That's easy to check. I knew your mention of Harold's passport earlier triggered some memory I couldn't quite retrieve. The records show he hasn't been beyond our borders since well before the sports day.'

'So no trip to France for ointment,' I replied. 'Right. So he's still in England.'

'Or Scotland or Wales or Northern Ireland. The system's not perfect, Dorothy. People have been known to slip through, but it's ninety-nine per cent foolproof.'

'Wait a minute! I've just thought of something.' I was getting excited. 'What about the Channel Islands? Does a British citizen need a passport to go there?'

Alan and Christopher looked at each other. 'No-o,' said Alan.

'At least I don't think so. It's a bit complicated; more so since Brexit. But in general, no, though the ferries and airlines do require some form of identification.'

'But they don't keep records, right? I mean, it isn't exactly travel within Britain, since the islands aren't a part of the UK, but it isn't exactly foreign travel, either.'

Alan sighed. 'No records, as far as I know, except perhaps a passenger manifest. So you're right, he could be on any of them. Or on the Isle of Man, for that matter. And checking up is tricky. The island authorities are a bit prickly about their independence and don't like to be bossed by Scotland Yard. We can inquire, but it might take quite a while to get any meaningful cooperation.'

'I can second that,' said Christopher warmly. 'Back in Cornwall, I once had to try to track down a thief who'd made his way to Alderney. Not too hard to spot on an island of that size, three miles long, population two thousand or so. Hah! Everyone was most courteous, except they were all deep in other concerns, would get back to me as soon as possible, happy to be of help. It was like trying to apply pressure to a half-filled water balloon – just kept slipping out from under. I was about to fly over there when they got tired of playing the game and turned the chap over to us. You expect that sort of thing when you're dealing with a foreign country that isn't too friendly to us, but not our own people!'

'But they're not exactly your own people, are they? And that's the point they want to emphasize. They won't actually ignore a request for assistance, or abet a criminal, but they won't treat it as an urgent matter, either.' I laughed. 'When Alan and I were there a few years back, we fell in love with the place and the people. Part of the appeal was the relaxed pace – that and the universal friendliness. But I imagine if you were in a hurry to get something done, you could go mad very quickly. I don't know if things are the same on Jersey and Guernsey.' I giggled. 'I'm sorry, but my first image when I think about those names is of pretty brown and white cows. That's all the words mean in America.

'But I digress. I'm sorry. My point was: do you think Harold could have fled to one of the Channel Islands? They're about as far away from Grasmere as you can get and still be – sort of – in the UK.'

'It's possible,' said Alan slowly. 'And there are a few things about Alderney, in particular, that might appeal to Harold. For one thing, it is, of course, a world centre for e-gambling. While I don't know that Harold is a gambler, it certainly seems in character. I could see him setting himself up in business there quite happily. That's if he was planning to stay. And the taxes are very low; it's regarded as a tax haven.'

'None of that would matter if he was just going to ground there,' I objected. 'And it's such a small place he'd find it very hard to hide. I'd think one of the bigger islands would suit him better. I've never been to Jersey, but it's the biggest, isn't it?'

'Helen and I visited them both years ago,' said Alan. 'From what I remember, Jersey's a fair-sized island, but there isn't a lot of undeveloped land, and not much to attract someone on the run. It's an international financial centre, with few opportunities for a scammer, if that's what Harold is. Where there aren't buildings, it's mostly agricultural, and you can't hide in a field of potatoes or a pasture.'

'Doesn't sound promising. What about Guernsey? I've never been there, either, except for that brief stop when we were en route to Alderney.'

'Smaller than Jersey, a lot bigger than Alderney. It does have rugged cliffs with a few caves, or near-caves, but there's a popular walking path along that shore that draws hundreds of energetic tourists in good weather. Again, not a very safe place to hide out.'

'Anything to make him want to stay there for a while?'

'Not much. As with Jersey, occupations are mostly in the realm of finance.'

I sighed. 'It seemed like such a good idea. Far away, none too cooperative with English authorities, no passport needed – but Alderney's too small, and there are few places to hide in the bigger islands.'

'It's still a good idea, love, and I'll suggest that Davies look into it.'

'Tomorrow,' said Christopher. 'Sufficient unto the day. We're not on the force anymore, chum.'

'You're right. And we're starving. We were just about to find a meal when everything broke loose. Join us for dinner?'

'Appreciate the offer, but we'd just sit and talk about the case, and I've had enough for the day. I'm off.'

'Alan, I've had enough, too. Can we leave it alone for one evening? As Christopher pointed out, you're not official anymore. You can take some time off. Maybe our heads will be clearer in the morning.'

So we found a place to eat and steadfastly talked about other things all evening. It wasn't the most stimulating conversation we've ever had, and we were bored enough to go to sleep early, in spite of our nap.

So I woke up early. After the obligatory trip to the bathroom, I crept back into bed next to my soundly sleeping husband. I had every intention of going back to sleep, but sleep eluded me, as it almost always does when I pursue it. The blasted hamster in my brain kept running on his wheel, chasing ideas into oblivion.

Where was Harold Thompson? Had he really killed Donald? Where was Sarah, and was she in danger? If we could find her, could she tell us any more about that puzzling 'blackmail' conversation? And would she, if she could?

Was Roger Taylor out of the woods? I thought he was innocent. Alan thought he was innocent. What about Davies and his minions, though? Oh, and weren't there some things we needed to tell him?

As I tried to remember, the hamster grew tired, yawned and jumped off the wheel. When Alan woke me with coffee, I was muzzy and thoroughly disgruntled.

'I was just about to nail down an idea,' I grumbled. 'Now it's gone.'

'Something important?'

'I thought so, in my dream. Now I'm not so sure.'

'Something about the glassblower's cat?'

The reference to one of the Lord Peter Wimsey books made me laugh, and I nearly choked on my coffee. 'Probably just about as useful. I think I was trying to remember something Inspector Davies should know, but I lost it.'

'So we're back to the problem, are we? More coffee?'

'Please. Yes, I can't leave it alone. I woke up early and couldn't get back to sleep and kept worrying at it like Watson at a toy, trying to work out where Harold and Sarah may be, whether she's in danger, and I thought of something we'd forgotten to tell Davies, but then I fell asleep for real and couldn't get the idea back.'

'Whatever it was, I'm sure Christopher has been in touch with the investigators and passed along everything we discussed.'

'Oh! I know what it was! It just came to me. What about London?'

'What *about* London?'

'As a hiding place for Harold! Any number of people could hide among London's millions. If I were going to hide some place, it would be there or New York, and given that I like London a lot better . . .'

'Quite right, my dear. Which is why . . .'

He let the comment trail off, and it didn't take me long to pick it up. 'Which is why it was the first place everyone thought of,' I said bitterly. 'Everyone but me. I suppose all the cops in London are looking for him, and he was even seen at St Pancras. And I thought I was being so smart! As a detective, I make a good football player.'

There being no answer to that, Alan didn't attempt one. 'All right, love. Breakfast here, or shall we go out?'

'Let's find a coffee shop. I'm getting awfully tired of hotel food, good as it is. What I'd really like to do is drive straight home, but I suppose we can't do that.'

He just looked at me.

'I know, I know. I don't really want to leave a job half done. Not even half. I just wish something would happen soon!'

You know the old saying about being careful what you wish for. Alan's phone rang while we were in the elevator.

'Christopher,' he said, looking at the display. 'What's up, old man?'

Then his side of the conversation consisted mostly of grunts. 'Right,' he finished. 'Twenty minutes.'

He turned to me. 'Change of plans. Sarah Atkinson's in hospital, in Keswick. Christopher's there with her, and she's asking for you.'

'For me? Whatever for? And why is she there? Is she hurt? Did someone—?'

'I can't answer any of those questions, love, but I think we'd better postpone breakfast and get there as quickly as we can. It's only about fifteen miles on a good road, so unless the traffic is horrendous, it shouldn't take too long.'

The day was picture-perfect, guaranteed to bring out the tourists, but in midweek there weren't hordes of them, so we made good time, taking only one wrong turn, and found the last parking space in the tiny hospital car park.

'I wish I knew what we were getting into,' I complained.

'We soon will.'

Christopher was waiting for us in the lobby of the hospital. 'I hope I didn't alarm you too much,' he said. 'Sarah's not in any danger, but they're keeping an eye on her. She was out in a wood all night, you see—'

'Outside all night!'

'So suffering from exposure to some degree. Fortunately it wasn't terribly cold last night, and there was no rain, but she was quite damp from the fallen leaves, and—'

'Christopher Prideaux, if you don't tell me this minute what she was doing in the woods, I'm going to stand here and scream!'

'Looking for her dog, of course. But here we are, so I'll let her tell you.'

Sarah was in a small ward, her bed in a corner. She was sitting up and looked, in fact, much better than I'd ever seen her. She was warmly wrapped in blankets and hooked up to an IV. Her hands were mittened, but her face was serene and smiling.

'Oh, Dorothy, I'm so happy to see you! They said everyone was worried about me, and I thought you could spread the word that I'm perfectly all right. They brought me here just to warm me up and make sure I hadn't suffered frostbite or anything like that, but they're going to let me go as soon as the doctor says. Tell Ruth and the others, will you?'

'Of course.' I wanted to ask why she didn't call Ruth in the first place, but maybe I knew. 'But why were you out all night? Did someone try to hurt you?'

'No, no. I was looking for Charlotte. She's the sweetest little dog! But she was very naughty yesterday. I found her at the shelter, so lucky. She'd just been brought in, because her owner was moving away and couldn't take her. She's so beautiful, bound to be snatched up in an instant, but I got there before anyone else, and took her home just before lunch. Then after we'd both had a bite to eat, I took her outside to play, and she bolted!'

'Oh dear. That must have been distressing.'

'I was devastated! I already loved her so much, and she had seemed to warm up to me, but she ran away from me!'

Christopher cleared his throat. 'They'll do that, the little spaniels. An interesting scent is like a magnet for them. One daren't let them off the lead until they're properly trained.'

'Oh, is that all it was? I thought she hated me and wanted to go back to her old owner. I called and called, and went out and looked everywhere. I was crying so hard I couldn't see very well, and I was afraid I'd miss her somewhere. Or maybe someone had stolen her. I suppose I was silly. I should have asked for help, but all I could think of was getting her back.'

'You've been through a very hard time,' I soothed. 'A time of loss and confusion. Of course you weren't thinking too clearly. But you found her in the end?' I was sure that was the case, or she wouldn't be smiling now.

'She found me. I don't know how long I was out there, only that it was dark. I'd somehow strayed into a wood, and I was so tired I sat down against a fallen tree, and the next thing I knew, there she was, yipping a little and licking my hand and sniffing my pocket. I'd put some treats in there, and the clever little thing had found them. I was so cold, and she was warm and sweet and cuddled up to me, and somehow we both fell asleep and didn't wake until a policeman found us this morning.' She giggled. 'I think he thought I was a tramp, and of course I didn't have any identification, so he took us somewhere to check up, and when I told him who I was, he brought me here.'

'And Charlotte?' I asked anxiously.

'They took her back to the shelter, to wait for me. I'll pick her up as soon as they let me go home.'

Christopher saw us out. 'I'll drive her home. She claims she's doing well, but she's very tired.'

'Did she do all that long trek on foot?' asked Alan.

'Yes, and it's probably a good thing. As upset as she was, she would have been a definite hazard on the road. The b— her

husband never let her drive the car, so she's had little
practice.'

'Even though the car was hers, I'm guessing.'

'No, he bought it himself. I imagine Sarah didn't question
where the money came from. Mind you, it's not quite what he
wanted, according to Ruth. He was looking for a Range Rover,
but he couldn't quite afford it, and apparently couldn't pry the
extra loose from Sarah.'

'Oh, and speaking of Ruth, has anyone told her Sarah is safe?
I'd hate to think she was still tearing her hair out.'

'Yes, but she's in a huff because I called you first. She thinks
of herself as Sarah's dearest friend.'

'And I'm sure she is, but she's a helicopter friend.'

Christopher quirked an eyebrow. Alan chuckled.

'She hovers,' I explained. 'Maybe it's just an American term,
usually used to describe mothers who never let their kids out of
their sight. Ruth tries to protect Sarah, which she probably needed
when Donald was alive, but now I think she wants to spread her
wings a bit.'

'And Ruth wants to keep her safe in the nest.' Alan shook his
head. 'Do you think that's as much for Ruth's sake as Sarah's?'

'I do, though I doubt she knows it. Ruth, I mean. She's lived
here only a short time, and her friendship with Sarah has given
purpose to her life here. And as to the question you're not asking,
either of you, I don't think it's at all a question of a lesbian
attraction, more like mother–child. Ruth is lonely, despite all her
community involvement. She thinks Sarah needs her. And I think
we need to deal with that somehow, but not right this minute.
I'm starving!'

We left the hospital and drove back to Grasmere, where we
breakfasted on a slab of the famous Grasmere gingerbread,
purchased in the village shop, and a cup of terrible coffee at
Davies' headquarters, where we'd gone to catch him up to date.

'Well, that's one less problem on my plate, at least,' he said
with a sigh. 'Would you say she's ready yet to talk about that
obscure blackmail conversation?'

'You'll have to ask her doctor if she's physically fit,' said Alan.
'Myself, I'd say she is. Whether she's able to concentrate on the
matter is another question.'

'All she's thinking about right now is her dog,' I said with assurance. 'Which is understandable. Based on what I've heard, I'd say that little creature is giving her the only real love she's had for years. No wonder she was beside herself when little Charlotte seemed to run away. I'm so glad Christopher explained it was just spaniel instinct kicking in. If I were in your place, I'd wait until at least tomorrow to ask her any questions. And yes, I do know time is of the essence in any murder investigation! Between the mysteries I've read for decades and the years I've spent married to Alan, I actually know quite a lot about police work.'

Davies sighed. 'I sometimes wish I'd gone into some other line of work. Computer tech, perhaps. Machines are a good deal more malleable than people.'

'And slightly more predictable,' Alan agreed with a rueful smile. 'We'll leave you to it, then.'

'And of course we'll let you know if we learn anything new.'

Davies didn't look especially grateful.

Alan and I went back to our hotel and had some lunch (the gingerbread not having sufficed as a real meal), then I sat and fidgeted, unable to settle to anything. In fact, I felt exactly as I had before we launched on this ill-fated holiday, uncomfortable in my own skin and without an imperious cat to snap me out of it.

I did, however, still have a husband.

'You're stuck, aren't you? No ideas, no trails to pursue, but you can't leave it alone.'

'You know me too well. If we were at home, I could go around and talk to lots of people and work out what to do next. But here—' I raised my hands and looked disgustedly at the unresponsive ceiling.

'Well, what's to prevent you doing exactly that here?'

I made an annoyed sound. 'But I don't know anybody here! I can't go around talking to perfect strangers!'

'Why not? That's exactly what you did that first time in Sherebury, when the canon was killed. You felt free to ask prying questions, because you were a stranger, indeed an American, and didn't count. Listen, dear heart. This is a very small community, much smaller even than Sherebury. Of course they're all gossiping about the murder, and Roger's troubles, and Harold's disappearance. The women at the church were willing to talk to you. Why not shopkeepers, and waiters, and anyone else you might run into?'

'They'll all know who I am.'

'So? You won't have to waste time explaining yourself. You're a visitor, you were actually there on the spot where Donald was killed, and you feel sorry for his widow. If that doesn't open the taps, I'll be very surprised. People find you easy to talk to.' He reached for his wallet and pulled out a credit card. 'Here. Go shopping. Take the car if you want.'

'Well . . . but what are you going to do?'

'I am going to empty my mind to let some new ideas creep in.'

'You're going to take a nap,' I accused.

'That, too. Now scoot!'

# TWENTY-SEVEN

I wasn't sure where to go first, but as I walked from the hotel to the main street, an attractive building caught my eye. Built of the multicoloured stone so typical in the area, its sign proclaimed it a bookshop. Aha!

Now some women are drawn as if by magnets to a jewellery shop; my oldest sister was one of them. Some men cannot pass by a shop selling tools or hardware. Me, I am totally unable to avoid a bookshop. I must go in, if only to browse and linger for a while amid all those riches.

Besides, unless the shop was busy, the proprietor was very likely to enjoy talking to customers. Most booksellers do.

The bell tinkled as I stepped inside, and a male voice from somewhere called, 'Feel free to look around. Let me know if I can help you find something.'

'Thank you,' I called back. 'Where can I find the mys— The crime novels?' remembering almost in time that the English prefer that term to 'mysteries'.

'Ah.' A grey head popped around a corner. 'Am I hearing an American accent? Or Canadian, perhaps?'

'American, but I've lived in England for years. I thought I sounded like a native by now!'

'Not quite, my dear.' The rest of the bookseller appeared from behind a shelf. 'You do speak the language very well, but you almost asked for mysteries. Which we have just round here.' He showed me the section. 'I confess I spotted you because I'm a transatlantic émigré myself, from Toronto many years ago. Now let me guess.' He looked me over. 'I'd say we're much of an age, so would you be an aficionada of Agatha Christie?'

I had to laugh. 'Yes, but more avidly of Dorothy L. Sayers. I've read everything by both those authors, though. How about P.D. James? I haven't read all of hers, and some are a little too dark for me, but she writes like an angel.'

'Oh, she's one of the best, and we have quite a good selection.'

Having established our similar tastes in fiction, I thought it might be time to bring up my real agenda, but he beat me to it. 'We've had a crime of our own, you know, a real one, right here in Grasmere. Have you been in the village for a few days?'

'A couple of weeks, and I do know about the death of Donald Atkinson. In fact, my husband and I were at the sports day when it happened, and as he's a retired policeman, he's been helping with the investigation. It's been a bit difficult because, as far as we can tell, the man had far more enemies than friends. Makes the field of suspects rather large. Or am I misreading the situation?'

'No, indeed. I do try to stay neutral in contentious village affairs. Well, a shopkeeper can't afford to take sides, can he? One is bound to offend somebody in a place the size of Grasmere. But as you don't live here, I can admit to you that I didn't have a lot of time for Atkinson, nor did I know anyone who really liked him.'

'I only met the man once, but I did get the strong impression that he liked himself so well, other people's opinions didn't matter much.'

'Now there you've got it wrong, if you don't mind my saying so. Yes, his ego was well-nigh unsurpassed, but it was important, nay *vital*, that everyone else agree. He'd a nasty temper and could be downright vicious with anyone who didn't worship at his shrine.'

'And yet he was planning to stand for Parliament. How could he imagine that anyone would vote for him?'

'Ah, you forget that the constituency is broader than just Grasmere, and it's been a safe Lib Dem seat for centuries. He was very good-looking, you know, and he spoke well, so that made him effective on television. There is an aura about someone who is convinced he is going to win that sometimes makes it happen. Although I've heard that he had gone off the idea a bit. It was never his idea, of course. His bear-leader pushed him into it, and I gather they had some sort of tiff shortly before his death.'

'Really! What about, do you know?'

But at that inopportune moment the bell over the door tinkled, and a family with three small, noisy children walked in. From my years as a teacher, I knew just how much damage unruly toddlers can do in any environment, but especially in a place where there are lots of things to be torn or soiled. These parents didn't seem able to control their little brats at all, so plainly the shopkeeper had no attention to spare for me.

I couldn't stand it. When the biggest child, chasing the smallest one, cannoned straight into me, forty years of classroom authority rose to the top. I grabbed the child by his arm and kept him in a tight grip. 'That will do, young man. This is not a place to run about, nor to shout. You might as well stop wriggling. I am not going to let go until you apologize for hurting me.'

'Mummy!' the child screamed.

'And your mother will say the same.'

'My daddy's a solicitor!'

'I don't care if your daddy is King Charles, you are still not allowed to plough into people and step on their feet.'

The father approached, looking harassed. 'I'm sorry, madam. The children are overtired.'

'I'm sure that's true, and I'm sorry they're such a handful, but I still require an apology from your son here. I'm going to have bruises. I had always understood that English children had beautiful manners.' I had allowed my accent to become pure American, and upper-class American at that. I let him take that in, and then requested his card. 'I believe you are a solicitor? Perhaps you can recommend someone to me in case I need to pursue the matter.'

'Oh, that won't be necessary, madam. I'm quite happy to reimburse any medical expenses you might incur. In fact' – he dug into his pocket – 'please accept this with my apologies.' He handed me a wad of banknotes. 'Adrian, tell the lady you're sorry you ran into her.'

'Won't.'

'Adrian.' This time the father's voice held a distinct threat.

'Sorry,' the child muttered in a petulant tone and broke away from my grasp. 'Want to go home. Want an ice cream.'

'No ice cream!' He towed the child away, collected his wife and the other two, who had been observing the scene with interest, and pulled them all out the door.

The shopkeeper had also been watching anxiously, hoping his stock wouldn't suffer. 'Goodness, how do you do that?'

'When kids aren't accustomed to firmness, a no-nonsense approach can do wonders. Those three have plainly never been disciplined in their miserable young lives. And today's experience won't help. They watched Daddy buy his way out of trouble and learned that money can solve any problem. Did the other two do any damage while I was reaming out dear little Adrian?'

'No, they were surprised into inaction. As you say, I doubt they'd ever seen retribution or heard the voice of authority. So I thank you for saving my books!'

'It was a reflex reaction. I truly can't stand back and watch kids run wild.'

'Did the little monster really hurt you?'

'Not badly. It's true I'll have bruises. I bruise if you look at me hard. Always have, and it's worse now that I'm older. But no real damage. If he'd broken any bones, I wouldn't have let Papa get by with a fistful of money.' I examined the money that was still in my hand. 'Goodness, there's over two hundred pounds here! I can buy lots of books.'

He led me to the mystery section. 'By the way, I never answered your question. I haven't heard what their row was about, Atkinson and Thompson, I mean. If I do, I'll let you know. Except I don't know your name.'

So we exchanged names and phone numbers, and I picked out as many paperbacks as I could for my little windfall, and we parted on the best of terms.

But I was no wiser about the murder.

I lugged my purchases back to the hotel and woke Alan to tell him about the encounter. He wasn't happy about the wayward child. 'He could have knocked you over!'

'I'm not that easily swept off my feet, dear. He was only about seven.'

'Still. Are you sure you're not hurt?'

'Quite sure. And his father did give me a bunch of money, which I promptly spent on books. Just look at them all! I'd have bought more, except I couldn't carry them.'

'And did you pick up any useful gossip?'

'Not a word, except that the shopkeeper said that Donald and

Harold had had a set-to just before the murder. And if he knows about that, the whole village knows.'

'Did he say what it was about?'

'No, drat it. I had just asked when the howling horde came in and I had to morph from Miss Marple into Mr Chips. Or no, he was kindly and gentle. Professor Snape? Anyway, definitely "she who must be obeyed". It worked, too. I haven't lost my touch after all these years away from the classroom.'

'You certainly keep me in line. Where's your next port of call?'

'Definitely not one of the gift shops. The only customers there will be tourists, who wouldn't know about village scandals.'

'There's always the staff. If you pose as a gullible tourist, you might be able to glean something there.'

I thought about that. 'You have a point. But only if it's not crowded. I can hardly start asking about a murder with lots of paying customers around. And maybe I'd better take the car. I managed to struggle home with all those books, but touristy gifts are apt to be heavy and awkward.'

Alan nodded. 'China models of Dove Cottage, replete with daffodils. Framed copies of his most famous poems. Coffee mugs.'

'Photos of daffodils. Watercolours of daffodils. Books about daffodils.' My voice was rising to a squeak.

'Until you never want to see another spring flower of any sort. I sympathize. But love, you don't actually have to buy all those things.'

'If I want to keep talking to the employees, yes, I do. At several shops, maybe. I can always use them for Christmas presents. I had some friends back home who were nuts about Wordsworth.'

We worked out a plan. Alan would drive me to the first shop, find a place to park, settle down with a book, and wait for me to call for a ride to the next place. 'And if I don't buy anything and can continue the shop-crawl on foot, I'll call when I've struck pay dirt and need a ride back to The Inn. I do wish I could still walk miles, the way I used to.'

He gave me a hug. 'But you can still indulge in other, more interesting forms of exercise. All right, which way do we go?'

We chose the farthest shop, the idea being to work our way

back and stop for tea if somewhere looked promising, and I set out.

It would be tedious to recount the fruitless visits and the amount of merchandise I avoided purchasing. It ranged from the tacky and overpriced to the lovely (and overpriced). The shops were full of tourists, giving me no opportunity to chat with the employees. I walked from one to the next, getting more footsore and discouraged by the minute. When the last shop promised more of the same, I phoned Alan. 'Nada, zero, zilch, and I've had it. Join me at the tea shop.' I told him which one and went in to get us a table and order a generous afternoon tea.

My patient husband arrived at the same moment as our tea. It was a bit late in the day for tea, most people beginning to think about supper, so the shop wasn't very full, and our server offered to pour our tea for us and stop to chat. She did a double take when she looked at me.

'Have we met?' she asked, sounding puzzled. 'Sorry, but you look so familiar.'

'My husband and I have been visiting for several days,' I said, establishing my credentials as a stranger and therefore negligible. 'Would you perhaps be one of the volunteers at St Oswald's?'

'Yes! That's where I saw you. You were wanting to talk about' – she looked around and lowered her voice – 'about the murder.'

I admitted it with what I hoped was a deprecating smile.

The server lowered her voice still further. 'I can't talk about it here, but we're closing soon. Could you – that is, would you care to – join me in about an hour?'

We offered to meet her in the lobby of The Inn, and she left us to finish our tea and speculate about what she might want to talk about.

'We'll soon know,' said Alan calmly, and got up to pay the bill.

# TWENTY-EIGHT

The evening was so lovely we sat on one of the benches outside the door of our hotel. We didn't have long to wait. The young woman had shed her cap and apron and looked much less like a waitress. Alan hailed her. She approached tentatively, glancing around.

'My dear, if you're at all uncomfortable about this, you don't have to talk to us,' I said quietly. 'We'll understand.' I hoped I didn't sound patronizing, but the woman was so young, scarcely more than a child, and I wanted to set her at ease.

'No, I want to tell you.' She was almost whispering. 'But not here; it's too public.'

'Then we'll go to a nice private pub we've found,' said Alan, taking control of the situation. 'We'd all be better for a wee dram, I'm sure. It's a bit of a walk, so we'll drive.'

Alan knew that meant he'd have to limit himself to a very small whisky or a half pint; English law is extremely strict about drinking and driving. However, I knew my husband's ways. He could nurse a modest drink all evening if necessary, meanwhile making his companions feel relaxed and talkative.

We went to the pub where Roger had taken us. The sheltered corner was just as sheltered, just as private as before. Alan went to the bar and fetched the bourbon he knew I'd want, the gin and tonic our new friend had requested, and a very pale whisky and soda for himself.

'Cheers,' he said, lifting his glass. 'I can't drink a toast to you, ma'am, as I don't know your name.'

'Jenny,' she said, still in that near whisper. 'Jenny Trelawny.'

'Then here's to you, Jenny, and a more Cornish name I never heard. Do you know my friend Christopher Prideaux?'

'Yes. That's one reason I thought I could trust you. He's a good man is Mr Prideaux, a kind man.'

'He is, and a good friend of mine for more years than I care to remember. Did you know him back in Cornwall?'

'No. I came here with my parents when I was only five.' She took a minute sip of her drink.

'And do you still live with them?' I took an equally minute sip of mine. I was trying to put her at ease, talking about herself until she was ready to talk about whatever she knew.

'No. My father died two years ago, and Mum couldn't bear to stay here without him. He was the one who loved this part of the country. Mum was from London originally and missed the big city. She wanted me to go with her, but I'd made friends here. And I'd heard stories about London . . .'

'Scary stories, I'll bet.'

'Not so much that; it just didn't sound like my sort of place. I'm more like Dad, I suppose. I like peace and quiet.'

'So you moved in with friends?'

'No, I got a tiny flat. I've been working at the café ever since I left school, and with that and a bit of money my father left me, I can manage.'

'And you hear things,' I prompted. 'At the café.'

She took a deep breath. 'Yes. No one pays attention to a waitress, you know. We're invisible. People will talk while I'm standing right there, not even considering that I'm hearing every word. That's how I heard about what Mr Atkinson was doing. He was a really rotten person, you know.'

'We do know.' Alan's voice and face were compassionate. 'What did he say in your hearing that gave him away?'

'It wasn't him. It was the other one, the one who was trying to get him into politics.'

'Harold Thompson?'

'I guess. I'd never seen him in the café before, so I didn't really know who he was until he started talking about Mr Atkinson.'

'Who was there with him, Jenny?' asked Alan. He tried to make it sound unimportant, so as not to scare her off. She was still pretty skittish.

'Nobody. I mean I don't know who he was talking to. He was on his phone.'

I groaned. 'And shouting, I suppose, as rude people so often do on their phones.'

'Not at first, but when he started getting mad, he did get loud.

And the language! The manager finally had to come and ask him to keep it down because he was offending other customers. But before that I heard a lot.'

I found I was holding my breath. I opened my mouth, but Alan laid his hand on mine in a restraining gesture. 'And it disturbed you,' he said gently.

'Yes, because he was talking about something dreadful. I couldn't tell what, but he was getting very upset about it. I heard the word "Atkinson", and then "I don't *know* how he found out. So long ago, and in London, for God's sake". Just like that, almost screaming. And then the other person must have said something, because he said, "He's got to be stopped. He's bleeding me white! And it's all so pointless. The bitch has been dead for twenty years" – sorry, but that's what he said – "and she didn't have any family to crucify me. But if it came out, I'd be finished. I've got to shut the bastard up!" And that's when the manager came to complain, and he stormed out.'

'Good heavens! How terrifying!' I finished my bourbon in a single gulp.

'And not just terrifying,' said Alan, 'but informative as well. A confirmation that he was being blackmailed – he actually said as much – and that he intended to do something about it. We knew about the blackmail, my dear, but now we have some idea about why. A crime long ago in London in which a woman died. That's not a great deal to go on, but it's more than we had before now.'

'You never heard him say for certain who the extortionist was?'

'No. I thought it was Atkinson because he'd mentioned that name. But can't the police trace calls or something?' asked Jenny. 'I don't understand about mobile phones, really, but I know they're not very private.'

'In certain circumstances the police can search phones, yes. It's complicated, legally, and there must be a very good reason. I'm not sure we have enough for that yet, though you've been an enormous help.'

'Oh. Well, I do know a bit more.' She was loosening up, whether from the gin or an interested, sympathetic audience. 'I told you Mum was from London. She married Dad and went to

Cornwall over twenty years ago, but she stayed in touch with some of her London friends. So I called and told her what I'd overheard and asked if she knew anything about a crime involving that horrible man all those years ago. A woman dead, a woman with no family – I thought it might have made some waves.'

'A very long shot,' I said, disappointed.

'That's what I thought, but I wanted to know. There was something so downright nasty about it. I mean, a woman died, and all this person can think about is how it might affect him! So Mum said she couldn't recall anything off the top of her head, but she'd text some of her friends. And here's where it gets downright spooky. Out of all the people in London, Mum found one who knew all about a story that seems to fit.'

'No! It's almost incredible.' I was becoming more and more sceptical.

Alan shook his head. 'You have to remember, love, that London, like most big cities, is really a collection of neighbour-hoods. A person who lives in Belgravia isn't likely to know someone in the East End, but the East Enders tend to know each other, at least to a degree. And of course people in the same line of business know each other.'

'That's it, you see,' Jenny chimed in. 'See, Mum was a nurse's aide at one of the small hospitals, so she got to know a lot of people in the medical profession and on the fringes. One she still hears from now and then was a doula. Well, still is, I suppose. Anyway, when she was just getting started in her work, this woman heard about a young teenager who fell pregnant and wanted to have the baby, even with all the problems. The usual story, I suppose. She wanted someone to love, someone who would love her.'

I shook my head sadly. 'Yes, the familiar dream. The sweet, cuddly baby. Never considering the costs, the fearsome respon-sibilities, the realities of motherhood.'

'All of that. But anyway, the father, who was something impor-tant in the City, said she had to have an abortion. The story was that he got abusive about it and forced the poor girl to get rid of the baby. His baby.'

Jenny lifted her empty glass and set it down again. 'He made her go to a place where they wouldn't ask questions. And something went wrong, and she died.' Once again she shot a longing look at the glass. 'She was fourteen.'

Alan went to the bar, fetched a glass of tonic and gave it to her along with a large handkerchief. When she had dried her eyes and blown her nose, she looked at us sorrowfully. 'Fourteen. And she died alone. Mum's friend said the poor child had no family. And of course the man was long gone.'

I took a deep breath. 'And the man was . . .?'

'Mum doesn't know. Her friend never said. Maybe she never knew his name, just that he was a rotter who thought he could do anything he liked.'

'"Something important in the City",' Alan quoted thoughtfully. 'A financier, then, one assumes.'

I knew that the City of London, as opposed to Greater London including Westminster, was the financial district, the Wall Street of England. The Bank of England is there, for example. 'There are lots of people working in the City besides the actual wheeler-dealers,' I said. 'Surely there must be lawyers. I never heard of a big business deal going forward without legal quibbles.'

'Hmm. Yes, at least some of the Inns of Court are located actually in the City, and though they serve barristers, not solicitors, the two do function together. And Harold Thompson is a solicitor. A possible link, but I'm afraid a very weak one, my dear.'

'Couldn't the Yard trace the dirty little story somehow? After all, the poor girl died. There must be records.'

'If the girl had gone to an NHS facility, there would certainly be records – confidential, to be sure, but accessible in a murder investigation. But the bastard took her to a back-street butcher specifically so there would *not* be records.'

'There's bound to be some record of her burial,' I insisted. 'There has to be *something!*'

'If she was buried. Your trouble, my love, is that you keep thinking of the way normal people do things. If you're a crooked doctor who has killed someone, actually two someones counting the baby, you're probably not going to ring up the nearest undertaker to deal with the body. London has a good big river.'

I slumped in my chair. So did Jenny. 'Then this isn't any help?'

'I didn't say that,' Alan soothed. 'It's a pointer in the right direction, but it doesn't look like any real proof will be easy to come by. What we need now is to find out who Thompson was talking to when you overheard him. I'll run this by Davies – he's the head of the murder investigation, Jenny – and see if he agrees that he'd be justified in asking for a warrant.'

'But wait a minute!' I objected. 'They don't have the phone. How can they search it, even if they do get a warrant?'

Even Jenny smiled at that.

'Quite easily,' said Alan. He succeeded pretty well at not sounding condescending. 'It'll be easier if it's an Android; iPhones are a trifle more secure, but not a lot. The fact is, my dear honest wife, that mobile phones might as well be made of glass, so transparent are they. Never say anything on your mobile that you don't want the whole world to know. Ask Nigel if you don't believe me.'

Nigel Evans, a young man whom I'd befriended years ago when I first moved to England, had the kind of brain I could only admire enviously. He ran the IT department at the university in Sherebury and could apparently make various electronic devices dance the cancan if he wanted to. He wrote the programs, repaired anything that needed repairing, taught everyone how to use them, and had even held my hand until I became fairly competent with email and other very basic electronic functions. Not only that, he had a gorgeous singing voice and a wide reper-toire of both classical and popular music. A Renaissance man, in fact. Yes, he would know how to tease out the secrets hidden in anyone's phone.

'Oh!' A thought suddenly occurred to me. 'So if they can do that, they can also find him, can't they? I mean, they can find out where he's making phone calls, right?'

'Possibly, if he's not gone to ground in a place where there are no transmission towers. But yes, there's a good possibility. So you see, Jenny, you've been very helpful indeed! We'd like to treat you to dinner.'

'Not just to thank you for your help,' I added quickly, 'but to get to know you better.' *And*, I added mentally, *because you don't have much money for food or anything else, and because you're lonely.* 'Do say you'll come.'

'I . . . Well, but I'll need to change into something nicer.'

'Not for supper at our hotel. It's very informal. Come along. I'm starving, and you must be, too.'

# TWENTY-NINE

We gave Jenny her choice: a 'proper' meal in the restaurant, or pizza or cold cuts in our room. Given her age, her preference for pizza was predictable. Alan and I chose the charcuterie tray. We chatted about her background, her goals, our life in Shrewsbury, everything but the murder and its attendant complications. Then Alan drove her home and came back to talk it all over.

'The first thing is to search that phone,' I said when he was sitting comfortably with an espresso in front of him.

'You're right. How do you think Davies will react if I call him at this hour?'

'It isn't even ten. And you know better than I do that policemen work all hours.'

'Yes, but he's an early-to-bed, early-to-rise man. Goes for brisk runs every morning.' Alan shuddered. 'I'd rather he were in a good mood, but it can't be helped.' He pulled out his phone. 'Did you take notes of the conversation?'

'Mental ones. She was nervous when she started out. I didn't want to alarm her. But I wrote down everything I could remember while you were taking her home. I think I got most of it.' I tore a couple of pages out of my notebook and handed them to him.

He glanced at them and placed the call.

His apprehension was justified. George Davies, who had been on his way to bed, was not best pleased at the idea of trying to obtain a warrant to search Harold Thompson's mobile.

When Alan had told him everything we had learned from Jenny, he acknowledged that a phone search was advisable in order to gain evidence, and was also the best way to try to find him, but he was peevish about it. 'It'll be hard to find a judge at this hour, and electronic warrants are dodgy at the best of times. No, no, not your fault, but I'm not a magician, you know. I'll do my best, but it might take time.'

I heard the last, and sighed as Alan clicked off. 'So much for that! Bureaucracy!'

'Simmer down, love. How would you like it if someone decided to burrow into your phone and find out everyone you've ever talked to?'

'Hah! I thought hackers could do that at the drop of a hat!'

'You have a point, but the police have to do it legally. Remember that any evidence they find will be presented in a court of law, and the prosecutors better be able to cite chapter and verse.'

'Oh, I'm sure you're right, and it's to protect everyone's privacy, yada, yada, yada. But it's so frustrating, now we finally have something to go on, that we have to sit and wait for a piece of paper. Do we have any wine left?'

'No, but how about some tea? "The cup that cheers but does not inebriate", as somebody said.'

I settled for tea, though I knew it would make me get up at least once in the middle of the night. It was soothing, I had to admit, so what with that and Alan's comforting presence, I managed to still the maddening brain-hamster and get to sleep, eventually.

I woke early, though, and fumbled to shut off the alarm before realizing it was the phone in the room. It seldom rang, since most people called on our mobiles. It was on Alan's side of the bed, and as he was still slumbering peacefully, I stumbled out of bed and reached the dratted thing just as it stopped ringing. Thinking blasphemous thoughts about Alexander Graham Bell and all his successors, I lifted the receiver and hit the code for the front desk. 'This is Mrs Martin. Did someone just call our room?'

'Yes, I'm sorry to disturb you so early, but there's a young woman here who wants to talk to you.'

I heard the phone being handed over, and then: 'Oh, Mrs Martin, I'm sorry, they said you'd still be asleep, but I have to be at the café in a few minutes, and I wanted to tell you something else I remembered. That man, Mr Thompson, he was talking to another customer about islands. No, I don't know why, but I heard him say islands are his hideaway. And he said something about Scotland. I thought maybe it might help. And I really, really have to go, or I'll be late for work.'

She hung up before I could ask any questions. I sat down on the edge of the bed trying to get my head straight.

The bed wriggled under me.

'Oh, sorry, Alan, did I sit on you?'

'Mmph.'

'I've just had a very interesting phone call.'

'That's nice.' His voice was slurred. 'Do you know what time it is?'

'No, but early. It's still dark. I'm going to turn on a light and make some coffee.'

'Mmph.'

But some of what I said must have gotten through the haze, because when I sat (on the chair) to drink my coffee, he said, 'Interesting phone call.'

'Oh, you're alive. Have some coffee.' He sat up against the pillows and reached out a hand for the mug.

'It was Jenny,' I went on. 'She called from downstairs, on her way to work. I guess we forgot to give her our numbers. Anyway, she remembered something else.'

'Mmm.'

That sounded a little more awake than 'mmph'. 'She overheard Harold talking to someone in the café about islands. Islands in Scotland. And he said something about islands being his hide-away. It might have meant nothing at all, but I just remembered that one of Ruth's painter friends thought Harold might have made for Scotland, just because parts of it are so remote.'

'Hmm. Islands in Scotland. The Hebrides?'

'Maybe. But there are also the ones to the north – the Orkneys and the Shetlands.'

'The Shetlands. Never been there. Too far north. But Orkney, now . . .'

We'd visited Orkney some time ago and loved it. 'Well, it's certainly remote enough. But not a place to hide, I wouldn't think. There are only two ways to get there – plane to Kirkwall or ferry to Stromness. And once you're there, only two very small towns, and the rest bare countryside. No trees, even.'

'One would have to know someone,' said Alan thoughtfully, 'a local, who could spirit you away somewhere. One of the other islands, perhaps.'

'Even then, the ferryman would know you were there. Remember what they told us about people leaving their keys in their cars, because a ferryman would know if anyone not the owner tried to drive it away.'

'It could be done, though. Arrive at Stromness on the big car ferry, in a crowd of tourists. Meet your friend at the dock, bundle yourself into his car wrapped in a blanket or whatever, and have him drive you to his home, preferably on one of the other islands, say Shapinsay. If he lived in a croft somewhere, there would be no neighbours to know you were there. Your friend might have to go off island to buy groceries, because the shop on Shapinsay is tiny and would know if he bought more than usual.'

'Seems like a lot of trouble, when he could just be hidden in some house on the Mainland.' (The biggest island is called the Mainland, which can be confusing.)

'Too many people around, too much chance of detection. And there's another disadvantage, too. The mobile service is reasonably good on most of the Mainland. I've been told that there are places on Shapinsay where there is no service at all, though I haven't been there recently enough to know for certain.'

'Ah. So that would make it much harder for him to be found. Oh, and, Alan! The police saw him in London, at St Pancras trying to board the Eurostar. But St Pancras is right next door to King's Cross, which is where you get trains to Edinburgh!'

'You're right! I wish Davies would call back.'

We left our phones on when we went down to breakfast. Nothing. We went for a walk to give the maid a chance to tidy our room. No call.

By mid-morning, when I was almost at nail-biting stage, Alan made a decision. He called Christopher. 'How far away is the nearest airport?' I heard him ask. After a pause, he said, 'Orkney.' Then: 'Right. What's the quickest way to get there?'

He had decided to take matters into his own hands. Great! I pulled out our suitcases and began to pack.

I wondered, when we at last set foot on the tarmac in Kirkwall, Orkney, if it would in fact have been quicker to drive the whole way. We had caught the very last flight out of Edinburgh, and once in Kirkwall had no place to stay for the night and no transportation.

'Now what?' I asked, once we were in the tiny terminal. 'The car-hire place is closed for the night. And anyway we've no place to go.' The café was also closed, and I was hungry and thirsty as well as tired and fed up.

'Seemed a good idea at the time.' Alan was plainly beginning to rethink his impulse. 'I hated sitting there waiting for something to happen. And we know Orkney a little. But maybe we're chasing wild geese.'

I caught sight of a lighted display case full of gifts one could buy if the shop were open. Most of the objects were beautifully crafted stoneware that I recognized at once. 'Alan! Call Andrew. He'll be able to help.'

On our previous visit, we'd made friends with genial Andrew Appleby, the extremely talented potter who lives near the Loch of Harray (pronounced like the name of the young wizard) and calls himself the Harray Potter. Andrew not only makes the most beautiful mugs and pots and wine glasses and what-have-you that I've ever seen, he's also one of the nicest men I've ever met. He'd help us out of our predicament, for sure.

Our luck was in. Andrew was not at home but actually in Kirkwall visiting friends. In minutes he was at the air terminal, hustling us into his car and dealing with our most immediate needs first. 'Not a lot of pubs in Orkney, but there's a pleasant one nearby.' It served excellent pub food and even better ale.

Once we were refreshed, he bought us after-dinner drinks – Highland Park whisky for Alan, of course – and allowed us to explain our sudden journey to his part of the world.

'So,' he summarized, 'you're looking for a person who may or may not have killed someone and may or may not have fled to Orkney to visit an unidentified resident who may or may not exist.'

I groaned, but Alan's drink had mellowed him. He roared with laughter. 'In a nutshell, yes,' he said when he could speak. 'Of course, we prefer to call it informed deduction rather than wild speculation.'

Andrew laughed, too. 'Actually, if your initial premise that he'd want to come here is true, the rest of your scenario makes a certain amount of sense. Shapinsay is a better place to hide than the Mainland, and yes, the mobile service there can be dicey. Now, how can I help?'

Alan was ready for that. 'You've already saved our lives. Now we need a room for the night, or perhaps several nights, and a car. Is Kirkwall the best place to find both those things?'

'Yes. The car-hire outfits open in the morning when the first flight comes in, and the hotels have shuttles to the airport. I can show you the best hotel tonight. It isn't posh or expensive, but I'm told it's comfortable and the service is exceptionally friendly. And if I may say so, you both look ready to drop, so shall we?'

# THIRTY

I woke the next morning to the usual sounds of a busy hotel. The room was dark and gloomy, so I was sure other people were getting a ridiculously early start on the day. Raising myself on one elbow, I got a bleary glimpse of the clock on the bedside table.

Almost eight.

Eight! When it looked like the darkness before dawn.

Coming back from the bathroom, I peered out the window and understood. Heavy clouds were dropping steady rain. The puddles on the street showed it had been raining for some time, and the pedestrians I could see were well wrapped up in sturdy raincoats and carrying stout umbrellas.

And it was cold! I had temporarily forgotten that Orkney was much farther north, and had a climate quite different from even the northern parts of England. Brr! I took a very hot shower, dressed, and made coffee, and by that time Alan was more or less awake.

'Who hit me on the head?' he muttered.

'Travel. And unease. They got me, too. Have some coffee.'

He looked at the clock. 'We've missed the first airport shuttle. And the first ferry to Shapinsay,' he grumbled, looking at the timetable he'd pulled up on his phone. 'But we can make the next one if we move fast. I'll call to book the nine forty-five.'

It was a tight squeeze. We had to get to the airport, hire a car, and get to the dock in a little over an hour. There was no time for breakfast, and by the time we drove onto the quay on Shapinsay, I was starving. 'Now what?' I whined, looking around.

'There's the castle,' said Alan, pointing. 'We'll go up and book a room if we can, but at least we ought to be able to get a meal.'

'At a castle?'

'Balfour Castle is a hotel. We'll give it a try.'

Alan can be very persuasive when he wants to, and he's quite distinguished looking. It took him a while, but eventually he had the desk clerk eating out of his hand and had procured some breakfast for us, even though they'd stopped serving. He also booked a room for us for one night, at a cost that made him gulp. 'But you can tell everyone we slept in a castle,' he said, eyeing his credit card to make sure it hadn't melted down.

'We did that in Durham,' I reminded him. 'A real castle, not a Victorian wannabe.'

We were getting settled in our room (much more comfortable than the one in Durham Castle), when Alan's phone rang.

'But Andrew said—' I began, but Alan hushed me.

His end of the conversation was not enlightening, but he was smiling when he ended the call. 'Davies managed to get the warrant. His people began the search, and the last call Harold the Horrible made was from Stromness to Stromness.'

'He is here!'

'At last sighting, yes. They're working on details now, but they did learn that the number he called in Stromness was listed to someone named John Smith.'

'Ri-i-ight.'

'There are people named John Smith,' he pointed out.

'Sure there are. Care to place a bet about how many of them live in Stromness?'

'No bet. Davies and co. are pursuing that right now.'

'And when they find out there's no such person, what then? Orkney isn't a huge place, but it does cover a lot of islands.'

'But we're on one of them, the one we thought was most likely as a place to hide. And I saved the best for last. Davies suggested that it might be a good idea for me to do a little investigating myself, hinting that he couldn't really authorize the expenditure involved in sending a team there, but if I cared to take a look, as I'd been there before, etc. I took great pleasure in telling him exactly where I was.'

'Now, I know this island a bit but not extensively. I'm going to ask the woman at the desk if there are guided tours of the island, which might be a start.'

'She'll probably offer to guide you herself. You've got her wrapped around your little finger.'

He leered and twirled his non-existent moustache. 'Ah, m'dear, it's my famous charm, you know.'

I stuck my tongue out.

The charm worked. In less than an hour, we were in a car headed out for an exploration of Shapinsay. I had explained to the driver that we wanted, of course, to see the beauty spots on the island, but we were also looking for a holiday let, preferably a remote croft to provide lots of peace and quiet for Alan's writing. (I had suggested painting, but he had drawn the line at impersonating an artist.)

Alan has long admired my talent for believable lies. The driver apparently bought it, because he took us to the loneliest parts of the island, tiny crofts with a few chickens and a vegetable garden, bigger tracts of arable land, sheep farms doubling as wind farms, and several structures that used to be houses but were now little more than piles of stone.

Some of the views were no doubt glorious on a fine day. With dark clouds lowering and the rain apparently prepared to continue till doomsday, I was less inspired.

Alan kept up a running trickle of conversation, asking who lived in the crofts, whether it was in fact possible to make a living on the island, what had happened to the people who had lived in the abandoned properties.

The driver was a dour Scot who answered in as few words as possible. Who lived in the crofts? Crofters. Could they make a living? Oh, aye, the land is rich. What happened to the other people? Died.

We came at last to the most desolate ruin of all. The four stone walls of the cottage still stood, but the roof was gone completely. Our driver came close enough that we could see the heap of rubble inside, broken and decayed beams, here and there a tile, all overgrown with weeds, dark and wet with the rain. I shuddered. This had once been someone's home. A peat fire had burned in that fireplace, warming the room and its inhabitants. I could envision a contented tabby cat stretched in front of what was now only a dark hole in the wall.

I was thoroughly sick of our quest and certain that it was fruitless, when our driver stopped the car and made a complicated sound apparently intended to show surprise. 'Will ye look at that noo!' It was his longest utterance so far. He pointed.

A shed on the property was still more or less intact, though in poor repair. There were several holes in the roof, but the walls were mostly sound. At one end a large door, big enough to admit a tractor, stood ajar, hanging from one hinge.

And in that doorway I could glimpse, even through the rain and gloom, the licence plate of a car.

The driver said something else I couldn't understand and made to get out of the car.

'No,' said Alan in his voice of authority. 'Take us back to the hotel immediately, please.' The 'please' softened it a bit, but the driver recognized it as a command. Grumbling, he put the car in gear and took off.

Alan kept trying his phone until we got close enough to the tiny village that he no longer saw 'No Service'. He called Davies. 'We may have found him,' he said. 'On the island of Shapinsay. Run a search for—' And he reeled off the licence number. 'He may have seen us, and if so, he won't stay here long. I'm going to have him held at the ferry if he tries to go off island. I'll need backup from Kirkwall.' Pause. 'Yes, I know, but we'll cross that bridge when we come to it. I'll try to stay within mobile range.'

He clicked off as we approached the quay. 'Stop, please,' he said to the driver, again in that voice that meant business.

Surly now, the driver stopped without a word. 'We can walk up to the castle,' he told the driver. 'Thank you for your patience.'

He nodded to me, and I pulled out my purse and gave him what I hoped was an adequate tip. He gave me a curt nod and drove off, and I waited in a small shelter while Alan talked to the man in the ferry office and then rejoined me.

'So that's all we can do for now,' he said wearily. 'There's a ferry due in soon. Well, you can see it.' He pointed to the shape approaching across the water.

'What was Davies worried about?' I asked. 'False arrest?'

'Something like that. He was most reluctant to send in officers from Kirkwall, but I think I convinced him. If we're all wrong and this isn't our man, I could be in big trouble, and so could Davies. We'll just have to hope.'

'If he isn't Harold the Horrible, he won't care if we saw him, and he won't come to the ferry, so there's no problem. But if he isn't a crook of some stripe, what would he be doing hiding out in that abandoned— Wait! Here comes a car. Is it the one?'

The car pulled to a stop in the small parking area near the quay, and out stepped Harold Thompson.

We never managed to get any lunch that day, either. By the time a second boat had pulled in behind the ferry, and the policemen aboard had taken Harold away, and Alan had filled out all kinds of paperwork and talked (and talked) to George Davies, it was more than time for dinner. Alan filled me in on the details as we sat peacefully sipping pre-dinner drinks.

'I was informed that quite a lot was happening back in Grasmere while we were, quote, "frolicking about in the islands", unquote. Once they obtained the warrant to search the phone, which happened late last night, they were able to trace the person Thompson was talking to when Jenny overheard him.'

'Who was it?'

'One of his mates. The name meant nothing to me. But when the police caught up with him, he told them all about the conversation. He and Harold have known each other since they both lived in London, and this man knew about the young woman who died, the whole sordid story.'

'Young woman! She was a *child*.' I took a gulp of my bourbon.

'As you say.' He, too, needed to wash the taste of it out of his mouth. 'Neither of them knew how Donald Atkinson got hold of the story, but when he did, he held it over Harold's head. Harold got tired of paying up and decided it had to stop. He told his buddy that he knew exactly how he could do it and run no risk of discovery. Unfortunately for the forces of law and order, he didn't explain the process, but we think we know, and the police are searching his home now for additional evidence.'

'Like that tube of Nitro-Bid, with his and Roger's fingerprints on it.'

'Exactly. He just may have been stupid enough to keep it. Confronted with what is known, and what the police will find out, he may confess to the crime. If not, there are plenty of people who can be asked to give us information. I think it will be a rather uninteresting trial.'

'Will we have to come back for it?'

'I hope not. If they want testimony about what we found, or

heard, or the like, we can try to get them to accept a deposition.'

'What will happen to him?'

'That's up to the judge. Quite a long sentence, I'd think. And I think they're telling us our table is ready.'

We had an excellent, leisurely meal in the castle's elegant dining room, finishing with the best sticky toffee pudding I've ever tasted, made distinctly Scottish with a wee nip of Highland Park in the sauce.

'Would you like to stay here a day or two and have a taste of real holiday?' asked Alan as we were getting ready for bed. 'We've spent the whole of our supposed holiday tracking down a murderer.'

'No. I want to go home. I want to see the animals and sit in front of our own fire and do nothing until Christmas!'

So Alan booked the ferry for the next morning, and by afternoon we were back in Grasmere saying goodbye to everyone, and on the next Sunday morning, we were in our familiar seats in our well-beloved Cathedral, vowing never to take another 'holiday'.

# AFTERWORD

The glassblower's cat mentioned in chapter twenty-six is a reference to Charles Parker's dreaming observation in *Clouds of Witness* by Dorothy L. Sayers.